BREAKING
COVER

ALSO BY J. D. RHOADES

Safe and Sound

Good Day in Hell

The Devil's Right Hand

BREAKING COVER

J. D. Rhoades

ST. MARTIN'S MINOTAUR
NEW YORK

BREAKING COVER. Copyright © 2008 by J. D. Rhoades. All rights reserved. Printed in the United States of America. For information, address St. Martin's Press, 175 Fifth Avenue, New York, N.Y. 10010.

www.minotaurbooks.com

Book design by Jonathan Bennett

Library of Congress Cataloging-in-Publication Data

Rhoades, J. D., 1962–
   Breaking cover / J.D. Rhoades.—1st ed.
      p. cm.
   ISBN-13: 978-0-312-37155-5
   ISBN-10: 0-312-37155-1
   1. Undercover operations—Fiction.   2. United
States. Federal Bureau of Investigation—Fiction.   I. Title.
   PS3618.H623B74 2008
   813'.6—dc22

                                                    2008013395

First Edition: August 2008

10 9 8 7 6 5 4 3 2 1

To David G. Crockett, the man who taught me that
"legal ethics" is not an oxymoron

ACKNOWLEDGMENTS

Thanks as always to Scott Miller of Trident Media Group for excellent representation and sound advice. Thanks as well to my editor, Marc Resnick of St. Martin's Press, for his enthusiasm.

There are a lot of people this year who've helped me get the word out. They include (but are not limited to): Jon and Ruth Jordan of Crimespree Magazine; Stacey Cochran; Alexandra Sokoloff, Margery Flax, and the folks at Mystery Writers of America (you finally got me); Sarah Shaber of MWA's Southeastern Chapter (and a damned fine writer her own self); International Thriller Writers; Joe Hartlaub of Bookreporter.com; Declan Burke; David J. Forsmark; Randy Johnson; Molly Weston; Anthony Rainone; Sandra Ruttan; Nathan Singer; Bob Morris; Zoe Sharp; Marshal Zeringue; Russ Heitz; Steve Allan; River Jordan; Josephine Damian; Joe Konrath; Dorothy Hodder; and James O. Born.

For support and advice, I am also indebted to Lori G. Armstrong and to the Honorable Companions.

Special thanks to my fellow bloggers at Murderati.com: Pari Noskin Taichert; Louise Ure; Ken Bruen; Robert Gregory Browne;

Simon Wood; J. T. Ellison; and Toni McGee Causey. It is an honor to be included in this kind of company.

Finally, thanks to my wife, Lynn. You keep it all together. Damned if I know how.

Just because you're paranoid
doesn't mean they're not really out to get you.

PART ONE

Under the Name of Sanders

CHAPTER ONE

HAVE YOU SEEN US?

THE FACES OF THE TWO BOYS WERE EVERYWHERE: stapled to roadside telephone poles, tacked to bulletin boards in Laundromats and grocery stores, taped to the sides of cash registers in convenience stores.

HAVE YOU SEEN US?

The pictures were grainy and blurred from repeated copying on creaky, overused public machines. The photo had been taken at a birthday party or some other festive occasion. The younger boy wore a cheap paper party hat with a tuft of plastic streamer jutting from the top. The older boy had his arm around the younger one's shoulders. The gap-toothed grins on the boys' faces contrasted grotesquely with the desperation of the hand-lettered caption.

HAVE YOU SEEN US?

Sanders's eyes flickered over the familiar poster as he waited in line. He knew who the boys were; everyone knew by now. The missing Powell boys, Evan and Earl, had seized as much news airtime as a dozen small wars. They had been taken from their suburban Raleigh home by someone invariably described as "an unknown assailant." There were also pictures of the unknown assailant, a drawing made by a police artist from the description of witnesses who had seen him talking to one of the boys. The boys were widely presumed to be dead, although no one would actually say this, least of all on the local news.

Sanders turned his attention back to the counter. The clerk was a bulky teenaged girl with bored eyes, a sullen mouth, and a gold stud through her tongue that flashed in the glare of the fluorescent lights when she spoke, which wasn't any more often than she could help. Her demeanor indicated a stubborn resistance to the idea of hurry. She rang up the gas purchase for the man in front of Sanders with short, erratic stabs of her fat fingers on the cash register keys.

"Mbackseeus," she mumbled at the customer, dismissing him from her consciousness as she said it and turning to Sanders in the same motion. "Atbeall?"

Sanders put a Mountain Dew and a pack of Nekot crackers on the counter. "No," he said, "I need to fill up on pump number four. Supreme."

"Leave the gas card," the girl said.

"Don't have one," Sanders said.

The girl looked at him in exasperation. "You gotta come back an' pay, then."

"I know," Sanders said. "But you won't turn the pump on until I come in and ask."

The girl heaved a heavy sigh and turned to the console that controlled the gas pumps. She punched the keys to turn on the pumps as if she were imagining poking Sanders in the eyes. She turned back. "Well?" she said, as if she were offended that Sanders was still there.

"I want to pay for the drink and the crackers now."

"You gotta pay all at once," the girl said.

"Says who?" Sanders replied.

"There some kind of problem, Alison?" a voice said.

Sanders turned. The man standing a few feet away was about the same height as Sanders, but he was slim and wiry where Sanders was stocky. It was hard to tell his age; he looked about forty at first glance, but his skin was lined and creased by long exposure to the outdoors and pockmarked with ancient acne scars. He had thinning sandy hair and a neatly trimmed mustache. He was dressed in a light brown deputy sheriff's uniform. The gold star gleamed on his right breast pocket. There was a rectangular gold name badge over the other pocket. Sanders could make out the raised black lettering against the gold background: T. BUCK-THORN.

"He's got to pay for the stuff all at once," Alison complained to the deputy.

"I'm thirsty," Sanders said. "I want to drink my drink while I fill the tank. I don't know why this is a—"

"Tell you what, Alison," the deputy said, "I'll walk out and keep an eye on him. I'll make sure he doesn't drive off without paying, okay?"

"Well . . ." the girl said doubtfully. People had begun lining up behind Sanders, and the way they were shuffling their feet and looking annoyed decided the question. "Okay," she said, giving Sanders a look of smoldering disgust as she rang him up.

Buckthorn was right behind Sanders as he walked out to his truck. It was a Ford F250, brand-new. Sanders got a new truck every year. He worried sometimes that maybe it was too conspicuous, but it was the one luxury he allowed himself. In another time and place, he had ridden a motorcycle, but pickups helped him blend into the landscape these days. Plus, the road he lived on tended to get tricky in bad weather, the kind of tricky that called for four-wheel drive.

Sanders popped the top on the Mountain Dew can with one hand while he took the gas nozzle off the hook of the pump. As he started pumping the gas, the deputy leaned against the metal light pole between the two banks of pumps. He took a toothpick out of the pocket of his uniform shirt and stuck it in his mouth. Sanders didn't look directly at him, but in his peripheral vision, he could see the man watching him.

"Alison's a sweet girl," Buckthorn said to Sanders. "She just doesn't want Jeff—that's the owner—to get mad at her. He's kind of particular about how he wants things done."

"Uh-huh," Sanders said.

"See, I know Alison. I know her family. I try to know everybody around here."

"I'm sure they appreciate that," Sanders said.

The deputy scanned him for a few moments, looking for sarcasm. "Thing is, Mr. Sanders, I don't know you. And what bothers me is that I can't seem to find out anything about you. Beth Anne at the Pine Lake Realty says you pay your rent on the old Jacobs farm in cash every month. Y'don't see that much. And you don't seem to have a job, so I'm figuring you're pretty well off."

"I have a trust fund," Sanders said. "My uncle died and left it to me."

"Lucky you," Buckthorn said. "But then, like you said back there, you don't have any credit cards. That's kind of odd, don't ya think?"

There was a clunk as the gasoline reached the level of the nozzle and it shut off. Sanders pulled the nozzle from the intake and set it back in its niche on the pump. "You do keep pretty well informed. Some folks might call that invasion of privacy."

Buckthorn shifted the toothpick to the other side of his mouth and smiled. "I call it good community policing. So do most of the folks around here. They don't mind me checking up. Makes 'em feel safer. 'Course, they've got nothin' to hide. You got something to hide, Mr. Sanders?"

Sanders began walking back toward the store. He saw the girl's pale face staring at him through the glass of the front window. It showed the most interest he had seen in her face yet.

He heard Buckthorn's footsteps behind him as he reached the door. He stopped and turned. "What do you want, Deputy?"

Buckthorn stopped and crossed his arms across his chest. "I want to know who you really are, Mr. Sanders. I want to know why you're here."

Sanders turned back to the door. "I'm here because I like peace and quiet," he said. He took hold of the door handle and looked steadily at the deputy.

Buckthorn uncrossed his arms. "Well, then, we should get along okay," he said. "I like that, too. Have a good evenin', Mr. Sanders." He flicked the toothpick into the nearby trash receptacle and walked off toward his cruiser, parked at the edge of the concrete lot.

Sanders took a deep breath and went inside. He tried to ignore the girl's stare as he paid for the gas. He felt her eyes on his back as he walked to the truck.

The deputy's car was pulling out as Sanders got behind the wheel. He started his own vehicle and pulled out behind, careful to keep below the posted speed limit. The little store was located on a country road a few miles outside of town. He pulled up to the stop sign at a crossroads. Straight would take him onto Main Street in the little town of Pine Lake. The left turn took him out the long two-lane country road to his house. The deputy's car pulled away, going straight toward town.

Sanders noticed his hands were shaking. Nobody was coming in either direction, but he sat there for a moment while he calmed down. *Just a redneck deputy throwing his weight around*, he told himself. *It's nothing.*

As he sat there, a white van came down the road from his left. It was unmarked, nondescript. If it hadn't been the only vehicle on the road, Sanders wouldn't even have noticed it. As he watched, the van went through the intersection and pulled over to the shoulder. Sanders saw that the rear windows of the van were covered with cardboard taped over the inside. His brow furrowed slightly.

Suddenly, the piece of cardboard was ripped away from the left rear window. Sanders found himself staring into a face he had seen before. He had just seen it on a poster in the store. He had seen it on every news brief and local news show on TV. It was the face of Earl Powell.

The boy's face was contorted with terror. He mouthed what looked like the word "help" before an unseen hand jerked him out of the window. The cardboard was replaced. There was a brief pause; then the van jerked back into motion.

Sanders sat for a moment, paralyzed with shock and uncertainty. He wondered if he had really seen the boy's face. His hand seemed to move of its own accord as he put the truck in gear. He fell in behind the van, following at a good distance. He passed the driveway to his house. He thought for a moment about stopping and calling the cops. Then he remembered Buckthorn and changed his mind. He didn't want to have to deal with the deputy again. He wasn't sure what he was going to do, but he reached behind the passenger seat and pulled out a black pistol, a Glock 9 mm.

TIM BUCKTHORN glanced in his rearview as he pulled away, watching Sanders sit at the crossroads for a moment. He saw the truck turn left after a white van passed. His fingers drummed restlessly on the wheel as he returned his eyes to the road ahead, his mind still on his conversation with Sanders. There was something about the man that still bothered him. It was illogical, he knew; he had never had cause to arrest Sanders or even suspect him of anything wrong. The man paid his taxes, took good care of his home, and kept pretty much to himself. Maybe that was it, Buckthorn thought. After all, didn't everyone say that after their neighbor turned out to have been a serial killer? *He was a quiet guy, kept to himself* . . . Buckthorn shook his head as his cruiser bumped over the railroad tracks at the edge of town. *Now you're thinking crazy, Tim,* he thought. He glanced left at the pine-fringed lake that had given the town its name. The sunlight glittered silver on the water, bringing a smile to Buckthorn's lips. The town had once been a prime vacation spot, the railroad bringing tourists from north and south to stay in the massive resort hotel that overlooked the big lake. An outdoor bandstand hosted big-name acts in the '30s and '40s. Benny Goodman was said by the town's older residents to have played there on several occasions. The place had fallen on hard times after World War II and had closed its doors in 1952. The once-grand structure had fallen slowly into rot and ruin, becoming a place children dared each other to sneak into, the biggest danger being that their parents whipped their behinds if they caught them taking the dare. A careless vagrant had burned it down with him in it in 1972, and the old bandstand had been torn down not long after. Now only the foundation stood among the tall grass near the water. The town's fortunes had also declined, the resort community bypassed by time and the interstate. Downtown had been struggling for years, with only the yearly Bass Festival and its related fishing tournament drawing tourists and money to the little community. Still, Buckthorn thought as the country road widened and turned into the tree-lined avenue of Main Street, it was a good place to live. There were good people here.

—

I SHOULD *call the cops,* Sanders thought. *This isn't my business. It's not my job* . . .

The phrase brought back a sudden memory, so vivid it was almost like a physical blow.

A pair of frightened eyes in a dark face, a high giggle, a voice behind him speaking in a high-pitched parody of a Mexican accent: "Ees not my yob, man . . ."

He steered with his elbows for a moment, racking the slide to chamber the first round. He saw the van ahead of him slow, then turn right. It looked for a moment as if the driver meant to steer the van into the trees that lined both sides of the road. Sanders noticed a deeply rutted dirt driveway coming out of the trees. The van disappeared as if swallowed by the woods. He drove past, not slowing down. He had passed the place before. The drive had been so overgrown, he had always assumed it was abandoned.

A half mile up the road, he stopped and made a three-point turn in the middle. He drove back to the hidden driveway and pulled in slowly. Branches scraped against the side of the truck. Gonna scratch my paint, Sanders thought. He stopped the truck and killed the engine. As he got out, he could hear the van on the road ahead, gears grinding as it tried to negotiate the corrugated road. "Dumb fucker," Sanders said out loud. "Should've got a four-wheel drive." He heard the engine stop. A door slammed. Soft clay mixed with pebbles squelched softly under Sanders's boots as he crept up the drive.

There was a small clearing at the end of the drive. Sanders faded back against a tree to scope things out. The van was parked about fifty feet away, in front of a single-wide trailer that looked at least thirty years old. The supports in the middle had given way, and it sagged in the center. Several of the windows were broken out and boarded up with plywood. The propane tank leaning at one end of the structure was badly rusted. The place looked as if it hadn't been inhabited in years.

Sanders heard the panel door on the other side of the van open. He heard a male voice grunt with effort, then a muffled squeal of pain.

"Shut up, you little bitch," a gravelly voice said. "I told you to stay still back there. Now you're going to get what's coming to you." Another grunt and another muffled sound of agony. Sanders heard the trailer door open, then bang shut. He started to move, but the sound of the door opening again stopped him in his tracks. He's getting the other kid, Sanders thought.

When Sanders heard the door slam shut again, he moved across the clearing. He crouched for a moment behind the van. From inside the trailer, he heard a man shouting, the same male voice he had heard earlier. He couldn't make out the words. He heard a sharp crack, then a cry. He slipped around the van.

The trailer door hung crookedly in its warped frame. A set of rickety wooden steps rose unsteadily toward the doorway, leaving a gap of several inches. Sanders sprang onto the steps and yanked the door open.

The first thing that struck him was the smell. The roof of the ruined trailer had leaked rain onto the cheap carpeting, giving the place a musty wet-dog odor. Overlaying that was a sharp smell of fear-sweat and body fluids, a throat-closing stench of misery and pain sealed into the small space. Sanders nearly gagged as he stepped through the doorway.

The door opened into what had been the trailer's living room. Someone had hammered sheets of plywood across the inside of all the windows, leaving the room as close and dark as a dungeon cell. The only illumination was provided by the harsh light of a battery-powered lamp that hung by a bungee cord from a dead ceiling fixture. The lamp swung as the violence of Sanders's entrance caused the rickety trailer to rock slightly. The illumination jerked and wavered, giving the scene before Sanders a surreal, hellish quality.

The man was bent over a small struggling figure on the floor. The boy had his hands fastened behind him with duct tape. More strips of the silver tape secured his ankles. The man had one hand hooked in the waistband of the boy's sweatpants, working them down over his buttocks. The other hand held a short knife that glittered and winked brightly in the unstable light. Sanders briefly registered another bound figure lying against the far wall. The man stood up, his eyes showing wide and white with shock in the jittering gloom. His mouth opened as if to say something. Sanders's first shot struck him in the chest, the impact shoving him up straighter for the second shot to drive him backward. The third shot went straight into his open mouth and sprayed blood and fragments of bone onto the wall behind. Another rank smell combined with the sudden coppery tang of blood in the air as the man's bowels and bladder let go. He collapsed like a house of cards to the floor.

Sanders crossed the room and stood over the man. He felt his heart pounding. His breath came in ragged gasps as he held the gun on the unmoving figure. After a long moment, he turned to the boy on the floor.

It was the older one; he couldn't remember if it was Evan or Earl. The kid looked up at Sanders. His eyes were wide above the duct tape wound around his head. Sanders bent down. "This may hurt a little," he said as he started looking for the end of the tape to rip it off. The boy lay terrified, unmoving. Sanders located the end and started to pull. It looked like the kidnapper had used almost an entire roll of tape on the boy's head alone. Sanders saw the knife lying a few feet away. He decided to try to cut through the tape. He bent over, put down the gun, and picked up the knife. The boy screamed behind the tape and tried to squirm away.

"Easy, kid," he said. "Take it easy. I'm not going to hurt you." The boy was beyond reassurance. He arched and bucked so violently that Sanders was afraid he'd hurt himself. "Okay, okay," he said. "Look, I'm putting it down, okay?" He dropped the knife back to the floor. The boy quieted slightly.

"Jesus,'" Sanders said under his breath. He looked over at the other bound figure. The kid's eyes were open, but they stared straight ahead, unseeing. Sanders went over and knelt down. He could see the rapid rise and fall of the small chest. The boy was alive, but out of it. Sanders hesitated for a moment, wondering what to do next. He bent down and started unwinding the tape from around the younger kid's head. It took some time, and the boy quivered slightly every time the tape took out a clump of hair. "Sorry," Sanders muttered whenever that happened. "Sorry. Sorry." Finally, he pulled the last strip off the kid's mouth. He still hadn't moved. Sanders pulled the tape from his hands, then his ankles. The boy immediately curled up in a ball against the wall, his arms wrapped around his knees, not looking at Sanders, not looking at anything. Sanders turned back to the first kid. "Okay," he said. "That took a while, and I need to get out of here pretty soon. You can see I'm not here to hurt you. I can use the knife to cut you loose, or you can wait for your brother to snap out of it and unwrap you." He picked up the knife and raised his eyebrows questioningly. The older boy hesitated, then nodded. It took Sanders only a minute or so to cut him loose. The boy immediately crawled to his brother. "Earl," the boy whispered. "Earl, come on, talk to me." Earl didn't respond.

"Come on," Sanders said. "Let's get outside."

The older kid—it had to be Evan—looked up. "Are you a policeman?"

"No," Sanders said.

He walked over to them. "Come on, let's get him outside. It stinks in here." He helped Evan get the unresisting Earl to his feet. They started walking him outside. Evan swallowed as he looked at the body on the floor.

"You shot the bad guy," Evan said. "Doesn't that make you the good guy?"

"Not exactly," Sanders said. "It's . . . kind of complicated." They guided Earl down the stairs. Evan blinked in the sudden light. Earl still didn't respond.

Evan looked at Sanders. "That guy," he said in a whisper. "That bad guy . . . he hurt my brother. He hurt him real bad." A single tear rolled down his cheek. "I tried to stop him, but . . . but I was too little . . ." His lip started quivering.

Sanders knelt down to look him in the eye. "Kid," he said. "Evan. Look at me, man." The kid's lip stopped quivering.

"Evan," Sanders said. "It's real important that no one knows I was here. You can't tell anybody about me."

Evan's look of despair turned to confusion. "Why?" he said. "You saved us. You shot the bad guy."

Sanders nodded. "Right. So you guys owe me, right? I did you a favor, you do me one, okay? Even Steven."

The invocation of the magic words of childhood justice got through to Evan. He nodded. Then his brow furrowed. "How are we going to get home?" he whispered. His lip started to quiver again.

"Shit," Sanders muttered as he stood up. He hadn't planned ahead. He walked over to the van and pulled the passenger side door open. The floor was littered with fast food wrappers and empty plastic bottles. There was a hole in the dash where somebody had pulled out the radio. Sanders finally located what he'd been looking for. He reached over and picked up a small black cell phone from the dash. It was one of the cheap models typically given out for free to people who signed a one-year contract for cellular service. He handed the phone to Evan. "You know how to use one of these?" Evan looked dubious. Sanders flipped the phone open. It was on, the indicator light showing a good signal. "Look, just dial 911. You know how to do that, right? Then hit this send button. When someone comes on the line, tell them that you're on Sutter Church Road. Can you remember that?"

"Summer . . ." Evan began.

"Sutter," Sanders corrected him. "Sutter Church Road. I don't know the number, but tell them about the trailer here. Somebody'll figure it out."

Evan looked alarmed. "Where are you going to be? You're not going to leave us!"

"It'll only be for a short time, kid," Sanders said. He started backing down the road toward the woods where his truck was hidden. "Go ahead," he called out. "Make the call. Your brother needs a doctor. And remember, I was never here." He saw the kid start to dial. Sanders turned and bolted down the road toward his truck.

CHAPTER TWO

G ABY!" HOWARD JESSUP'S DEEP BASS voice cut through the din of the newsroom like a foghorn. "The cops just got the guy that took those two boys!"

Gabriella Torrijos sprang from her desk, nearly spilling her coffee in the process. She crossed the room to the cubicle where her videographer was holding a phone to his ear. "Sounds like he tried to shoot it out with the cops," Howard said, scribbling furiously on a notepad. "The guy's dead."

"Where?"

"Pine Lake."

Gabriella checked the map tacked to the wall over the scanner. The map showed the entire area reached by the WRHO-TV transmitters, with the station's ADI (area of dominant influence) outlined with a heavy black border.

"Right," she said. "Thirty miles south. On 43."

"Yep," Howard said. "Home of the Bass Festival."

Gaby pulled on her suit jacket. "I didn't know you fished."

"I don't," Howard said. "Bob's been the grand marshal last couple years." Gaby grimaced at the mention of Bob Caulfield,

WRHO's chief anchor. "Be nice, girl," Howard said, a grin on his craggy dark face. "Our Bob is a North Carolina institution. Beloved by all."

"Especially bartenders and nineteen-year-old interns."

"Mee-yow, baby," Howard said.

Michael Ellis, Channel 12's news producer, came skidding around the corner of the cubicle. "Gaby—"

"I'm already gone," Gaby interrupted. Howard was grabbing his dark blue windbreaker with the WHRO logo stenciled on the back. "Get me a live feed set up so we can break in as soon as I find out what's going on. Any word on the kids?"

"Yeah," said Howard, "sounds like they're all right—"

"Walk *and* talk, Howard. Walk *and* talk . . ."

By the time they got to the parking lot and the waiting news van, Gaby was puffing from trying to keep up with Howard's long-limbed strides.

"Who called it in?" Gaby said as she climbed into the van.

Howard turned the key and stomped the gas as soon as her door slammed shut, the acceleration momentarily pressing her back into the seat. He spun the wheel one-handed, slewing the van around a car entering the station's parking lot. "Brian knows some dispatcher down at the county EMS office. They've lit up the switchboards for three counties. Everyone wants in on this."

"I'll bet," Gaby said. Then Howard's words sank in. "Wait a minute," she said. "It was one of *Brian's* sources that called?"

"Come on, come on," Howard muttered in the direction of a vehicle at an intersection ahead that was slow pulling away as the light turned green. "Why all you white people drive so got-damn slow?"

"Howard," Gaby repeated. "Answer me. Was it a source of Brian's who called?"

Howard refused to look at her. "They called the *station*, Gaby," he said. "You were there."

"Brian's the senior correspondent," Gaby said. "This is a big story. He's not going to be happy about this."

Howard shrugged. "You do a good job on this, girl, ain't nobody going to care if Brian's happy or not."

She looked at him for a long moment. "Thanks, Howard," she said.

Howard whipped into a right-turn-only lane to pass a line of slow-moving cars, then yanked the van back into the travel lane. Horns honked. "Don't thank me," he said. "I ain't the assignment editor. You were there, that's all." He gave her a quick grin. "You're always there."

"I was wondering if anyone noticed," she said.

"I do," Howard said. "Michael does. Pretty soon so will everyone else."

They hit the off ramp at fifty miles an hour, then swung onto 43. Soon the parade of shopping centers and gated subdivisions began to thin out, replaced by older homes set farther back from the road, then by farmland. Howard picked up speed as the traffic thinned out. When they got closer to the town of Pine Lake, Gaby turned on the police scanner. The red LEDs had barely begun their rapid back-and-forth pulse before the speaker crackled to life. Out of the static and garbled chatter, Gaby picked out the name of a road. She reached behind the seat and pulled out a plastic shopping bag, crammed full of clumsily folded county maps. She rustled through them until she located the one she wanted, grimacing at the creases and coffee stains. "Jesus," she muttered. "What is the deal with men and folding maps?"

"Sexist," Howard said.

"Here it is," Gaby said, stabbing her finger down onto the map. "Sutter Church Road. There's an exit for Pine Lake, then a right about three miles down. That's Sutter Church. That's where they are."

The scanner crackled and squawked. It did sound like every lawman and rescue worker for miles was converging on Sutter Church Road. As Howard took the exit for Pine Lake, a green and white ambulance rocketed past in an explosion of flashing lights and blaring sirens. Howard fell in behind it and pressed the gas pedal to the floor.

They saw the lights from almost a mile away on the flat, straight road. It looked like a carnival midway seen from a distance, with red, blue, and white lights strobing chaotically on both sides of the road. A wild hodgepodge of vehicles lined the shoulder: sheriff's cars, black and silver Highway Patrol cars, town cops, EMS, even a fire truck. A few civilian vehicles, mostly 4×4 pickups, sported flashers on their dashboards. A hard-faced highway patrolman in a uniform that matched the colors of his car motioned them to a stop.

"No press," he barked.

Gaby leaned over and gave him her best professional smile. "Officer," she said, "I'm Gabriella Torrijos from WRHO NewsNow."

He wasn't buying the smile. "No press," he repeated. "Keep moving, please."

"Yowsa, boss," Howard said. The highway patrolman gave him a hard look, but Howard was already moving.

"What are you doing?" Gaby hissed.

Howard pointed ahead. Gaby looked. A pickup was pulling out, leaving a space open on the side of the road. "Don't want to lose our parking space." Gaby looked nervously in the rearview mirror for the highway patrolman, but he had apparently dismissed them from his thoughts and was busily directing traffic with abrupt hand motions.

Howard and Gaby piled out of the news van almost before it had stopped moving. Howard yanked open the side of the van and flicked a switch. There was a grinding of motors as the white pole of the microwave antenna raised out of its holder on the side of the truck. Howard yanked his camera out and began settling it on his shoulder as Gaby hooked up her microphone. The highway patrolman noticed then and began approaching, waving his arms angrily.

"Howard . . ." Gaby said.

"Don't worry, girl," Howard murmured back. "These days, the cops're almost as scared of a black man with a video camera as they are of one with a gun. I'm thinkin' of carryin' one everywhere I go." The antenna rose to its full height and began unfolding.

"I thought I told you—" the red-faced patrolman began.

Gaby turned to the officer, still holding the mike.

"Officer," she said, "can you tell us what's going on?"

The patrolman stopped dead in his tracks. "Ma'am," he said, "you can't be here."

She ignored him. "Is it true the police have a suspect in custody in the kidnapping of Evan and Earl Powell?"

He snapped to attention. "Ma'am," he said in an official voice, "we're not able to make any comment at this time." He turned on his heel and walked away.

"The power of television," Howard said.

Gaby laughed. "He's just gone to find somebody with enough juice to make us go away."

"We better finish setting up, then," Howard said.

They were set up within five minutes, in communication with the newsroom via the microwave relay towering above the van. Both Howard and Gaby were linked with the control room by tiny earpieces.

"Gaby?" a calm female voice came through her earpiece. Some of the tension went out of Gaby's shoulders as she recognized the speaker.

"I'm here, Stella," Gaby replied through the tiny mike attached to the earpiece. Stella Darby was one of the show's best producers. Gaby had never heard her raise her voice, never seen her lose her cool, even during the most glitch-plagued broadcasts. Gaby sorely needed Stella's granite steadiness right then.

"Howard?" Stella asked.

"Stellaaaaaaa!" Howard grinned at his own bad Brando imitation. He shouldered the camera and adjusted the focus on Gaby.

"That joke gets funnier every time I hear it, Howard," Stella said. "Okay. We got you loud and clear. We're breaking into *Seinfeld* right after the commercial."

"Which episode?" Howard asked.

"The one where you're not funny anymore, Howard," Stella said. "Okay, twenty seconds."

"Wait!" Gaby said, sudden panic washing over her. "I just got here! I don't really know anything yet!"

"Doesn't matter," Stella said. "We need to get something on the air. Just tell them there's been a break in the case, that

WHRO will be keeping you updated, blah blah blah, then pitch it back to Bob. Ten seconds."

Gaby took a deep breath and composed her face into the mask of the TV newsperson, professional, yet concerned.

Stella started counting down. "Five . . . four . . . three . . . two . . . and go."

Gaby heard the familiar horns and kettledrums of the WRHO NewsNow theme and the prerecorded announcer informing listeners: "This is a Special Report from WRHO NewsNow, Where North Carolina Gets Its News First." She heard Bob's voice: "It appears there has been a dramatic development in the saga of Earl and Evan Powell, the two young boys kidnapped from their North Raleigh neighborhood five days ago. With more on the story, we go live to Gabriella Torrijos."

The red light on the front of Howard's camera came on. "Bob, law enforcement officers converged today on this tree-lined road near the tiny town of Pine Lake, south of Raleigh. We don't know a great deal yet, but we have heard from sources that the two kidnapped boys have been recovered and that they are both okay. We'll be bringing you updates on this story as it develops. With the WRHO NewsNow team, I'm Gabriella Torrijos. Bob?"

There was a short pause, then, "We're clear," Howard said. He shifted the camera slightly, peering at her from around the viewfinder. "Tiny town? What, they all dwarves or something?"

"Oh, God," she groaned. "Did that sound totally stupid?"

"Naw," Howard said. "But you ain't gonna be winnin' no awards from the local chamber of commerce." He noticed the stricken look on Gaby's face, and his teasing grin turned to a look of contrition. "You did fine, girl," he said. "Now let's go get some actual information." She gathered up a coil of the mike cord that linked her to the camera gear hung all over Howard. The two of them wove between the vehicles lining the side of the road toward what looked to be a break in the trees. Bright yellow police tape was strung across a dirt driveway. As they approached, there was a sudden commotion among the trees. A man in a dark green jumpsuit with an EMS patch on the shoulder lifted the tape. Two more appeared, carrying a stretcher. There was a body on the stretcher, covered with a blanket. Gaby pulled up short. "Howard . . ." She whispered.

"I'm gettin' it," Howard's tight voice came back. She stole a look at him. The red light was on. Even though they weren't live, she knew, they were still connected. She prayed that the recorders back at the station were on and working properly. The EMS men didn't seem to be in any particular hurry. They carried the draped body within a few feet of the camera, to the open doors of a waiting ambulance. They slid the stretcher into the back and closed the doors with a thud.

"That's a money shot, right there," Howard murmured.

"Gaby," Stella said in her ear, "is that—"

"I don't know who it is," Gaby whispered.

"Go find out."

"On my way." As Gaby turned, another man came out from under the police tape. He was dressed in a brown deputy sheriff's uniform. He noticed Gaby and the camera as he straightened up. Disgust rippled across his face. Then he sighed and began trudging toward them, running a hand through his thinning hair before replacing his Smokey Bear hat. By the time he reached Gaby and Howard, his professional mask was back in place. "Lieutenant Tim

Buckthorn," he said. "Gibson County Sheriff's Department. What can I do for you folks?"

"Lieutenant Buckthorn, Gabriella Torrijos, WRHO News. Can you tell us, are the two Powell boys all right?"

Buckthorn nodded. "Evan and Earl Powell were found today after apparently escaping from their abductor. They used a cell phone to call 911. They appear to be in good health, but they're going to be taken to a hospital to be checked out."

"Is the person who abducted them in custody?"

Buckthorn glanced involuntarily at the ambulance pulling away. "No comment" was all he said.

"Lieutenant," Gaby said, "was the body just taken out of here under that blanket the person who kidnapped the Powell boys?"

Buckthorn's face hardened. "That's all the comment I can make right now," he said. "We'll have a full statement later." He walked off, leaving Gaby and Howard behind.

"Gaby," Stella's voice came through the headset, "do you think the cops killed the guy who took those boys?"

"I don't know," Gaby said. "I don't think so. He—that Buckthorn guy—he said they'd escaped. If it was the police that did it, he would have said they'd been rescued."

"Jesus," Stella said. "What if it was one of the *boys* who killed him?"

Howard and Gaby looked at each other. There was nothing to say to that.

THE PARTY WAS IN FULL SWING, ebbing and flowing around the guest of honor parked to one side of the living room. All of the old crew were there, flying their colors on their sleeveless leather jackets. There were some faces Johnny didn't recognize. A few of the men had their girls with them, but it was a mostly male crowd. The music, a mix of heavy metal and southern rock, was loud to the point of being painful. Johnny sat in his wheelchair, watching, savoring the aromas of beer and pot smoke that filled the room. He'd been gone a long time.

Every few minutes, another reveler would approach. There would be some variation on the theme of "welcome home" combined with an awkward pat, sometimes on the shoulder, but more often on the back of the chair, as if the well-wisher were afraid to touch him, as if paralysis were contagious. Some would not even meet his eyes. Johnny kept his face empty, the way he had learned to do inside. He hated them. He was surprised at how deeply he hated them all.

"John-*nay!*" A body crashed heavily into the lounger next to the wheelchair. A heavyset young man with his dirty blond hair cut short and spiked grinned drunkenly at him. A joint dangled from one corner of his mouth. You havin' fun?"

"S'okay," Johnny Trent said.

"You looks tired, my bruth-ah," his cousin Clay replied. "We needs to get you a little pick-me-up." He lit the joint, took a long drag, then put it between his cousin's lips. Johnny inhaled as deeply as he could. The smoke burned his lungs, but he held the hit in, not wanting to seem weak. Clay's grin got wider. "There you go. It's gonna be just like old times, man." Johnny started to cough violently, the smoke exploding between his lips into Clay's face. Clay flinched, then made a grab for the still-burning joint as it fell into Johnny's lap. Clay beat at the sparks as Johnny coughed. A few people nearby stared. A couple laughed. "Always knew you two had a thing for each other," a voice said from the crowd.

Clay stood up, his face suddenly purple with rage. "Who said that?" he demanded. Then, louder, *"Who the fuck said that?"* The crowd fell silent, leaving only the music blasting.

"Clay," Johnny croaked, his cough subsiding but his voice still ragged. "Ease up, man." Not that he cared if Clay beat the fuck out of the comedian, but he knew it wouldn't stop there, any more than a hurricane would stop before its fury was spent. "Dude. It was a joke, it's nothing." Clay continued to stare at the crowd for a moment, his expression promising mayhem. No one looked back.

After a moment, Clay looked back at Johnny and his face broke into another grin, a little more forced this time. "Okay, cuz," Clay said. The jollity in his voice was as forced as his smile, but the crowd accepted it with a visible ripple of relief. Conversation resumed.

"Sorry, dude," Clay said as he sat back down. "But da-yum, we got to get you back into shape."

"Guess I just can't do what I used to," Johnny said.

Clay leaned forward, his eyes suddenly blazing. "Don't say that, man," he said in a low, intense voice. "Don't ever say that. It's gonna be just like it used to. Nothing's changed, man, nothing."

Johnny stared at him for a moment. The harsh buzz of the doorbell interrupted him before he could speak. Clay's expression lost its intensity. Now his eyes were dancing with mischief. "You'll see what I mean in a minute." He stood up and walked to the door. He gestured to someone across the room, who turned the music down. "Who is it?" Clay asked in an exaggerated singsong falsetto.

"Pizza delivery," a female voice answered. Johnny was puzzled to see a couple of the other guys in the group nudging one another and grinning. Clay threw the door open with a flourish.

A young woman stood there, holding a pizza box at shoulder height. There, however, the resemblance to a delivery person ended. She was heavily made up, her brown hair moussed and sprayed to a stiff cloud around her face. She was dressed in a long brown trench coat that fell to below her knees. "Hot delivery for Mr. Johnny Trent," she cooed as she sashayed into the room. Several of the guys pointed at Johnny, snorting with laughter. A couple of the girlfriends looked upset. The professional smile dropped off the woman's face; she glued it quickly back on. Someone fumbled with the CD player, and then the opening chords of a DMX rap number blasted through the room. The "pizza girl" dropped the box and shucked off the trench coat in one movement. She was dressed in a sheer red teddy and a bra and garter belt. The men and a couple of the women whooped. One of the girlfriends stormed from the room as the dancer began moving toward Johnny. He pasted a leer on his face, hating her, hating Clay for his stupidity. *Or is it?* he thought. *Is that cocksucker dissing me?* He saw the sloppy grin on Clay's face and decided. *No. He's not smart enough. He thinks he's doing me a favor. Dumb-ass.* His hatred was a general, impersonal thing, nurtured and grown inside the prison hospital like a rare orchid in a hothouse. He hated anyone with functioning legs.

The girl was right up on him now. She had shed the teddy and her bra and was waving her tits in front of him. They were rigid and unmoving despite the girl's undulations. Obviously a boob job, and not a good one. She smelled of powder and cheap perfume. He took a deep breath, taking pleasure in a scent he hadn't experienced in over five years. Some of the guys were chanting now: "Lap dance! Lap dance!" they crowed.

Johnny looked up at the girl. The smile had slipped a notch. She had a trapped, almost panicky look in her eyes as she gripped the arms of his chair and wiggled. She was wondering how to settle herself down onto his crotch. He savored her discomfort more than her scent. He had a brief fantasy of taking a flamethrower to her, to all of them, hearing them scream, watching them burn and try to run and fall down, burning . . .

Something must have slipped though into his eyes. The girl stepped back. She stopped dancing. There was a rumble of discontent from the crowd.

"Um, look," the girl said, shouting a little to be heard over the beat. "I'm sorry, but no one said nothing to me about no cripple . . ."

The whooping and jeering fell silent; only the music still blared. Clay walked over to her, no longer smiling, and backhanded her across the face. She screamed and collapsed at Johnny's feet, bleeding from a cut on her cheek.

Johnny noted that the few women who'd remained after the girl started dancing had now fled as well. The atmosphere in the room had changed. The previous good-time aura had been replaced with a darker, more menacing feeling.

"Bitch," Clay said, his smile gone, "what did you call my man here?"

The girl looked up with the glazed expression of an animal in a trap. She knew the drill, knew that any answer would bring another blow.

But so would no answer. Clay kicked her brutally in the ribs. "*Answer me!*" he screamed. She grunted and tried to curl up. Clay bent down and grabbed a handful of her hair. She screamed in pain as he used her hair as a handle to yank her onto her knees.

"I think you owe my man Johnny an apology," he said, his voice silky and dangerous.

"I . . . I'm sorry," the girl stammered, tears running down her cheeks. She looked at Johnny's face, searching for a hint of compassion. She found none. "I'm *sorry!*" she sobbed.

Johnny stared down at her. Five years ago, a scene like this would have given him a hard-on the size of the *Hindenburg*, but he hadn't felt anything below his chest for that whole time. He wanted to kill her. He wanted to tell Clay to break her fucking neck. But he didn't know everybody here. He didn't know who could be trusted to keep their mouth shut. So he swallowed the anger, adding it like fuel to the furnace of rage inside him.

"Clay," a voice said. All heads turned. A man was standing in the doorway. He was in his early fifties, with streaks of gray shot through his thick black hair and beard. He was dressed in a subdued but expensive-looking gray suit. A diamond pinky ring glinted on his finger. His lined face bore an expression of long-suffering exasperation.

"She said she was sorry," the older man said. "Don't fuck her up so bad she can't work."

Clay released the girl's hair like a child dropping a stolen cookie. He looked down sullenly. "You said you weren't coming over till later," he mumbled.

The man ignored him. He walked over to the girl and lifted her chin with his finger. He examined the swelling bruise on her cheek. He tsk'd at her. "Chloe, isn't it?" he said conversationally.

"Y-yes, Mr. Trent," the girl whispered.

"You're a pretty good earner, I hear," Nathan Trent said. "And now my idiot son has let his temper get away from him again. You can't dance like that." He dropped her chin and turned to Clay, who was still staring at the floor. "Her earnings are coming out of your pay till she gets back to work," he said. "Understand?" Clay mumbled something. "Understand?" Nathan roared.

Clay looked up, his face expressionless. "Yes, sir."

"Good," Nathan said. "Now, I need to talk to Johnny for a bit." He looked around to where the rest of the men were shuffling their feet and looking uncomfortable. "The rest of you boys have fun." He noticed the girl picking up her clothes from the floor. "What the fuck do you think you're doing?" he said mildly.

She looked up, a panicky expression on her face. "I . . . I was just leaving . . ."

Nathan Trent sighed the sigh of an employer surrounded by idiots. "I said you couldn't dance," he snapped. "I know damn well you were hired for more than that." He turned to Clay and raised a warning finger. "Remember," he said, "no more marks."

Clay's eyes glinted. "Don't worry, Dad," he said. He looked down at the cowering girl, smiling unpleasantly. "Just good clean fun and games."

Nathan smiled thinly. "Good," he said. "Come with me," he said to Johnny. He walked down the hallway toward the back bedrooms.

The motorized wheelchair whirred and groaned as Johnny used the joystick to maneuver down the hallway behind his uncle. The chair was slow; Nathan was seated on the edge of the bed by the time Johnny got there.

"It's good to see you," he said.

Johnny nodded. "Thanks for all you've done," he said.

Nathan waved a hand in a dismissive gesture. "I'm just sorry it took so long," he said. "Five years is a long time to spend in a prison hospital."

"Yeah," Johnny said. "It is."

Nathan sighed. "Compassionate release should have been a no-brainer considering . . . well. Considering your condition," he said. "But there were people who thought they could use you as leverage to get to me. Some of them may have thought you'd give me up in order to get out."

"I didn't," Johnny said.

"I know," Nathan said. "And believe me, I appreciate that kind of loyalty. And I reward it."

"I don't want you to think I don't appreciate it," Johnny said. "Not only arranging the CR. The other stuff. The van, the ramps at the house. All that."

Nathan nodded slightly. "Anything you need?"

Johnny leaned forward slightly. "You know what I want," he said. "There's only one thing in this world I want."

Nathan sighed. "I know, Johnny," he said. "You're not the only one he fucked over, you know. He took off with a shitload of my money."

"He didn't take your legs," Johnny spat.

"I know, John, I know. We've looked for him. All over. It's like he disappeared off the face of the earth."

"Maybe he went into witness protection," Johnny said.

Nathan shook his head. "No," he said decisively. "He never testified. Besides, if he'd gone that route . . ."

"What?"

"I'd have known," Nathan said. "Just leave it at that."

"Still got your guy on the inside, then?" Johnny said, too casually.

Nathan's voice sharpened. "I said leave it," he snapped. Then he smiled. He stood up, straightening his cuffs as he did so. "Believe me, Johnny, we'll find him. He'll fuck up. He'll do something to call attention to himself. And when he does . . ." He made a quick slashing motion across his throat.

"I don't want him dead," Johnny said.

Nathan looked surprised. "You don't?"

"No," Johnny said. "I want you to take his legs from him. Like he took mine. I want him to live like I live."

Nathan's smile was the grin of a shark opening its mouth to devour. "Damn," he said, "but I like the way you think, Johnny. You always were the one with the brains. Not like . . ." He stopped, sighed, and moved to the door. "I need to see if we can find you something," he said. "A mind like yours can't go to waste."

Johnny knew it was an empty promise. There was no work in the Brotherhood for a man with a pair of useless legs. At that moment, Johnny Trent hated his uncle most of all.

CHAPTER FOUR

S ANDERS'S HOUSE STOOD AT THE TOP of a tall ridge, dead center in the middle of what was still known as "the Jacobs land." In the 1930s, Arlie Jacobs had been the largest landowner in Gibson County, making his considerable fortune farming tobacco and hay. Harsher times, hapless descendants, and rising property taxes had caused the land to fall away and out of the family, until what had once been practically a plantation was whittled down to just an old farmhouse in the center of ten acres. The house had originally been built in 1863, but it was still solid.

Even though he didn't farm the land, Sanders kept the fields clear of brush and weeds, mowing the grass twice a month with the tractor-pulled mower that he kept in the barn. He had also removed all the shrubbery, including a stand of crepe myrtle that had been the previous owner's pride and joy. From his windows, Sanders could look away down the long slopes of the ridge, at greenery trimmed as close as the fairway on a golf course. Some of the locals found his obsession with keeping such a huge plot of land so neatly groomed to be more than a little odd; others nodded with approval. It wasn't a desire to be tidy that kept

Sanders at the hot, dusty task of mowing, though. No one could approach the house unseen.

Sanders drove up the long driveway, a plume of dust rising behind the truck. He stopped under one of the huge oak trees that flanked the front porch. He took a deep breath. His hands were clenched so tightly on the wheel that they were almost numb. Slowly, he unwrapped his bloodless fingers from the wheel. He leaned back and closed his eyes. He could feel himself begin to shake, as if a fever were robbing him of muscle control. He let it wash over him. He knew it would pass; it always did. He regarded it as the payback his body took for not betraying him in moments of high stress.

After a few minutes, he felt the trembling subside. He opened his eyes. As the adrenaline slowly drained out of him, he felt logical thought return. What the hell had he been thinking? Did he really expect the two kids to keep quiet about the man who had burst in with a blazing gun and killed their kidnapper? Still, he thought, they didn't know him. There was nothing to connect him with anything local.

He looked at the house. It wasn't a particularly lovely structure; Arlie Jacobs had been a blunt, plain man with little patience for aesthetics. It was a utilitarian two-story box. Further, it had been a major pain in the ass to get back into shape. The previous owner, a grandson of the builder, had had a long decline before he had gotten bad enough to move to the hospital, where he died six weeks after leaving the land. The house had gone downhill with him, and Sanders, unused to handyman work, had sweated and cursed and done himself half a dozen minor injuries before the place had become halfway livable. Yet for some reason, Sanders found himself strangely unwilling to leave. The feeling surprised him. He had never been sentimental about places.

Sanders got out of the truck. He decided that there was no need to run from this place just yet. Still, there were preliminary steps he could take.

He went into the house. The interior design was as simple and uncomplicated as the outside. A wide entrance hall divided after a few feet into a stairway on the left and a hallway on the right that ran to the back of the house. A doorway off the hall to Sanders's right led to a small parlor. He fumbled a key out of his pocket and unlocked one of the cabinets that lined the walls of the room. He removed a rifle with a telescopic sight and a web sling. He slung it over his shoulder. A short-barreled pump-action shotgun was next, and he slung that over the other shoulder. He went upstairs to the bedroom. He leaned the rifle against the dresser next to the bedroom window. The shotgun went next to the bedroom door. He went back downstairs. He took another rifle and shotgun out of the cabinet and laid them on the rough wood table in the dining room to the left of the hallway. He returned to the cabinet and equipped himself with a pair of 9 mm pistols, brothers to the one in the truck. He slung them into a pair of shoulder holsters and went to a hall closet underneath the stairs. He pulled out a duffel bag, already packed. The bag contained several changes of clothing. It also held a set of identification papers—driver's license, Social Security card, and passport—in a name different from Sanders. He shouldered the duffel bag and walked outside to the barn.

The old tobacco barn had been unused for an even longer time than the house. Like others of its type, however, it had been tightly constructed to hold in the heat generated by brick furnaces during the four- to five-day process of curing freshly harvested tobacco. Even after farmers had all switched to the blocky metal bulk barns, the old structures still dotted the landscape, too sturdy to fall of their own accord and too much trouble to pull down.

Sanders ducked his head slightly to avoid the rusting tin roof of the gallery that wrapped around the old building like a hoopskirt. He entered the barn, stopping to give his eyes time to get accustomed to the dim light. A bulky shape beneath a bright blue tarp dominated the interior. He pulled the tarp aside.

The vehicle beneath the tarp was a 1985 Ford LTD. It looked undistinguished on the outside. Sanders had repainted it to remove the Florida Highway Patrol markings and removed the light bar from the roof. Under the hood, however, was the same police package—5.0-liter V-8 engine, stiffened suspension, enhanced cooling system—that it had used in its younger days.

Sanders popped the trunk. He reached in and took out a pair of large canvas bags with cloth handles. He placed the duffel bag in the trunk where the canvas bags had been, then carried the bags back to the house. He set them down next to the single white-painted rocker and wiped his brow. He went inside and got a bottle of Corona out of the fridge, rubbing it against his sweaty brow as he came back out. He sat down in the rocker and pulled one of the bags to him. A flap on the front of the bag opened to reveal two side-by-side compartments. Sanders reached into the right-hand one first and checked its contents: a roll of insulating tape, a roll of wire, a small plastic device that looked like a pistol grip and trigger with no gun attached. He reached into the left-hand compartment. It contained only one object: a rectangle of smooth, molded green plastic, slightly curved, with a complex set of indentations and protrusions along one side. Sanders repeated the process with the other bag, satisfying himself that all the necessary components were there. He had done so before, and he knew that no one had disturbed his packages since. But he would no more have skipped the checklist than he would have ignored the warning embossed on the front of each of the green rectangles: FRONT TOWARD ENEMY.

Sanders closed the bags and took a sip of his beer, looking down the long slope toward the trees that hid the farm from the road. He wondered if he was being overly paranoid. He wondered if, in his situation, "overly paranoid" was a term that had any meaning. He decided that he would take the two mines into the house, but he wouldn't take them out of the bags and set them up. Yet.

BUCKTHORN RUBBED HIS EYES, pinching the bridge of his nose in frustration. The two boys were hiding something, he knew it—but how the hell was he supposed to interrogate a couple of traumatized kids? The parents hadn't let him talk to them alone for a moment, and they steadfastly refused to bring them back to the sheriff's department for questioning. They had retained a lawyer to back them up. He couldn't blame them, he supposed, but sitting on the designer couch in their expensive North Raleigh home, Buckthorn was the one out of his natural element, and it was making him cranky.

"Okay," he said, "let's go over this again."

"I'm sorry, Deputy," the lawyer said smoothly, from where he sat perched on the edge of the couch between Buckthorn and Evan Powell, "but I don't see where this is getting us. These boys have already told the FBI everything they know."

"We still haven't gotten anything on the guy that shot their kidnapper." They had run the prints and discovered that the dead abductor was one Crandall Biggs, a lowlife with a series of sex offenses on his record. They hadn't turned up anything about known associates. Buckthorn was beginning to lose faith in the FBI's pet theory that Biggs had been shot by an accomplice angry over how the spoils of their crime—the two Powell boys—were divided.

"Mr. Mullens." Buckthorn addressed the lawyer. "I appreciate that your clients have been over this before. I'm just hoping maybe one of the boys will come up with some detail that might mean something to me. I grew up in the area. Lived there all my life, except for my time in the service." He looked at Evan, who was staring down at his own feet. "Evan," he tried again, "did the other guy that was with Biggs . . . with the guy that took you—"

"They weren't together," the boy said. "I don't know who the other guy was."

"I know they scared you. But if you help us catch the other guy, I can promise you we won't let him hurt you. Or anyone else, ever again."

"I told you." Evan's voice broke as if he was about to cry. "I never saw the other guy before he came through the door and started shooting."

"I know what you said, Evan." Buckthorn kept his voice level. "But you can see how it doesn't make much sense that a total stranger would come through the door, shoot this guy dead, then disappear without a trace."

"I'm not lying!" Evan said. Now he was crying. His mother came rushing in and gathered him into her arms. She looked at Buckthorn as if he were the child molester.

Mullen stood up. "That's enough, Deputy," he said.

Buckthorn stood up as well. "Counselor—"

"You can see yourself out," the lawyer said.

Buckthorn gritted his teeth. The dentist had warned him against the habit, telling him he'd started to develop a webwork of hairline cracks in his enamel that was going to cost him thousands in dental work someday. He turned and walked out. On the way to his car, he flipped his cell open and hit a number on the speed dial. After a couple of rings, a voice answered. "Blauner."

"It's Tim Buckthorn."

"Let me guess," the FBI man said, "you got nothing."

A headache was forming at Buckthorn's temples. "Right."

"I hate to say I told you so—"

"Then don't," Buckthorn snapped.

"Okay," Blauner said equably. "We've got another request for you, anyway."

Buckthorn had climbed behind the wheel of his cruiser. "What?"

"We've been going to the stores in the area, trying to get any surveillance videos they have. We're trying to see if our Mr. Biggs might have showed up in one of the local places to get gas or supplies."

"Okay," Buckthorn said. "What does that have to do—"

"One of them, a guy who owns a convenience store, won't cooperate. He won't give us the tape."

"Let me guess," Buckthorn said. "Jeff Slocum."

"You know him," Blauner said.

"I know everybody. And I'm not surprised. Jeff still thinks you guys shot JFK."

"It was before my time," Blauner said, "but I'm pretty sure that was the CIA."

"Yeah, well, Jeff doesn't see that much difference."

"Anyway," Blauner said, "we could get a court order, but we figured he might cooperate better with one of the locals."

"Okay," Buckthorn said. "I'm headed back. I'll stop by on the way."

"Thanks, Deputy," Blauner said.

Buckthorn sighed as he shut the cell phone. No, the lovers' quarrel theory, as he privately called it, was looking more and more like a dead end. As for a theory of his own, he didn't have squat. He was reduced to running errands for the FBI boys. He didn't like it, but it seemed to be the only way he could make himself useful. He had to stop himself from grinding his teeth again as he started the car.

———

"HOW CAN you eat those things?" Gaby asked.

Howard grinned as he fished another Vienna sausage out of the can. Gaby nearly gagged at the sight of the gelatinous goo that still clung to the pale pink cylinder.

The NewsNow van was parked on the far side of the parking lot, away from the convenience store where they'd bought their improvised lunch. Gaby was seated in the open side door of the van. Howard leaned against the passenger side door. He popped the sausage into his mouth with exaggerated relish. "Mmmmmm," he murmured. "Delicious *and* nutritious." He took a long drink from his can of RC Cola.

Gaby made a retching noise, then took a bite of her peanut butter cracker. "You know what goes into those, right?"

"Nope. Don't want to, either." He tossed the empty can into a nearby metal trash bin. "So what next?"

Gaby finished the last cracker and tossed the empty wrapper

into the bin. "I don't know. The FBI guys have clammed up. The family won't let us near the boys." She rubbed her eyes. "Maybe that deputy again?"

Howard shrugged. "You're the boss."

"Okay," Gaby said. She looked up at Howard. "So how bad is it?"

His face was expressionless. "Not sure what you mean," he said.

"You know what I mean, Howard," she said. "Just how pissed off is Brian?"

Howard gave her a thin smile. "Well, for a few minutes there, it was lookin' like our star reporter was going to have that brain aneurysm the production staff has been hoping and praying for. But he settled for pitching his standard hissy fit."

She sighed. "He can make it hard for me, you know."

"Girl," Howard said, "you got this story fair and square. Michael knows that. That's why he gave it to you. If Brian gives you any shit, Mike's a good enough news director to back you up. Have a little faith." He looked across the parking lot. "Huh," he said. "Looks like we don't have to chase that deputy down."

Gaby followed his gaze. A sheriff's car had pulled up at the doorway of the store. She recognized the deputy getting out as the Lieutenant Buckthorn she had met the day before.

"See what I mean?" Howard said. "Have a little faith and the Lord will provide." They saw Buckthorn enter the store. "Now that," Howard says, "is not the walk of a cop who's just here for the doughnuts." He reached inside the van and grabbed his camera.

"Let's set up and wait outside," Gaby said.

"You got it."

After a few minutes, Buckthorn came out. He was holding a small black object in one hand. As they walked toward him, Gaby saw it was a videocassette. "Lieutenant Buckthorn," she called. He stopped for a second. The look that crossed his face was anything but welcoming.

"Gabriella Torrijos, NewsNow," she began as she pulled up to a stop, Howard behind her in position with the camera running.

"No comment," Buckthorn mumbled. He began walking toward his car.

"Lieutenant, I see you're coming out of the Stop-N-Go Mart with what looks like a videotape. Does that videotape contain a lead in the investigation surrounding the kidnapping of Evan and Earl Powell?"

He had reached the door to his cruiser. "No comment," he said more strongly. He opened the door and tossed the tape onto the seat. Howard swung the camera to get a shot of it through the car window.

"Does that tape contain an image of the kidnapper?" she persisted. Buckthorn didn't answer. She stepped back as he started the car.

Gaby lowered the mike as he drove out of sight. "Well, hell," she said.

"Wonder what's on the tape?" Howard said.

"You and me both," she replied.

—

BUCKTHORN DELIBERATELY relaxed his jaw, willing himself not to grind his teeth as he drove away. With everything else going on, he really didn't need the stress of having to duck the girl reporter who seemed to be dogging his steps. He took a deep breath and tried to relax.

———

HIS ENCOUNTER with Blauner, however, did nothing to improve his mood. The FBI man was cordial as he took the tape from him, but when Buckthorn offered his assistance in identifying anyone local who might be on the tape, Blauner's condescending smile had set his teeth to grinding again. "We'll let you know if we need you, Deputy," Blauner said, then turned around and walked back into the tiny offices they'd "borrowed" from a pair of disgruntled detectives. The dismissal was unmistakable.

Buckthorn stood there for a few minutes, fuming silently, before taking a deep breath and walking back to his own office. *I'm behind on the paperwork anyway,* he thought. His position as chief deputy saddled him with far more administrative crap than he liked, and it was constantly piling up until guilt drove him into a desk-clearing frenzy of work that had driven veteran secretaries to the point of mutiny. Janine, the secretary in the front office, was in the middle of informing him in no uncertain terms that the fact that he'd allowed his work to pile up didn't obligate her to work through lunch when there was a knock at the door.

"Yes?" Buckthorn managed—barely—to keep it from turning into a snarl.

Blauner opened the door. There was a strange expression on his face, as if he had seen something he didn't quite understand. "Lieutenant," he said, with more deference than he'd shown so far, "can you come take a look at something for a second?"

Buckthorn got up and followed the agent down the hall. Inside the cramped office, a playback unit had been set up on a folding table, with a small black-and-white monitor beside it. An image had been frozen on the screen: a short, stocky, bearded man standing at the counter of the Stop-N-Go, a canned drink in one hand. He was dressed in a leather jacket and jeans.

Blauner's partner, Ross, was seated a few feet away, talking in a low voice on a cell phone. "Yeah," Buckthorn heard him say. "I'll hold."

"Do you know this man?" Blauner asked, his voice curiously expressionless.

Buckthorn leaned forward and squinted at the screen. "Looks like that Sanders guy. The one who rents the old Jacobs place." He straightened up. Blauner and Ross were looking at each other. "What?" Buckthorn said.

It was Blauner who replied. "How long has this Mr. Sanders lived there?"

Buckthorn felt a strange feeling crawling up the back of his neck. "About four years. Why? Is he on some list?" They didn't answer. "Look," Buckthorn said, "if this guy's any kind of threat, in my county, I need to know about it."

Blauner continued to stare at the screen. Ross spoke into the phone. "Right. Wolf. SAC Kendra Wolf."

The name seemed to snap Blauner out of his reverie. "Thanks, Lieutenant," he said, "we'll call you again if we—"

"Like hell!" Buckthorn exploded. "Listen, goddammit, you can't pull me in here, show me a picture of someone who lives here, look at him like he's just stepped off a goddamn alien spaceship, then march me out the door. I want to know what the hell's going on!"

Ross spoke again into the phone. "Yes, ma'am, he's right here." He handed the phone to Blauner. Blauner took it and motioned with his eyes toward Buckthorn.

"Lieutenant," Ross said, "if you'll just step out with me—"

"Fuck you," Buckthorn said calmly.

Ross sighed. "I can explain some things to you right now. Outside. But before I can give you the whole story, my partner has to clear some things with some people. And he can't do that with you in the room." He opened the office door. "Please, Lieutenant," he said.

Reluctantly, Buckthorn followed him out. Blauner began talking in a low voice before he'd even cleared the doorway.

"Just tell me," Buckthorn demanded as the door closed. "Is this guy some sort of terrorist? Is he going to blow up the bank or something?"

"No, sir," Ross said. "It's nothing like that." He looked around as if searching for prying ears. "If it's the man we think he is," he said, "he's one of ours."

"Excuse me?" Buckthorn said. "He's FBI? So what's the problem?"

"The problem is," Ross said, "the last time I saw that man's picture, it was on the memorial wall at the Hoover Building." He looked back at the door to the office. Buckthorn could barely hear Blauner's voice through the door.

"That man," said Ross, "that guy who calls himself Sanders, was killed in the line of duty four years ago."

———

"THANK YOU, Agent Blauner. I'll get back to you."

Special Agent in Charge Kendra Wolf stared at the office wall as she hung up the phone. It was the standard "glory wall," covered with awards, accolades, and photographs of Kendra with various dignitaries. She saw none of them.

He's alive.

Emotions roiled through her, each one fighting for primacy: shock, relief, bewilderment, anger.

He's alive.

So what do we do about it?

The "we" shocked her mind back into analytical mode. It was comforting. It felt safer to treat this as another problem to be solved. She'd deal with the other emotions later.

There was a knock at the door. Without waiting for her answer, Agent Brett Harper stuck his head in. "Hey, beautiful," he said. "I talked to my friend at the wine store. He's holding us a bottle of Duckhorn Estate Cabernet. The 2002. I figured for our six-month anniversary—" He stopped. "Hey," he said as he saw the look on her face. He came the rest of the way into the room. "What's wrong?"

She looked at him and hesitated. But she knew she owed him the truth.

"It's Tony," she said. "An agent working a case in North Carolina saw his picture on a surveillance camera from some country convenience store."

With detached amusement, she saw the same mix of emotions that she had felt flash across his face. *Well, maybe not relief,* she thought. *Poor Brett. He never was able to keep a poker face.*

"So . . ." he said. "What does that mean?"

"First off," she said, "we . . . I . . . need to call the deputy director. This is a decision above my pay grade." He started to say something, but she silenced him with a raised hand. "I know what you really meant," she said softly. "And the answer to that question is . . . I don't know."

"I guess that means our anniversary dinner is off," he said. He was trying to look calm and failing.

"I think I'm going to be working late," she said. "All of us are." He nodded. Without another word, he turned and left the room.

Kendra sighed and picked up the phone. She hesitated before dialing. In her mind's eye, she saw an image. A plastic stick, sitting on the edge of the bathroom counter at home. The small plus sign in the tiny window at the end. It was such a small thing, to mean so much. *Guess I wouldn't have been able to drink the wine anyway*, she thought ruefully.

She owed Brett the truth—but right now, she couldn't bring herself to tell him the whole truth.

CHAPTER SIX

THE VAN BOUNCED AND JOLTED its way up the pitted road, tires occasionally spinning in the mud left by a recent thunderstorm. Clay was at the wheel, a cigarette dangling from the corner of his mouth. He was humming tunelessly to himself. It was making Johnny nuts, but he kept hold of his temper.

"Fuck," Clay said without heat as the van bottomed out in a particularly deep hole. The impact jarred Johnny's teeth together, and he nearly overbalanced. He kept from toppling over only by grabbing the strap above the door. He glanced at the wheelchair in the back of the van. It was still upright, secured to the floor by bungee cords. Through the rear window, Johnny could see their escort: four Harleys, traveling two abreast. Johnny could hear the low rumble of their engines over the higher whine of the van's motor. It was a sound so distinctive that the motorcycle company once tried unsuccessfully to register it as a trademark. The men on the bikes were helmetless, long hair and beards trailing in the wind. This part of the state, no one was going to stop a member of the Brotherhood for a pissant helmet violation.

The road ended in a broad clearing surrounded by tall pines. A single wide trailer slumped at the far edge. A long, low, crudely built shed ran down the left side of the clearing, at a right angle to the trailer. The bare ground surrounding them was cluttered with old appliances, car parts, and unidentifiable pieces of scrap metal.

A pair of chained mastiffs started barking wildly as they pulled to a stop, with the Harley riders taking up flanking positions on either side. The riders dismounted. After a brief exchange of words, the largest biker, a massive, cue-ball-headed man named Stoney, approached the door. The dogs' barking and growling climbed in pitch. Stoney reached for something in the waistband of his jeans. Johnny rolled down the window. "Stoney!" he called. The man stopped and turned. Johnny could see his hand on the butt of the huge .357 revolver stuck in his pants. "The dogs're tied up, brother," Johnny said. "Leave 'em." Stoney looked at the dogs and shrugged. His hand fell away from the gun.

He turned and walked to the door. His huge hand pounded on the metal framed door once, twice. There was no answer. Stoney knocked again, harder this time. Johnny heard a voice from inside. Stoney's answer was also inaudible, but there was no mistaking the command in the tone. After a moment's hesitation, the door opened. Stoney's hand shot inside the open doorway and hauled a figure out. The other man was about five-five, with thinning hair and a straggly Pancho Villa moustache. He wore ragged jeans and a T-shirt that tore in Stoney's hand as he used his momentum to propel the man toward the van.

"Hey, man!" the man from the trailer said as he stumbled and barely caught himself. "What the fuck—" He looked up and saw Johnny in the window of the van, watching him calmly. A look of shock crossed his face, and was wiped away as quickly. He straightened up with as much dignity as he could muster and walked the rest of the way toward the van under his own power. Stoney followed a few steps behind, his hand on his gun. He looked amused. The other three bikers fanned out around him. As the man drew near, Johnny could read the words on his T-shirt. DAYTONA BIKE WEEK, the shirt read over a stylized picture of a bug-eyed drooling monster on a Harley. Underneath was the slogan: FIVE THOUSAND BATTERED WOMEN, AND HERE I'VE BEEN EATIN' 'EM RAW.

"Nice shirt, Eugene," Johnny said.

"Thanks," Eugene said. He looked at Clay, who was getting out of the van. "Didn't know you were out," he said to Johnny.

"Guess not," Johnny replied. He gestured toward the shed. "Heard you went into business for yourself."

"Aw . . . naw, man," Eugene said. "Weren't nothin' like that. Made a li'l extra for, you know, personal use. Nothin' that would cut into you or your uncle's business. You know."

Johnny drummed his fingers lightly on the door of the van. "Funny," he said. "That's not what your cousin Larry told us."

"Larry?" Eugene scoffed. Johnny could see a thin sheen of sweat on the man's brow. "That fucker wouldn't know the truth if it bit 'im on the ass. Shit, he tells lies just to hear himself talk."

Clay spoke up for the first time. "I don't know," he said. "Larry was pretty anxious to tell us the truth." He walked past Johnny and unlatched the van's sliding door. "After a while, that is." He pulled the door open and reached inside. He pulled out a round object and tossed it on the ground. It took Eugene a few moments to realize what the object was that lay at his feet. In that brief

interval, four bikers drew their weapons: two giant hogleg re-
volvers, a sawed-off shotgun in a shoulder rig, and a Glock 9 mm
automatic. Finally, Eugene recognized what was left of his cousin's
face on the severed head in front of him and screamed, a high,
keening sound of terror and despair.

The door to the trailer slammed open, and a woman appeared.
She was short and chunky with disheveled dirty blond hair. She
was carrying a shotgun. She fired once, wildly. The bikers ducked
as the shot whistled past overhead. The four men fired at once,
the blasts reverberating across the clearing. None of them hit
their target. The woman screamed and racked the slide on the
shotgun. The barrel was on its way down, coming to bear on
them, when Clay pulled a stubby Uzi machine gun from the cargo
compartment of the van. In a smooth, practiced motion he raised
the weapon calmly to his shoulder and fired off a three-round
burst. Then another. The first round caught the woman in the
belly and hammered her backward. The barrel rode up with the
recoil so that the second burst smashed her in the chest and upper
throat. She fell against the trailer, then slid sideways and toppled.
The dogs were going insane. Clay tracked the weapon toward
them, then grinned. "Woof woof," he said. He giggled. He turned
back to Eugene, who was on his knees on the ground. The man
was dry heaving, having thrown up the entire contents of his
stomach onto the muddy earth. Some of it had spattered his late
cousin's head.

Eugene looked up at Clay. He saw no hope there. Then he
looked imploringly at Johnny. "Please, man . . . brother . . . We
rode together. We flew the same colors. That ought to count for
something."

"That's over now," Johnny said evenly. "For a lot of reasons." He looked over at where the woman had fallen. "Pity," he mused, then shrugged. "Least the dogs won't starve."

"*Please!*" Eugene shrieked. He tried to spring to his feet. Stoney shot him through the left kneecap from behind. Eugene fell to the ground, howling like his dogs. Clay nodded to Stoney and one of the other bikers, an enormously obese man called, of course, Slim. He pointed at a nearby stump. "Over there'll be good," he said. They dragged the sobbing, pleading man over to the stump and threw him over it, facedown. At Johnny's order, they arranged him so his head was facing Johnny in the van. Slim grabbed Eugene's head and pulled it up so Johnny could look him in the face as Clay approached, holding a burlap bag. He had pulled a cheap yellow coverall over his clothes.

Johnny had to raise his voice to be heard over the snarling of the dogs. "I got a chance to do a lot of reading when I was inside," he said. "You know how the Vikings used to deal with traitors?" Clay took a hammer and chisel out of his bag. "They called it the Blood Eagle." Clay grabbed hold of Eugene's shirt and pulled. The flimsy thing ripped away easily. Clay straddled Eugene's body from behind, his weight bearing down against Eugene's futile squirming and bucking. He placed the chisel just to one side of the helpless man's spine, probing gently beneath the skin. He found what he was looking for and raised the heavy mallet. When he brought it down, there was a loud crack, followed by a renewed shriek of agony from Eugene as the chisel plunged deep, separating the rib from the backbone.

Johnny went on, heedless of the fact that it was unlikely anyone could make out his words over Eugene's screaming and the baying of the dogs. "When all your ribs are cut away," he said, "Clay will reach in." Another crack, another scream. "He'll pull your lungs out from behind and spread them over your shoulders like wings." Eugene hardly sounded human by this time. His eyes were full of madness. Johnny was disappointed in that. He wanted the traitor to feel every bit of his suffering with a clear mind, so he knew what he was being punished for. Still, it couldn't be helped. Johnny went on. "That's why they call it the Eagle. I hope you don't die before that."

He didn't. It was only when Clay reached into Eugene's chest cavity from behind and started clawing that the man expired. It proved harder than anticipated to actually pull the lungs out, however, and Clay gave up after a few minutes.

"Fuck it," he said eventually. "We made our point." He looked up at Johnny and grinned. The front of his coverall was soaked in gore. His sleeves were scarlet to the elbows. "This'll put you back on the map for sure, cuz," he said. "Don't think any of the dealers are likely to feel froggy after this."

Johnny nodded. He gestured toward the shed. "Burn the lab," he said. "Get the money out of the trailer. Then burn it, too."

"What about the bitch?" Stoney asked.

"Throw her in with the dogs."

CHAPTER SEVEN

"WELL, TIM," SHERIFF HENDERSON Stark drawled, "seems to me this is the sort of thing I depend on you to take care of."

Buckthorn gritted his teeth, then relaxed them again by a sheer effort of will. "Yes, sir," he replied, "but I figured with something this important . . ."

"I understand," Stark said, with the indulgent tone of an uncle humoring a favorite nephew, "and I do appreciate you keeping me informed. Let me know if anything else develops, okay?"

"Yes, sir," Buckthorn said. He walked out of the sheriff's office, followed by Blauner and Ross.

"Not what you'd call a real hands-on type of manager," Ross observed. Buckthorn didn't answer. He knew that Stark's talents were all political, which was why he'd won the last five elections for sheriff. No one even bothered to run against him anymore. Buckthorn knew he was the one who handled all the actual law enforcement duties, which suited both him and the sheriff of Gibson

County just fine. However, Buckthorn felt no real need to explain that to these outsiders.

"So," Buckthorn said. "What do we do now?"

"We don't do anything right now," Blauner replied. "We're waiting for instructions from SOG."

"SOG?"

"Sorry," Blauner said. "Seat of government. Washington."

"I don't get it," Buckthorn said. "I thought you guys would be happy to find one of your own people is actually alive. Unless he really is dangerous and you two are blowing smoke up my ass."

"I assure you, Lieutenant," Blauner said, "he's no immediate danger. At least not that we know of."

"Great," Buckthorn said. "Not that you know of."

"It's . . . complicated," Blauner said. "We'd like to be able to tell you more. And I hope I'll be getting a phone call any minute now telling me that I can tell you the whole story." Buckthorn still looked unconvinced. "Look," Blauner said. "If it makes you feel any better, put someone on him. Just keep an eye out. Let us know what he's up to. Where he goes."

"Agent Blauner," Buckthorn said, "my people aren't trained in any kind of covert surveillance. They're uniformed officers. They're good at it, don't get me wrong. I make damned sure of that. But the cloak and dagger stuff is up to you guys."

Blauner just shook his head. "I'm sorry," he said, "but right now, we're waiting for instructions."

"What about the kidnapping investigation? Did this guy— whoever he is—have any kind of role in the—"

"I would be very, very surprised if the subject in question had

any kind of role in any kind of kidnapping or child molestation."
He raised a hand as Buckthorn started to speak. "And no, I can't
even tell you why I'd be surprised." Buckthorn growled an unintelligible reply, turned on his heel, and walked out.

He stepped into the tiny cubicle that held the dispatch center.
The young woman on duty was surrounded by computer screens
and radio gear. She wore a small flimsy-looking headset. "Hey,
Tim," she said distractedly. "Forty, be advised." She spoke into the
headset mike. "Ten-twenty-six that missing person, subject ad-
vises his grandmother didn't wander off, she was next door having
a cup of coffee." The voice on the other end acknowledged. She
looked up. "What can I do you for, Tim?"

"Tina, who's working sector three?"

She glanced at a clipboard hanging on a nail. "Ollie. He
swapped with Lewis so Lewis could go to his cousin's wedding."

"Get him on the line for me, will you?"

"Sure," Tina replied. She keyed the mike. "Two-seven, this is
County, stand by." She took the headset off and handed it to
Buckthorn.

"Two-seven, this is Buckthorn. I need you to keep an eye on
the old Jacobs place." He searched his memory for the correct address. He squinted up at the map hanging on the cubicle wall.
"1104 State Road 4507."

There was a pause, then the voice of Ollie Arrington came
back. "Ten-four. Anything in particular?"

"No," Buckthorn responded. "Just let me know if anyone comes
or goes. And try not to be too obvious. Don't park at the end of
the driveway. Just cruise by a few times."

"Ahhh . . . ten-four" was the reply.

"He sounds a mite puzzled," Tina said.

"That makes two of us," Buckthorn muttered.

———

"HUH," HOWARD said. He reached down and adjusted the volume on the news van's police scanner.

"That's weird," Gaby added. "Why would the chief deputy ask someone to keep an eye on a house, without anything more?"

"That Buckthorn dude's knee-deep in this kidnapping investigation," Howard said. "Wonder if—"

"Me, too." Gaby grabbed the county map off the dashboard. She ran her finger across the map until she located the address. "Let's go take a look."

"You got it," Howard said as he started the van.

———

"YOU'RE SURE about this?" Deputy Director Paul Dunleavy said.

Kendra felt rather than saw the eyes of everyone in the room turn toward her. She kept her voice level. "Yes, sir," she said. "I'm sure. It's him."

"Well," Dunleavy said, "you would know. He was . . . I mean is . . . your husband, after all."

"Yes, sir," Kendra said.

Dunleavy turned to SAC Pat Steadman, seated at Kendra's right. "So tell me, Pat," he said with deceptive mildness. "Just how do you manage to lose an agent for four and a half years?"

"Sir," Steadman said, "I don't think that's quite fair . . ."

The mildness in Dunleavy's voice evaporated. "I really don't give a fuck if you think it's fair or not, Agent Steadman," he spat. "I want to know who fucked up this situation, why they fucked it up, and how we're going to unfuck it. I suggest you start at the beginning."

Steadman kept his face expressionless, but Kendra could see the muscle in his jaw twitching with the effort. Steadman opened a file folder. "Tony Wolf was one of our best undercover assets," he said. "Former Green Beret. Top of his class at Quantico."

"Yes," Dunleavy said. "If I remember correctly, Agent Wolf here was one of his instructors." He looked at Kendra, who stared straight ahead.

"We've been through that already, sir," Steadman said. "They were never, ah, seeing each other until after his graduation. And he was never in her chain of command." Dunleavy just grunted, as if he didn't really believe it but didn't consider it worth arguing about. There was a brief, uncomfortable pause; then Steadman went on. "Back to Wolf. The guy was absolutely fearless." He took out a picture and slid it across the desk. It was a much clearer portrait of the man in the surveillance photo.

"Wolf was working an operation in western Kentucky," Steadman went on. "We had word that an outlaw motorcycle gang called the Brotherhood was moving into more serious crimes. They started as another bunch of rednecks with loud bikes and bad attitudes. Back in 1987, though, they elected this man as club president." He took out another photo and slid it to Dunleavy. It was a mug shot of a young man in the inevitable beard, long hair, and glower. "His name is Nathan Trent. This is what he looks like now." Another photograph. This one was taken outdoors, presumably with a long lens. It showed the same man, somewhat older. This time his beard was neatly trimmed and he was dressed in a suit.

"Moved up in the world, I see," Dunleavy observed.

Steadman nodded. "Trent saw the potential of having a small army of highly mobile foot soldiers who'd sworn loyalty to his organization. When methamphetamine started coming into the picture, he was ready. Club members became producers and distributors, working out of the bars and strip clubs they frequented. Before long, Trent branched out into prostitution, which he used as both a profit source and a means of keeping his people in line."

"Explain," Dunleavy said.

"Loyal members who'd done well were rewarded with 'freebies,'" Steadman said. "But people who got out of line, owed them money, whatever, might find their wives or girlfriends, sometimes even young daughters, forced into 'working off the debt.'"

"Trent's a nasty piece of work."

Keen grasp of the obvious, Kendra thought. Steadman just nodded. "And he was getting bigger every year. So we decided we'd put someone on the inside to take him down."

"And you picked Wolf."

"No, sir," Steadman replied. "He volunteered."

Kendra spoke up. "He'd been working in CACU," she said, using the acronym for the Crimes Against Children Unit. "Trent was starting to branch out again, this time into pornography. We believe some of the subjects he was using were as young as ten years old."

"Hmmm," Dunleavy said.

Kendra didn't like his tone. "Crimes against children were an obsession with him, sir," she said. "He'd seen some of Trent's 'product.' He wanted him taken down. Hard."

Dunleavy looked at her for a long moment, then turned back to Steadman. "So what happened?"

"We're not sure." Steadman grimaced. "Something went wrong. There was an explosion at one of the methamphetamine labs.

When the fire department got there, they found Trent's nephew, Johnny, on the scene." Steadman took out another photo. "He'd been shot, but he was alive." He pushed the photo toward Dunleavy, who picked it up and studied it.

"So young Mr. Trent was in prison?" Dunleavy asked, noting the federal prison system number on the photo.

"Yes, sir," Steadman said. "He was let out on compassionate release about a month ago."

Dunleavy arched an eyebrow at him. "Compassionate release? Why?"

"The bullet severed his spinal column," Kendra said. "He's been in a wheelchair ever since he was shot."

"What does this have to do with Wolf?" Dunleavy asked.

"We think Wolf was at the lab when everything went haywire. A quantity of blood was found at the scene that matched his blood type. We found his car by the side of the road a few miles away. There were motorcycle tracks all around it, and more blood in the driver's side. One tire was blown out. We think they caught up with him. Or at least that's what we thought until today."

"And now what do you think, Agent Steadman?"

Steadman took a deep breath. "After Wolf's disappearance and Trent's arrest, we closed the operation. We had a major player in custody, and we figured our inside man was blown. But we still had some secondary sources. We started to get word that the Trent organization had suffered some sort of major catastrophe. Johnny Trent was his uncle's heir apparent. In many ways he was the one driving the push into new areas. So his injury and his incarceration were a major blow. But it was more than that, and more than the loss of one meth lab. Our other sources had heard of a large quantity of cash that had gone missing."

Dunleavy glanced at Kendra. She sat rigid, her lips in a tight line. He turned back to Steadman. "You think he may have taken the money and run? Gone into business for himself?"

Steadman hesitated. "We have to consider that possibility, yes, sir."

"And you don't consider that a possibility, Agent Wolf?" Dunleavy's voice was back to that deadly mildness.

She looked him in the eye. "No, sir," she said. "I don't."

"Which is why," Dunleavy said, "I'm reluctant to put you on this matter at all, Agent Wolf. You're too close to it."

"Sir," Kendra said, "in one of the last communications Tony Wolf got to us, he mentioned that he had some concerns. There'd been some talk about a leak. In our organization."

"Excuse me?" Dunleavy said.

"Agent Wolf had expressed some, ah, suspicions he'd had. Some wild talk about a leak in the FBI. Someone feeding information about investigations to the Brotherhood."

"Really," Dunleavy said.

"He couldn't give us much more than that, though," Steadman went on. "And"—he glanced at Kendra—"some of Agent Wolf's later communications indicated that . . . um . . . well, it seemed that the strain was beginning to work on him."

"That's bullshit," Kendra said flatly.

"Undercover work is mentally draining," Steadman said. "The cognitive dissonance involved in pretending to be someone you're not, coupled with the fear of knowing what will happen if you're discovered—"

"Tony Wolf did not go crazy," Kendra said. "He'd been in combat, for Christ's sake."

"A much more straightforward type of stress," Dunleavy observed. "No, Agent Wolf, I don't think I can put you into any kind of supervisory role on this one."

"Sir," Kendra said, barely suppressing her desire to scream at him, "I'm a SAC. I worked hard for it—"

"And you've done a stellar job," Dunleavy soothed. "But I can't let you run this operation, Agent Wolf, any more than a hospital would let a surgeon operate on his own wife or child. You have no objectivity in this situation, and no one would expect you to. You're only human, after all." Dunleavy still managed to make the last sentence sound like a personal failing. He turned to Steadman. "It's your ball, Pat," he said. "Take whoever and whatever you need. Find out what's going on with Tony Wolf. And bring him back, even if you have to do it in handcuffs."

"Sir," Kendra tried again.

"That's all, people," Dunleavy said. "I'll brief the director. And I don't think I need to tell you that we need to keep this matter out of the public eye as much as possible."

OUTSIDE, STEADMAN turned to her. "He's right, you know," he said gently. "There's no way you can run this op."

She stared at the floor. "At least put me on the team," she said. "He'll talk to me."

"How do you know that?" he demanded. "He hasn't contacted you in over four years."

She looked up. "I know him, Pat," she said. "I can at least advise you."

"Are you sure, Kendra?" he said. "Are you sure how well you know him?" He sighed. "Okay. Dunleavy'll probably scream, but he said it's my ball to run with. You can come."

She smiled. "Thanks, Pat," she said. "I owe you."

"Yes, you do," he said. "And you can start paying it back by getting on the phone and rustling up an aircraft. We'll need"—he thought—"room for you, me, and two others."

"Who else?"

He pursed his lips. "Simmons," he decided, "and Harper." He saw the expression on her face. "What's wrong with Harper?"

She willed her face back into neutral. "Nothing," she said. "Nothing at all." *Oh, shit,* she thought. *You think I've got a conflict of interest.* She knew she should say something to Steadman. Her career would take a blow, she knew, if her relationship with an agent below her in rank became known. But so would Brett's, and she didn't know if his could survive it.

"Come on," Steadman said, "we've got to get going. I want us wheels up within the next two hours."

With that, she felt the opportunity pass.

CHAPTER EIGHT

TONY WOLF, THE MAN THE TOWN OF PINE Lake knew as Sanders, slowed as he approached his driveway. He could find no obvious reason for the vague feeling of unease as he approached, but he'd learned to trust the feeling. He saw a sheriff's car approaching from the opposite direction. That in itself wouldn't be out of the ordinary. But then the car slowed. Wolf could see the face of the man behind the wheel. The deputy was looking straight at him. When the deputy pulled his radio mike to his face and began talking, Wolf's vague sense of wrongness turned into a jolt of adrenaline as if an alarm bell had begun clanging in his head. The sheriff's car slowed a bit more, then sped up and drove away. Wolf turned in to the driveway. He saw an unfamiliar white van parked at the front steps.

"God *damn* it," he muttered. He considered turning and driving away at top speed, then rejected the idea. He could still put them off. There were things he needed before he could run.

Two people were standing outside the van as he pulled up: a dark-haired young woman and a lanky black man with short graying hair. There was a TV camera rig on the ground next to him.

As he got out, he noted the woman's thick glossy black hair, the fineness of her features, the big dark eyes . . . then he noticed the microphone in her hand, and all that became insignificant. The man had raised the camera to his shoulders. Wolf saw the red light above the lens go on.

"Mr. Sanders?" the woman asked.

"Turn that thing off." Wolf's voice was deadly calm. He held up a hand between himself and the lens. The cameraman deftly stepped to one side to keep Wolf in the shot.

The woman held up the mike. "Mr. Sanders," she repeated, "I'm Gabriella Torrijos from Channel 12 NewsNow. Can you tell us what—"

"I said *turn that goddamn thing off!*" he bellowed. He could see the cameraman's grin. The bastard was enjoying himself. Wolf stepped back to the car and opened the door. As he ducked back inside, the woman tried again. "Mr. Sanders, can you tell us what connection you have with the kidnapping of the Powell brothers and the . . ." She trailed off as Wolf came up holding the Glock. The cameraman's grin faded. Wolf swung the gun on him. "Turn. It. Off."

The red light went out. "Be cool, man," the cameraman said. His voice shook slightly. "Just be cool."

"Take the tape out," Wolf said. "Slowly." As the cameraman set the camera down on the ground, he swung the gun back toward the woman. "Turn the mike off."

She stood there, wide-eyed, her mouth open as if frozen in midword.

"I don't want to shoot you," Wolf said in that same deadly calm voice. "But I really don't want to be on television."

"Yeah, I'm kinda gettin' that," the cameraman said. "I got bad news, though."

Wolf swung the gun back to him. "What?"

"There ain't no tape. It's all digital now."

"Fuck," Wolf muttered. "Can you erase it?"

"Yeah," the cameraman said. He looked as if the words left a bad taste in his mouth.

"Do it."

The cameraman sighed and bent down. He began fiddling with the camera. After a moment, he straightened back up. "Done," he said. "Now what?"

Wolf turned the gun on the woman. "Now," he said. "You two are going to get back in that van and get the fuck off my property. I'll keep the camera, just to make sure that there's nothing on there."

"Okay," the woman said. She had one hand up in a placating gesture. "Just please. Put the gun down."

Wolf shook his head. "Sorry," he said. "I really wish I didn't have to do this."

"Yeah, us, too," the cameraman said. "C'mon, Gaby." He was staring to move toward the truck when another vehicle appeared at the bottom of the driveway. All three of them turned to see the sheriff's cruiser slow, then stop.

"*Fuck,*" Wolf spat. He could see a tall deputy with close-cropped black hair getting out. The deputy's gun was in his right hand.

Wolf covered the distance between himself and the woman in a few quick strides. The deputy was yelling something. Wolf couldn't make it out, but he got the gist. Put the gun down, step away, etc. He yanked the woman in front of him and put the gun to her head. She screamed. The deputy leveled his gun.

"No closer!" Wolf yelled.

The deputy called out again. This time Wolf could hear. *"Put the gun down, sir!"*

"In the house," Wolf ordered in a low voice. He began backing toward the door, keeping the woman between him and the deputy. The cameraman was just standing there. *"Move!"* Wolf snapped.

The cameraman turned and looked at him. "Let her go, man," he said. His voice sounded rusty. "Take me. C'mon. I'll stay. But let her go."

"Sorry," Wolf said. "I need all the insurance I can get." He backed closer to the door. "You both come in with me, and I promise you this. No one gets hurt. I meant it when I said I don't want to shoot anybody." The man looked at him for another moment, then followed. "Get between us and the cop," Wolf ordered. The deputy was back inside the car, on the radio. "We haven't got a lot of time."

CHAPTER NINE

"SHIT!" BUCKTHORN YELLED. Blauner and Ross came piling out of the borrowed office in time to catch the full blast of his rage.

"Your goddamned 'dead' agent just took a TV reporter and her cameraman hostage." They glanced at each other in confusion.

"We just got off the phone," Ross said. "There's a team on the way."

"Well, they're going to be late for the party," Buckthorn said. He stormed out and into the communications room. "I need all units," he barked. "We've got a hostage situation, so we need full tac gear. Out at the Jacobs farm. Establish a perimeter. They know the drill." *At least I hope they remember,* he thought. The department had done a training exercise dealing with a simulated hostage situation, but that had been a year and a half ago.

"Ollie wants to know what he should do," the dispatcher said.

"Tell him to stay put. Don't approach. Wait till I get there."

"Got it." She began relaying the instructions in a tight, clipped voice. She, at least, was staying cool.

—

THEY HAD made good time into the Raleigh-Durham airport. Steadman had abandoned the effort to get a chopper, after considering the cost versus the small time saved on what would be a relatively short hop. A pair of black Ford Tauruses sat on the tarmac near where they were debarking from the airplane. "Simmons, Harper," Steadman said, pointing at one of the cars, "you take that one. Wolf, you're with me. You've got the map?"

"Yes, sir," Kendra said. She was secretly relieved that she wouldn't have to ride with Brett. It had been hard enough being on the plane with him. She could feel him staring at her from time to time, and she still didn't know what to say. Everything was just happening too fast for her to sort out.

The interior of the car was cooler than the heat on the tarmac, but not by much. Steadman started the car and cranked the AC up all the way. "So," he said as he pulled out, "what's with you and Harper?"

Kendra gave him a startled look, then slumped into her seat with a resigned sigh. "Which one of us gave it away?"

"Both of you," Steadman said.

She was relieved to see that he didn't seem to be particularly angry. Then again, that was never his way. Steadman was a man who assessed situations rather than reacting by instinct or emotion. He gathered information, then calmly, some said coldly, planned and strategized, whether the situation was a case or a career move.

"Harper couldn't stop looking at you," he went on, "and you wouldn't look at him. That says one thing to me."

"Yeah. Okay," said Kendra. "We've been dating."

"How serious are you?" Steadman asked.

"That's none of your—" She stopped. "Okay, I guess it is your business. It's your team."

"Good." He kept his eyes on the road. "You haven't totally lost your objectivity."

"Yeah, well, I learned that from the best."

"Flattery won't keep you from having to answer my question."

She sighed. "It's pretty serious." She was damned if she was going to tell him about the baby. That was strictly need-to-know, and right now, as much as she admired Steadman and as much as she knew she owed him, this was something only she needed to know.

"Can you work with him?"

She thought a moment. She knew her only hope of staying off her mentor's shit list was total honesty. "It wouldn't be my first choice," she said, "but yeah. I can."

For the first time, he showed emotion. He sighed. "I can't help you, Kendra," he said, "if I don't know what's going on."

"I know, Pat," she said, "and I'm sorry. It was my mistake." He was silent. She went on. "I owe you a lot. You've been a big help to my career."

"You're a good agent," he said. "Possibly one of the best I've ever seen. I wouldn't consider the directorship out of your reach." He glanced at her, then back to the road. "But you've got to get your personal life under control."

She flushed with anger, hating herself for doing it. It was bad enough he was talking to her like a child, but letting herself react like one . . . When she answered, she kept her voice steady. "I know."

"I managed to contain the fallout over what happened with

Tony the first time. Now . . ." He shook his head. "Well, we'll see."

Holy shit, she thought. *He's worried.* And if the situation could rattle SAC Patrick Steadman, then it damn sure worried her.

Steadman's cell phone rang. He snapped it open with more force than was strictly necessary. That worried her even more. "Yes?" He listened for a long time, his face absolutely blank. Then he answered, "We'll be there in a little under an hour." He closed the phone. He didn't look at Kendra.

"What?" she said.

"Tony just took a TV reporter and her cameraman hostage."

———

"WHAT'S YOUR name?" Wolf asked. He finished duct-taping the cameraman's ankles to the arms of the antique dining chair he had dragged into the front hallway.

"Howard," the man said. "Howard Jessup."

"I'll tell you this, Howard," Wolf said. "That was pretty brave, offering yourself up like that."

"Just let the lady go, man," Howard said. "How many hostages you need?"

Wolf glanced at Gaby. She was sitting on the floor where he had put her, her back against the door. Her knees were drawn up to her chest. He could see her legs shaking in fear, see the whites of her eyes showing.

"You're not a hostage, Howard," he said. "She's a hostage. You're a diversion." He stepped out of the hallway for a second. When he came back, he was carrying a burlap sack. "Were you ever in the service, Howard?"

Howard swallowed. "No," he said.

Wolf took an object out of the bag. "Okay. Let me tell you what this is." He did.

"Oh, shit," Howard said.

H E WENT IN THE HOUSE, SIR," the deputy told Buckthorn. "He took two people in with him. A man and a
woman. Haven't seen nothing since."

"Good work, Ollie," Buckthorn said. Other cars were
beginning to arrive, both the on-duty vehicles and the personal
vehicles of off-duty officers who'd heard the news and were showing up to help. Buckthorn was pleased to see them deploying by
the numbers, just as they'd practiced. They were arriving in good
order, arming themselves with the rarely used assault weapons and
Kevlar vests from their trunks, and forming a decent perimeter.
Not bad, he thought to himself with savage satisfaction. He was
acutely aware of the presence of the two FBI men, Blauner and
Ross. Ross sat a few feet away in Buckthorn's car, talking into his
cell phone. Blauner stood a few feet away, not speaking. When
they'd run their first practice session a year and a half ago, the
State Bureau of Investigation had sent an instructor down to
teach them the proper technique. The SBI man had been a pa-
tronizing little prick from Raleigh, and his barely concealed scorn
had driven Buckthorn to drill his teams without mercy, till even

the most gung-ho of the young guys had their tongues hanging out from exhaustion. Now that practice was paying off in front of the Feds.

"Sir?" Arrington said.

"All teams," Buckthorn said into the mike clipped to his shoulder. "Report."

"Team one," the deputy in charge of the three covering the front door said. He was in the car next to Buckthorn's, the two vehicles blocking the driveway. He was close enough that Buckthorn could hear him without the radio. "In position."

"Team two." The voice was scratchy over the radio, but Buckthorn could hear that the man was out of breath. *When this is over,* Buckthorn promised himself, *we're going to see about getting Reggie Comer on the treadmill a few times a week.* "Moving . . . into position," Comer panted. Through the speaker, Buckthorn heard a grunt of surprise; then a loud hissing sound erupted from the woods on one side of the house. Everyone flinched as a bright white ball of flame erupted from the tree line, arcing high into the sky.

"*Shit!*" someone yelled. Out of the corner of his eye, Buckthorn saw the nearest weapons tracking toward the disturbance.

"*Hold fire!*" he bellowed into the radio. "*Hold fire!*" He could feel the tension crackling in the air like dry lightning, but no one fired. "What the hell was that?" he barked into the mike.

"Some kind of booby trap," Comer panted. "I tripped over a wire or something."

"Then he knows we have a team headed for the back," Arrington said glumly.

"If it's the guy we think it is," Blauner said, "he will have figured it out already. He knows the doctrine. Close off the perimeter, then negotiate."

"That's what worries me," Buckthorn said. "He knows too damn much."

"What worries me," Blauner said, "is that that alarm rocket had to be preset. Your guy said he hasn't been out since taking the people indoors. He couldn't have seen this coming, so he had to have had that rocket in place before any of this happened. He's worried about people sneaking up on him through the woods. Why?"

"So we could be dealing with some sort of paranoid? A mental case?" Buckthorn demanded.

"A very highly trained and competent mental case," Blauner said.

"Great," Buckthorn muttered.

"Team two in position," Comer said. "We've got the back door sealed up."

"Any sign he may have already bolted?"

"Negative," the reply came back. "There's lots of brush and leaves back here, and a creek running at the foot of the hill. Nothing looks like it's been disturbed."

"Ten-four," Buckthorn said. "Now for phase two." He picked up the mike.

CHAPTER ELEVEN

WOLF HEARD THE VOICE BOOMING from the loud-speaker down below. "We have the house surrounded," the voice said, the words echoing from the tree line.

He tore the last strip of duct tape with his fingers and patted it into place at the back of the cameraman's head. "Can you breathe all right, Howard?"

Howard glared at him over the tape that covered his mouth and chin. He nodded his head in a quick angry jerk.

In the kitchen, the phone rang. "That'll be the negotiator," Wolf said. "Everybody works off the same playbook." He turned to the woman. She was still seated where he had put her, back against the wall. "Time to go," he said.

She looked up at him, her face a picture of terror and misery. "Go where?" she said softly.

Wolf walked over to a door at the end of the hallway where Howard sat, bound to a chair. He pulled the door open. Howard tried to turn his head at the sound but couldn't get turned around enough to see.

"The basement," Wolf said.

The woman shook her head. "No," she said. "No way. I'm not going down there with you." Howard's muffled protest behind his gag of duct tape indicated he didn't think much of the idea, either. The phone kept ringing.

Wolf sighed. He drew his pistol from his waistband. "Miss . . . Torrijos, is it?" She nodded.

Wolf pointed down the darkened stairs with the pistol. "I'm going to ask nicely. But I'm only going to do it once. Stand up and walk down those stairs. Please."

Slowly, the woman got to her feet. She shuffled toward the door as if it had an electric chair behind it. Wolf stood back to let her pass, far enough that she couldn't reach him.

As she started down the stairs, Wolf turned to Howard. "They'll be here soon," he said. "Just sit tight."

Wolf couldn't clearly make out what Howard replied through the duct tape, but it sounded a lot like "Fuck you."

⸻

"HE'S NOT answering," Ross reported.

"He's not shooting, either," Buckthorn said. "That's something."

"He's not shooting *yet*," Blauner said. "You'd best sit tight and wait for our team to get here."

"How long will that take?" Buckthorn asked.

"They just went wheels-up from Andrews Air Force Base," Ross said. "They should be at Raleigh-Durham in an hour, hour and a half. Then figure forty-five minutes to an hour drive. If they can't locate a chopper. I'm working on that now."

Buckthorn considered. "And then what?"

"Then they'll probably want some intel about what's going on inside. Dispositions, locations of hostages, stuff like that."

"Right," Buckthorn said. "I'd like to know about that myself." He raised his voice. "Duane!"

A short, slender deputy with a dark complexion trotted over. He was dressed head to toe in black tactical gear. He had a stubby CAR-15 assault rifle slung on his back. He was grinning like a child taken to the zoo for the first time. His nameplate read WILLIS.

"What you need, Tim?"

"You think you can get up close to the house? Maybe take a look-see?"

Willis looked toward the house. "Don't see anyone in any of the windas," he observed.

Buckthorn nodded. "If we see him, we'll let you know. If he looks to be making a hostile move, we'll lay down suppressing fire."

Willis nodded. "You be sure and do that, hear?"

"Don't worry," Buckthorn said. "I let anything happen to you, your mama won't bring me any more of those good tomatoes from her garden."

Willis grinned. "Roger that." He started toward the house, unslinging the rifle.

"Duane," Buckthorn said. "No shooting. Recon only."

Willis looked unhappy but nodded and slung the rifle across his back. He moved toward the house in a low, nervous crouch. Nothing moved behind the windows. Buckthorn realized he was holding his breath as Willis picked his way slowly up the driveway. He forced himself to take slow, even breaths, but as Willis reached the porch, he found that he had stopped again.

Willis crept onto the porch, avoiding the field of fire from the front door. He drew himself up to a sitting position beside the door, took something from a pocket, and fiddled with it for a moment. When he was done, he was holding an extensible metal rod with a mirror on the end. He held the mirror up to the front door glass. Nothing happened for a few moments. Then Willis lowered the mirror and keyed the mike on his shoulder. His whisper came through the cheap speakers as a harsh rasp. "No sign of our subject," he said. "But we got a problem."

"What is it?" Buckthorn said.

"He's got a hostage tied up in the hallway. And there's something sitting on the floor in front of him."

"What?"

There was a pause. "I think it's a claymore mine."

"Holy fuck," Buckthorn said.

Blauner looked at him. "What's that?"

Buckthorn shaped a semicircle in the air with his hand. "Antipersonnel weapon," he said. "It's a shaped plastic explosive charge with, like, ball bearings imbedded in the front. When it goes off it sprays a whole area like a giant shotgun."

Blauner looked at Buckthorn soberly. "If that thing goes off right in front of a hostage," he said, "they'll be scraping him off the walls."

"Duane," Buckthorn said into the mike, "are you sure?"

"Pretty sure," the answer came back. "I worked with 'em when I was in the marines. Nasty little critters."

"Ask him if he can see the trigger," Blauner said. "Is it wired to anything?" Buckthorn passed the question on.

"I can see a string or wire or something leading to it," Willis came back, "but I can't see where it goes."

"He's probably got it wired to the door," Ross said.

"Shit," Buckthorn muttered. "This guy is nuts."

"But where is he?" Blauner said.

W HAT'S HAPPENING?" Gaby asked. "Why are we down here? What's going to happen to Howard?"

The man didn't answer. He prodded Gaby gently in the back with the pistol. "Go sit over there," he said.

She looked where he was pointing. The cellar was damp and cool, with brick walls that looked ancient. The floor looked like clay.

"I'm not sitting on that floor," she said positively. She took hold of the lapel of her suit jacket. "This is a Donna Karan. It cost me damn near a month's salary."

The man stared at her for a moment in disbelief; then he laughed sharply. "Okay, then," he said. "Stand. But be quiet." He walked over to a wooden rack on the wall. Various rusted tools and dusty glass jars lined the shelves. He set the pistol on one of the shelves and stepped to one side. Gaby tensed slightly, trying to decide whether to try to flee. He whipped the gun off the shelf so fast she barely saw the movement until the weapon was pointed at her again. "Don't" was all he said. She froze. He put the gun back down and began tugging at one side of the shelf. It slid away from the wall slowly, the glass jars rattling and clanking against one another. Gaby saw a door-sized hole gaping in the wall behind it.

"Wh—what's that?"

"It's the reason I rented the house," he said. He picked up the gun and reached into the darkness. He came out with a flashlight in one hand. He turned it on. There was a tunnel in the wall. The flashlight beam only pierced the dusty gloom for a few feet.

"After you," he said.

"I can't go in there," Gaby said. "It looks . . . it looks snakey in there."

"It's safe," the man said, "and there aren't any snakes. At least not the last time I checked it." He motioned with the gun again. "We need to get a move on," he said. He held the flashlight out to her. "You go first."

Gaby considered turning and running and taking her chances. She considered grabbing the flashlight and trying to club the strange man with the gun. She remembered his quickness, however, and knew it would be suicide. She walked to him and took the flashlight. She shined it into the tunnel. It was lined with the same old brick as the cellar. "Where does it go?" she asked, struggling to keep her voice steady.

"The old toolshed, behind the barn," the man said. He poked her in the back with the gun, not too hard. She took a deep breath and walked inside. The ceiling was low and the walls close, and Gaby fought back a swelling of panic.

"Interesting story, actually," the man said. His voice was matter-of-fact, as if he were giving a lecture in a schoolroom. It was a deep voice, almost soothing. Gaby tried to focus on it as she picked her way down the tunnel.

"The house was built in 1864," the man said. "During the Civil War. News was coming in about a Yankee general named Sherman, rolling across the land with an army, tearing stuff up, stealing everything that wasn't nailed down and most of the stuff that could be pried up. The guy who built it decided he wanted a way to get his woman and children out if the Yankees came calling."

"How do you know this?"

"The real estate agent told me," he said. "She spun it as some sort of legend, said she'd never seen the tunnel herself. But I poked around a little and found the loose bricks where they'd tried to wall it up. I figured it might be useful."

It seemed to Gaby as if they'd been walking for hours, even though she knew it couldn't have been more than a few minutes. The tunnel suddenly ended in a wall. There was a wooden ladder attached to it. The ladder looked as if it had been built recently. Gaby looked up. There was a brick shaft above. She felt the gun in her back again. "Up," he said.

"I don't think I can climb in these shoes," she said. She heard him sigh. "I didn't expect to be doing this sort of thing, you know!" she snapped.

"Okay," the man said. "Take the shoes off. I'll carry them up."

She was numb with terror and fatigue. She slipped the shoes off and started to climb. The wood felt rough beneath her feet, but she didn't catch any splinters. There was a wooden hatch over the top of the shaft. She pushed at it experimentally. It moved easily, silent on well-oiled hinges. She emerged into the cool darkness of a small wooden building. Fading light came through chinks in the wood siding. A sudden thought occurred to her, and she whirled to slam the lid back down on the shaft and run. But the man was so damned fast! He was already up and sitting on the edge of the shaft. He grinned as he handed her her shoes.

"Now what?" she said.

"The barn." He gestured to the door with his gun.

The small tool shed was directly behind a bigger structure. "We need to be quiet," he told her. He opened a door in the back wall. At his gesture, she preceded him into the barn. The large space inside was mostly empty except for a rack of tools on the wall, a homemade work bench beneath the rack, and the car that sat near the closed front door. The man went to the door and peered out through the cracks. He nodded in satisfaction. He walked to the back passenger side and opened it. "Get in, please," he said. She got in, ducking her head as she did so. Just as she noted the fact that the rear doors had no inside handles, the man reached into his jacket pocket and pulled out a pair of handcuffs. She tried to push her way past him, out of the car, but he had locked one cuff around her right wrist. She struggled briefly against him, opening her mouth to scream, but then the gun was at her temple. Tears ran down her face as she let her wrist go slack. He fastened her wrists together.

"Please," she whispered. "Please . . ."

The man put a finger gently against her lips. "Shhhhhh." The man quietly opened the driver's side door and slid behind the wheel. He picked up a small object like a remote control from the front passenger seat. As he turned the car ignition with one hand, he pressed a button on the device with the other. There was a sudden flurry of loud noises from outside.

CHAPTER THIRTEEN

BUCKTHORN'S STOMACH SEEMED TO LEAP into his throat as a series of bangs and flashes erupted inside the house. It was like a thunderstorm behind the downstairs windows.

"He's killing the hostages!" someone shouted. Everyone was yelling at once. Buckthorn keyed his mike. "All teams!" he barked. "Move in! Take the door!" Two of the black-clad figures near him bolted for the house, awkwardly carrying a heavy iron ram between them. Others kept their weapons trained, moving back and forth, searching for targets or fire to suppress. But no fire came from the house. The next noise they heard was the roar of a large automobile engine, coming from the small barn off to one side. Then the barn door seemed to explode off its hinges as the vehicle inside burst into view. The assault teams stopped dead in their tracks. The covering teams hesitated, confused by the threat coming from the unexpected direction. By the time the first deputy recovered his wits enough to fire, the car was halfway down the drive. The first shots went wild, and by then the car had veered off the driveway into the grass. They could see a figure in the backseat, a woman with dark hair. One of the hostages.

"*Hold fire!*" Buckthorn bellowed instinctively, then reversed himself. "*Aim for the tires!*" The conflicting commands only served to increase the confusion, and the guns fell silent. The car threw twin rooster tails of earth and grass behind it as the tires clawed for purchase in the soft grass beside the blocked driveway. Then it was past the barricading cruisers and slewing back onto the drive. Now it was clods of dark red clay that sprayed behind the roaring vehicle. There was a scream of rubber as the car hit the hard road in a vicious turn that caused its rear end to fishtail wildly before the driver stomped the gas pedal and straightened out. The vehicle roared and was gone.

In the silence that followed, Buckthorn stood, looking back and forth from the house to the road. He had the poleaxed look of a man experiencing total sensory overload. The he shook his head and started barking orders. "Somebody get after him!" he snapped. The deputies looked at each other, unsure of which one he meant. "Arrington!" Deputy Ollie Arrington jumped as if he'd been kicked. He dove into the driver's seat of the nearest cruiser and cranked the engine. "Secure the house!" Buckthorn ordered the assault team lying prone on the front lawn. "But don't open that front door," he added. Slowly, the team got to their feet, looking at the house uncertainly. Buckthorn resisted the temptation to throw his hat on the ground and curse. He could see Blauner approaching. "Don't you say a goddamn word," Buckthorn snarled at him.

CHAPTER FOUR

CHAPTER FOURTEEN

OLLIE ARRINGTON HAD ALWAYS LIKED to drive fast. Even before he'd gotten his license, he'd snuck out with his daddy's car and gone tear-assing down the back roads of Gibson County, loving the vibration of a big engine and the rush of acceleration on the straightaways, the gut-dropping shiver of delicious fear that ran through him when taking a curve, putting the car right on the edge of losing control. But he was cocky; he knew his abilities and the vehicle's, and like any young man, he knew deep in his bones that nothing bad would ever happen to him. Lucky for him, he'd gone to school with most of the guys in local law enforcement, and the rest knew his family. It was all that had kept him from getting worse than a series of warnings. Then he'd gone on the sheriff's department, where sometimes he was actually expected to drive fast, and that was about the coolest thing he could think of. Like now. He was doing at least a hundred down the long straight ribbon of State Road 1282, hanging a mere dozen yards off the back of the Ford. *Dang*, Arrington thought, *what the heck's he got under that hood?* He considered his options. The easiest thing to do would be to simply punch the gas, give the Ford's rear bumper a little pop, send him into a spin. He'd gone to the law enforcement driving school up in Salemboro; he knew how to do it. But it looked like the driver had a hostage with him. So that was no good. He could try to get ahead, muscle the other car off the road with his own, but he frankly didn't know if the cruiser had enough juice and weight to pull that off. He saw the brake lights come on, so he backed off a few more yards. They were coming up on the curve by Otter Pond. The brake flashed again, then stayed on. The back of the car began to drift as the wheels locked. Arrington tensed up and backed off farther. *He's losing it.* At the last second, the Ford straightened out and accelerated through the turn. *Dang,* Arrington thought again as he entered the turn. *This guy's good.* He realized too late that he'd gotten distracted. He stomped his own brakes and jerked the wheel over, a second too late. The cruiser's tires shrieked as he began to spin. He let up and stomped the gas. Still too late. The back tires were still trying to get ahead of the front. The car went sideways, the back half off the road. Finally, the tires grabbed in the soft dirt and the cruiser roared back onto the road. But the front was no longer pointed straight down the road, and the acceleration carried it across and off the other side at an angle. Arrington jerked the wheel again, but not before the tires on the right side caught in the drainage ditch on the inside of the curve. The car slewed sickeningly and went the rest of the way into the ditch. There was a horrible crunch of rending metal as part of the front grille struck a concrete culvert. A huge white fist seemed to come out of nowhere and punch Arrington backward into the seat. The back of his head rebounded off the headrest. Everything went gray. He could hear the hissing of steam. It seemed to be coming from a long way away. There was another sound as well, a deep rumble that seemed to vibrate beneath his feet. *Radiator's busted,* he thought muzzily. *Radiator's busted. Engine's on. Turn it off.* The big white fist that had hit him was gone. He tried to lift his arm, but the limb seemed to be receiving garbled instructions from his brain. It moved slowly, spastically.

The door to his left was jerked open. He turned his head slowly. The face of the person standing there was familiar, but Arrington couldn't quite place it. The name was on the tip of his tongue, but his tongue seemed as uncooperative as his arms. Then the name came to him, and a blast of cold fear set him shaking.

"Don't kill me, man," he whispered. "Please."

"I'm not going to kill you," the man Arrington knew as Sanders said. He reached over and turned the key. The engine died, leaving only the sound of escaping steam in the quiet. Arrington looked down. There was something white lying in his lap like a huge deflated balloon. *The airbag,* he thought. *It was the airbag knocked me silly.* A sudden thought came to him, and he reached for his weapon. It was gone. He looked back at Sanders and saw with a sinking feeling that his pistol was tucked in the other man's waistband.

"Don't kill me," Arrington said again. Sanders didn't answer this time. Instead, he reached out and gently pried Arrington's left eyelid up. He was too terrified to resist. Sanders repeated the process with the other eye. "Can you walk?" he said. He reached across and unbuckled the seat belt.

"I think so," Arrington said. He wiggled his feet experimentally.

"Then you'd better haul ass," Sanders said. He stepped back. "The gas tank's ruptured, and this thing could go up in a second."

The words sent a blast of adrenaline through Arrington that blew the last of the cobwebs away. He leaped out of the seat, lost his balance on the slope, and fell back against the car. Sanders drew the pistol from his waistband. Arrington put a hand up. "No," he said weakly.

"Run," Sanders said.

Arrington ran, back the way the car had come. He ran blindly, waiting for the shot that would kill him. *This is it,* he thought. *Please, Jesus,* he prayed, *please have mercy* . . . but there was no pain, no blackness. He kept running. There was a giant *whoomph* as the gas ignited. He didn't look back.

CHAPTER FIFTEEN

SON OF A BITCH," BUCKTHORN SAID. He stood over the hostage, still bound to the chair. The black man's eyes glared furiously at him. The doctor knelt by him and began to cut gently at the duct tape wrapped around the man's head and covering his mouth. Buckthorn looked at the deadly little claymore mine sitting in front of the chair. His eye followed the string that reached from the mine's trigger. It ran from the back of the device to the wall next to the door. It was secured there with a hastily applied piece of the same duct tape that covered the hostage's mouth. "Son of a *bitch*," Buckthorn said again. "It wasn't wired to the door at all."

"It wasn't even armed," the hostage said as the doctor pulled the last strip of tape away from his mouth. "He told me before he took Gaby away."

"That asshole," Buckthorn said.

"Hey," the hostage said. "You'd be happier if he'd set the motherfucker up for real?" He worked his jaw as if trying to get feeling back in it. "Man," he said. "That hurt." He looked at the doctor. "You mind cuttin' me loose the rest of the way, Doc?" he said.

"I gotta piss like a racehorse." The doctor got back to work with his scissors.

The door opened. A man and a woman entered. Buckthorn turned, savagely grateful for the opportunity to vent his frustration. Before he could speak, however, they both produced badges from inside pockets.

Great, Buckthorn thought. *All I need is more Feds in my life right now.*

"I'm Agent Steadman," the man said. He nodded, indicating the woman. "This is Agent Wolf."

It was the woman who stepped forward, extending a hand. "Sorry to barge in on you like this, Sheriff," she said, "but I think we have a bit of a situation here."

Buckthorn looked her up and down. She was a good-looking woman, he thought. Tall, slender, with short blond hair framing an angular face. The only things marring the first impression were the dark circles under the striking gray eyes. She looked like she hadn't slept in a while.

"You could say that," he answered her, but not as irritably as he'd first intended. "Are you two the ones authorized to tell me what's going on?"

Steadman avoided the question. "I understand the subject got away."

Buckthorn nodded, trying to keep the bitterness out of his face. "Yeah," he said shortly. "Distracted us by a fake threat to the hostage here." He nodded toward Howard, who was getting up from the chair and rubbing the circulation back into his wrists. "Then he got out through some kind of old tunnel under the house. Took his car and went through the perimeter."

Steadman nodded. He reached into an interior pocket and took out a snapshot. He showed it to Buckthorn. "Is this the man?" Buckthorn took a brief look and nodded. "Don't feel too bad, then," Steadman said. He smiled wryly. "Surprising people is sort of a specialty of his." He glanced at the woman, who looked away. "Come outside," Steadman told Buckthorn. "We need to talk in private. Agent Wolf, you debrief the hostage." She nodded, still not looking at him.

"What's her problem?" Buckthorn asked as they walked outside. He saw other men in suits talking to his officers. His boys stood with slumped shoulders, looking at the ground and giving short answers. Ollie Arrington was sitting in the open door of a patrol car, his arms wrapped tightly around himself as if he were freezing, staring at nothing.

"Let's sit in your car," Steadman said.

"Hang on," Buckthorn said. He walked over and stood by the car.

Arrington looked up at him miserably. "I'm sorry, sir," he said in a low voice. "I lost him. He just flat outdrove me."

Buckthorn put a hand on his shoulder. "Don't worry, son," he said, "we'll get him."

"He coulda kilt me," Arrington said. "But he didn't. He coulda just left me behind, but he didn't do that, either. He come and got me out of the car before it blew up. Who *is* this guy, sir?"

"I'm about to find out," Buckthorn said grimly. "And I'm also going to kick someone's ass for not letting us know sooner. If we'd known what we were up against, none of this might have happened."

CHAPTER SIXTEEN

I DON'T GET IT," THE REPORTER SAID from the backseat. Her voice was still shaky, but she had stopped crying. It was the first time she had spoken to him since they had left the farm. "I don't get *you*. You killed Howard, but you let that deputy—"

"I didn't kill Howard," Wolf said.

"But—"

"I'd wired up a bunch of fireworks, rigged them to go off by remote control. The mine wasn't even armed."

"It was a trick?" she whispered. "He's okay?"

Wolf shrugged. "Unless your friend had a bad heart or he got popped by a deputy by mistake," he said. "But I did everything I could. I didn't want anyone dead."

"You had all that stuff wired up? For how long?"

"Pretty much since I moved in," he said. "I tweak it now and then. Try to improve it. Work on the plan."

"Why?"

He shrugged again. "Man's gotta have a hobby."

"Some hobby," she said. "Wiring up your own house like that, clearing out secret tunnels . . . you sound like you'd been expecting someone to come after you for a long time."

He looked in the rearview mirror at the road behind them. "I have."

"Why?"

"Long story."

"I'm good with long stories," she said. "Why don't you tell me yours?"

He laughed. "Always the reporter," he said.

"Yeah," she said. "Well, it beats sitting back here being scared."

"Maybe later."

"Tell me this much," she said. "The guy who was killed. The kidnapper. You did that?"

There was a long pause. "Why should I answer that?"

"For one thing, the cops think you might have been his partner. The theory is that you guys had a falling-out—'lovers' quarrel,' I believe, is what one of my sources called it."

His hands tightened on the wheel until the knuckles turned white. He took a deep breath and relaxed. "We weren't partners," he said shortly. "I'd never met him before . . ." he trailed off.

"Before you shot him," she said.

"Be quiet now," he said. "Let me drive."

"Look," she said, "if you killed a man who was kidnapping and raping little boys, there are some people who'd call you a hero. Why not let them know?"

"Do I have to put you in the trunk to shut you up?" he snarled.

She recoiled back against the seat as if he'd struck her. She was silent for a long time. "Are you going to let me go?" she said finally.

"In a little while."

"Where are we going?"

"I've got to pick some stuff up. It's in a safe place. I'll take you to another place and drop you off. I'll make sure there's a phone you can use after I'm gone."

"Okay." There was another long silence. "So what happened to the guy who built the tunnel?"

"Jesus," he said, "do you ever stop asking questions?"

"Not really. It's why I went into this business. Even as a kid, I drove my parents crazy."

"I'll bet," Wolf said. Then he laughed softly. Despite himself, he was starting to like her. Of course, he thought, that might be just what she was trying to get him to do by talking about her family. Still, he hadn't had anybody to talk to for a while. It felt good to hear another voice. It worried him a little how good it felt.

"From what I read in the local library," he said, "the Union army finally came through. They didn't go near his house. But one day he and his family went into town. A Union soldier made some remark to the guy's wife he didn't like. He knocked the soldier down. The army held a five-minute trial and hanged the guy in front of the courthouse."

"Huh," she said. "After all that work . . ."

"Yeah. Best-laid plans."

CHAPTER SEVENTEEN

YOU HEARD ANYTHING ABOUT GABY?" Howard asked. They were seated at a rough-hewn dining table in a side room.

"Who?" Kendra replied.

"Miss Torrijos. You know, the hostage?"

"Oh. Sorry. I didn't know the nickname." She paused.

"So?" Howard asked after a few moments.

She shook her head as if she were just now coming awake. "So . . . oh. Sorry. No news yet. Apparently, the . . . the subject got away with her still in the car. We've put out a BOLO on the vehicle." She looked at him. "Be on the lookout," she translated.

"I know what it means," Howard said. "You mind if I ask you something, Agent?"

"What?"

"You been doing this long? 'Cause I've got to tell you, I been questioned by the cops before, and this ain't the way it usually goes."

She stared at him for a moment, then laughed softly. "Maybe it's a new and improved technique."

He smiled back. "Gettin' interrogated by a pretty lady beats bein' put under bright lights and gettin' called nasty names, I guess. But ain't you supposed to be asking *me* questions?"

Her smile lost a fraction of its warmth. She picked up her legal pad and went down the page with her pen. "You're sure you didn't get any footage of the subject?"

He glanced over to where his camera sat on the hardwood floor. "Like I told you," Howard said. "He ordered me to erase it all. He really didn't want his picture taken, I guess. Some people are funny that way."

There was a bustle of activity and raised voices outside. Kendra got up and opened the door. "You can't come in here," a voice was saying. "This is a crime scene—"

"The First Amendment gives me the right to be here, Officer!" someone said.

Howard rolled his eyes as he recognized the voice. "Awww, shit," he said.

Kendra looked back at him over her shoulder. "What?"

He looked at her with pity in his eyes. "Lady," he said, "your day just got way more aggravating."

There was a bright light in the hallway that suddenly turned on Kendra. She took a reflexive step back. "Brian Mathers, Channel 12 NewsNow," the unseen voice barked. "Do you have my cameraman in there?"

"I ain't no way *your* goddamn cameraman, Beav," Howard muttered.

"He's being questioned," Kendra replied. "We'll be done in a few more moments—"

"By what authority are you holding my people incommunicado?" Brian demanded. "Is Mr. . . . Mr. . . . ."

"Jessup," another voice volunteered. "Howard Jessup."

Howard stood up and waved. "Hey," he said. He could see Brian's face over Kendra's shoulder. "I'm good, man. I'm okay."

Brian acted as if he hadn't noticed. "Is Mr. Jessup a suspect?" He tried to push forward.

Kendra didn't budge. "Mr. Jessup is a witness. Now, step *back*, sir."

"I have a right to speak with—"

"One more word, *sir*, and I'll have you taken into custody for interfering with a federal investigation." Brian opened his mouth as if to say something. Kendra leaned forward, pointing at her own right eye. "You think I'm bluffing, sir," she said in a low deadly voice, "just look right here."

Brian's mouth snapped shut so quickly, it was audible from where Howard stood. The camera light behind him died. Kendra stepped back and slammed the door shut. "I am *not* in the fucking *mood*," she said in a savage whisper at the shut door. When she turned back to face Howard, he was shaking with silent laughter and applauding softly.

She smiled, a little embarrassed. "Sorry about that."

"Oh, no," he said. "Don't be apologizin' to me. That there nearly made this whole day worthwhile." His voice softened. "But unless I miss my guess," he said, "somethin' about this case's got you on edge. Somethin' personal about this one?"

She shook her head. "I really can't discuss—"

He held up a hand. "I know, I know. I just want you to know it's kind of personal for me, too. That girl, Miss Torrijos, is a friend of mine. Find her. Please."

"We will, Mr. Jessup," she said. "And for what it's worth,

and"—she glanced at the door—"totally off the record, if this subject is who I think he is, she's in no danger."

"I don't s'pose you can tell me—"

"No." She opened the door.

Howard picked up his camera. "I find out anything else," he said, "you'll be the first to know. You got a card?"

She took one out and scratched a number on it. "My cell phone," she said. "It's always on."

"Got it," he said. "I'm gonna need my camera back, by the way." She looked over at it, frowning uncertainly. "There's nothing on it, like I said. And if I show up back at the station without it, ma'am, they'll have my ass in a sling."

She nodded. "Okay. But if you find anything . . ."

"I'll call. Promise." He picked up the video camera on his way out.

When he walked out onto the porch, he saw a man sitting on the steps, smoking a cigarette. He was a thin man, with long hair and a wispy beard. A sturdy video camera case was sitting on the ground next to him with the lid open and the camera nestled in the thick gray foam inside. Howard sat down next to him, setting his own camera on the porch.

"There he is," the other cameraman said. He shook a cigarette out of the pack and handed it to Howard.

Howard took it and the offered book of matches. "Thanks, Spider," he said.

"*De nada*," Spider replied. "What's it feel like becoming part of the story, dude?"

"Not great." Howard took a puff on the cigarette. "How's the Beav?"

"He's not real happy. That lady FBI agent kinda disturbed his *wa*."

"His what?"

Spider blew out a long stream of smoke. "His *wa*, man. His inner harmony."

"The Beaver has *wa*?"

"He'll have even less of it if he hears you call him that."

"Man, fuck him."

"I'd rather fuck that lady FBI agent," Spider said. He grinned around the cigarette. "Fiery. Must be a Scorpio." Howard just grunted noncommittally. "So how about it?" Spider said. "She bring out the thumbscrews? The rubber hose? Whips and chains? Don't normally swing that way, mind you, but for that one . . ."

"Man, you a freak." Howard laughed.

"Hey, I go with the flow, dude. Only way to be."

"Naw," Howard said. "She was okay. I actually hated to lie to her."

Spider raised a bushy eyebrow. "Lie to her? How?"

Howard patted the camera. "Well, I didn't exactly lie. I told her that the guy—" He stopped for a moment, suddenly unable to speak. "The guy who took Gaby told me to erase all the footage I had of him. I told her I did it."

"Whoa. Man, you're gonna get in trouble. What'd you do that for?"

"Because if I told them I had pictures, they'd take the camera and I'd never see it again. When I get back to the station, I'll run them off a copy. Tell 'em I pulled it out of the chip buffer or something."

"The chip buffer? What kind of bullshit is that?"

"They'll probably figure it's bullshit. But they'll have their pictures, and so will I. And when Gaby gets back, so will she."

"They'll go to Brian, dude," Spider said. "It's his story now."

"Yeah, well," Howard said. "We'll cross that bridge when we come to it."

CHAPTER EIGHTEEN

BUCKTHORN STARED OUT THE FRONT WINDOW of the sheriff's cruiser for a little while after Steadman finished talking. "You think," he said finally, "that it might have been a good idea to let local law enforcement know that the guy they had in the house wasn't just an FBI agent, he was an agent who might've gone bad?"

"Well, Deputy," Steadman said, "we're still not sure about that. In fact . . ."

Buckthorn looked at him and gave him a tight, humorless grin. "In fact, you were just as thrown by this whole thing as we were." Steadman didn't answer. "We're all just sort of making this up as we go along. And he"—he gestured out toward the world beyond the car window, the world where Wolf was out there running—"he had everything planned." He turned to Steadman. "So what's your plan now?"

"We're putting out a BOLO for the car and for Wolf. Every law enforcement agency in North and South Carolina—"

"You don't think he's planned for that, too?" Buckthorn

demanded. "He's one step ahead of you, every step of the way. And he's got a hostage."

"We're reasonably sure he won't harm her. He had plenty of chances to kill or injure people, but he's gone out of the way to avoid those."

Buckthorn nodded. "But you saw what he had in there. If he'd wanted to, he could have probably killed all of us. And the hostages, too."

"Like I said—"

"I know what you said, Agent Steadman," Buckthorn cut him off. "But what happens if he changes his mind?"

"WHERE ARE we?" Gaby said.

It was getting dark. Wolf had left the main highway about a half hour before. They were out in the middle of nowhere, she thought, houses scattered infrequently among the wide flatness of the fields.

Wolf didn't answer at first. He was scanning the road ahead, eyes slightly narrowed, even raising a little bit up off the seat as if the inch or so of extra height would give his vision a longer range. Finally, he seemed to locate what he was searching for and dropped back down with a satisfied "Ha!"

Gaby looked out. They were pulling into a deserted gas station. Weeds sprouted in the concrete of the parking lot, and the plate glass windows in the front of the building had been replaced by giant sheets of plywood. Someone had tagged the plywood with spray paint, a riot of unknown symbols fighting for space on the light brown panels.

"What are we doing here?" Gaby asked.

Wolf gestured across the parking lot. A blue phone box sat on top of a white pole speckled with rust. "Check and see if that phone works," he said. "But wait till I'm gone to call someone to come get you."

"This is crazy!" she said. "I don't know where the hell I am! You can't leave me here!"

"Call 911," Wolf said. "They'll be able to pinpoint where you are."

"You can't leave me out here," she insisted. "It's getting dark." She gestured at the signs on the plywood. "And I'm pretty sure those are gang symbols."

He glanced at them, and his shoulders slumped a bit. "Yeah," he said. "M-13. And Folk. What the hell are they doing way out here?"

"Haven't you heard? Gangs are moving into the rural areas. I did a series on it last fall. Immigrants are—"

"I don't have time to hear it, okay?" He was gritting his teeth. "Shit," he muttered under his breath.

"Look, you don't have to drop me off. I want to hear what you have to say, okay? I know there's a story here . . ."

It was the wrong thing to say. His back stiffened and he turned to glare at her. "It's not a goddamn news story. It's my life."

"People are wondering if you're a criminal. People are wondering if you're some kind of nutcase. I can give you a chance to tell your side of it."

He looked out the window. "You don't understand."

"I want to. And I want other people to understand. You're not a bad person. I can tell that. Let me tell other people."

He looked at her and laughed. "Oh, you're good," he said. "You're very good."

She grinned at him, her heart in her throat. "You have no idea," she said.

He shook his head decisively. "No," he said. "It's too danger-ous." He hesitated. "It's not just the cops I'm worried about. There are some very bad people who'd like to know where I am."

"Can your story help put them away?"

"That's just it," he said. "I think some of the people I used to work for may be working for these bad guys . . ."

She sat up straighter. "Wait a minute. You're a cop?" He didn't answer. "Of course," she said. "It makes sense . . . the things you know . . . the way you act. And you think these bad people may have contacts—accomplices—in law enforcement?"

He laughed again, as if against his will. "Look at you," he said. "You're shaking."

She ignored the jibe. "And that's why you don't go to the cops. You don't know who to trust."

"Well, good. Obviously, you've got it all figured out, so you don't need me. You can go on and file your story and—"

"Not without you I can't." She put a hand on his arm. "You can trust me."

"Right."

"No, you can. And you know why? Because this is the biggest story I've ever told. It's going to be huge. And if I don't tell it right, then that's my ass on the line. You can trust me to tell it right because it's in my interest to do so. Make sense?"

"Sure. But you've left out one thing."

"What?"

"What makes you think I want this story told at all?"

"Because right now, these bad people, whoever they are, think they're safe. They're in the shadows, under cover, and they think as long as they're under that cover, they can do anything they want. You shine a light on them and they're not safe. And the less safe they are, the safer you are."

"You tell this story," he said, "and you're not safe, either. You ever think of that?"

"Remember the story you told me? The guy who went to all that trouble, dug that tunnel? And he died anyway." He was silent. She held her breath.

Finally he stuck out his hand. "My name's Tony Wolf," he said.

She took the hand. "Gabriella Torrijos," she said. "My friends call me Gaby."

"Ms. Torrijos," he said, "we've got to get out of here. I need to change cars."

CHAPTER NINETEEN

THIS IS GOOD STUFF, HOWARD," Michael Ellis said. He was standing behind Howard, leaning over his shoulder and peering at the image frozen on the screen. The man was just bringing his gun up, and his face was contorted in anger. "Good stuff," Ellis repeated. "We're talking award winner."

Howard grunted. "That's not the best frame," he said. "It makes him look kinda crazy."

"Are you kidding? It makes him look like the devil himself. People are going to eat this stuff up."

Howard looked back over his shoulder. "That guy could have killed me—" he started.

"And he's still got Gabriella," Ellis said. "He could be doing God knows what to her now." He straightened up. "Download that still. We'll use it as the OTS for Brian," he said, referring to the graphic electronically placed over the shoulder of the reporter reading the story. "He'll lead in, then go to voiceover behind the tape of the guy pointing the gun. Make sure the sound's off while the guy's cursing."

"Brian's got the story," Howard said, his voice without expression.

"I know you don't like him, Howard," Ellis said. "Just deal with it."

"So where is the Beav?"

"He's at the home of those kids who got kidnapped. He's got a hard copy of that shot. If they can tie this guy to the kidnapping, we're talking local Emmy. And stop calling him the Beav, okay? If word gets back to Brian, he'll blow a gasket."

"Mike," Howard said, "I don't think that guy was in on the kidnapping of those kids."

"Yeah, you mentioned that," Ellis said. "But how else would he have known where the guy was? And why get involved if he wasn't already involved?"

Howard shrugged. "I don't know. It just feels wrong."

"What, you don't think the guy's capable of kidnapping someone? Do I need to remind you he's got Gabriella?"

Howard sighed. "No," he said, "you don't have to remind me."

"Just put the visuals together," Ellis said. "You let the reporters figure out how to spin it."

CHAPTER TWENTY

EVAN POWELL WAS CRYING.

"He made me promise," he sobbed. "He made me promise not to tell."

"Evan," Brian Mathers said in his most soothing voice, "you know that when a grown-up tells you not to tell another grown-up about something, then it's probably something you really should tell someone, right? They taught you that in school, right?"

Evan looked confused. "What?"

Brian held the picture up again. It was blurry from the computer printer, but it was good enough to make out the face of the man with the gun. "Is this the other guy from the trailer? The guy who shot Crandall Biggs?"

"Who's Cran . . . Cran . . . Who's that?"

Brian tried to keep his voice down. "The guy that hurt your brother." The words must have come out harsher than Brian thought, because Evan flinched away.

"Mr. Mathers," the boy's mother piped up nervously, "I really think you should stop now. My husband will be home soon, and our lawyer . . ."

And as soon as either of them comes through the door, Brian thought, *my chance of getting anything out of these kids goes right out the window.* He ignored her. "Evan," he said again. "This is important, okay? Is this the guy that shot the man that hurt your brother?"

Evan looked miserable for a moment, then nodded. Brian straightened up. A rush of adrenaline hit him. He resisted the urge to pump his fist and shout "Yes!" Instead, he said, "Thank you, ma'am. And thank you, Earl," as he headed for the door.

Outside, he ate up the distance to the waiting van with long strides. His cameraman was leaning against the van, smoking a cigarette. Brian fished his cell phone from his jacket pocket and hit the speed dial.

The phone on the other end barely rang once before it was answered. "Hello?"

"It's him," Brian snapped. "The guy in the picture is the second kidnapper."

"Great work, Bri," Michael Ellis answered. "You'll be doing the live feed from there?"

Brian looked over. The cameraman—Scooter? Shooter? Brian couldn't remember—was already hauling the camera out. He was humming a tune that Brian couldn't quite hear.

"Yeah," he said. "We're setting up."

"Great," Ellis said. "And CNN called. They want to go national with your coverage."

"Oh, that's awesome," Brian said.

"Be ready," Ellis said, "we're leading the six with you."

"We'll be there," Brian said.

The cameraman—Spider! That was the name—had begun singing softly.

"There's no business like show business . . ."

CHAPTER TWENTY-ONE

T HERE'S A SET OF KEYS IN THE GLOVE BOX," Wolf said. "Can you get them out for me?"

Gaby opened the compartment and took out the keys. "Where are we?"

Wolf took them. "East Bumfuck," he said.

They were parked in front of the gate of a chain-link fence. Behind the fence sat rows of corrugated metal storage units perpendicular to the road, ranging from small units the size of a closet to giant ones the size of a two-car garage. There was a small metal building off to one side. A crudely lettered wooden sign that read OFFICE hung on the door, but there was no light inside.

Wolf got out and opened the gate, which slid aside easily. He got back in the car and pulled inside, the tires crunching on the gravel driveway. When they were inside, he got back out and closed the gate.

"We staying a while?" Gaby asked as he got back in.

"Not too long," he said, "but I don't want any attention."

"Paranoid much?" she said.

"Yeah," he replied. "I am."

He drove slowly down the driveway, then turned down one of the rows. These were larger units, and the row seemed to stretch for miles.

"Jesus," Gaby said. "This place is huge."

"And anonymous." He stopped in front of one of the larger units and got out. This time, she got out with him. He fumbled with the padlock for a moment, then slid the door up as it, squeaked on its seldom used metal tracks.

"Wow," she said.

A huge black Chevy Suburban dominated the space, looming in the dimness. Gaby could make out boxes stacked neatly in the back of the unit, halfway to the ceiling. There was a toolboard running down one side, with a workbench below. There were objects hanging on the toolboard that Gaby couldn't make out. Wolf flicked the lights on, and she gasped.

The room was an arsenal. At least a dozen pistols hung on the board and at least a dozen more long guns lay on the workbench. She couldn't tell what was in the boxes at the back of the room, but in the clearer light, the dark green metal containers had a military look about them.

"My God," she said. "Are you planning to start a war?"

"No," Wolf said as he pulled the door of the Suburban open, "but if someone does start one, I'm planning to be the one that finishes it."

Very macho, Gaby thought. She was trying to sort out her impression of this guy. When he stopped to talk, he seemed to be someone who really had a story to tell. He intrigued her in moments like that. But then he'd suddenly show her this side of himself. She began to think maybe he was some sort of off-the-wall militia type. "Where do you get all this stuff?" she wondered.

"I know people. Where I've been, you make some interesting friends." He got out of the Suburban again, stuffing a leather wallet into his back pocket. "Come on," he said, walking to the back of the truck. She followed as he opened up the tailgate. The rear seat was folded down, leaving a large empty cargo compartment. Wolf picked up one of the boxes in the back of the unit and worked a latch on the top. The box popped open. Gaby's eyes widened with shock as she looked inside.

The box was full of cash, large bills in neatly wrapped bundles. He took a few bills off the top and closed the box back up. The wallet came out again and the bills went into it.

"How . . . how much money is in there?" she said.

"A couple hundred thousand," he said, sliding the box to the front of the compartment, "give or take." He picked up another box.

"Is that one full of money, too?" she asked.

He nodded and slid the box next to the first one.

"Do I want to ask where all this money came from?"

"Of course you do. The question is, do I want to answer."

"Well?" she said, "do you?"

"I'm still making up my mind about that." He leaned down to pick up another box. This one seemed heavier than the other two. He grunted slightly with the effort.

"More money?" she said.

He shook his head. "Ammo." He picked up a large flat case and set it on the tailgate. He popped it open and raised the lid. The weapon inside looked strange. It had the rough shape of a semiautomatic rifle, but it was much bigger, with a wider stock and receiver than any rifle she'd ever seen.

"What is that thing?" she asked.

"Automatic shotgun," he replied. He pulled a couple of large circular drum magazines out of the case and raised the lid on the ammo box. It was full of red shotgun shells, arranged in neat rows, facing up. He began taking shells out of the box and sliding them, one by one, into the drum.

"For someone who's not planning to start a war, you seem awfully prepared for one."

"May not be up to me," he said as he slid another shell into the drum.

"You want me to help you with those?" she offered.

He shook his head. "What you can do," he said, "is take that bucket." He nodded to where a white plastic bucket sat in the corner. "There's a spigot about halfway down the row there, for when they have to wash out a unit. Fill the bucket about half full and bring it back."

"What are you going to do," she said, "take a bath?"

He grimaced. "I wish." He rubbed his hand over his beard. "This has got to go," he said. "Your pal back there may have been bullshitting me about erasing my picture. And in any case, there are quite a few people who can give a description of me, and some of those are cops. But"—he rubbed his beard again—"they all know me with this. And it doesn't match the picture on my new IDs."

Gabriella took the bucket and went outside. The sun was going down, and there was the first hint of fall chill in the air. She found the water spigot, on top of a rusty iron pipe sticking up out of the ground, and began filling the bucket. She seriously contemplated just taking off, running as far and as fast as she could to get away, but she had no idea where she was. He could probably catch her, and while he seemed calm enough, she decidedly did not want to see him angry. Besides, there was still a story here, if she could get it out of him. The bucket sloshed a bit as she hauled it back to the storage unit, but she managed to keep from getting any on her shoes.

When she got back to the unit, he was standing by the workbench, a small mirror propped up in front of him. A towel, an electric razor, and a plastic basin sat on the bench as well. He was cutting chunks out of his beard with a pair of scissors. "Thanks," he said. "Just put it down over there."

"Look," she said, "can I make a phone call?"

He stopped for a moment, then resumed cutting. "To who?"

"I just want to let people know I'm all right."

"No," he said. "They've gotten better at tracking cell phones."

"Who's this *they* you're so afraid of? The government?"

"Part of it."

"Jesus, you're paranoid."

"Just because you're paranoid," he said, "doesn't mean they're not really out to get you."

"But I mean, this . . ." She gestured around the unit. "The armory, the stash of money, the fake ID—you've been planning this for a while." She stopped. "My God . . . you're not some kind of terrorist, are you? You're not planning to blow up the Brooklyn Bridge or something?"

He snorted. "Not hardly. If I was, you'd be lying in a ditch right now with a bullet in your head."

"You want me to thank you?"

"No, but I would like it if you'd shut up for a minute and let me think." He put down the scissors and picked up the shaver but didn't turn it on right away. After a moment looking in the mirror, he sighed. "Okay. When I'm done, you can call your friend. The camera guy. You'll have thirty seconds to tell him you're all right. But then we ditch the cell phone."

"That phone cost me almost two hundred dollars," she protested. "I'm not going to—"

"Suit yourself," he said, "but then you don't get to make the call." He turned the shaver on and started shearing off the remains of the beard.

She stood there fuming for a moment, then spun and headed back to the car. She was reaching for the door when she felt the pistol at the back of her neck. She hadn't heard him coming.

"What are you doing?" he said, his voice deadly calm. She froze, unable to answer. He answered for her. "You were trying to get your cell phone. You were trying to show me I couldn't order you around, couldn't tell you what to do. But see, the thing is, I can. Because I've got the gun."

"You won't shoot me," Gaby said. "I don't think you're the kind of man who'd shoot an unarmed woman."

"That's where you're wrong, Miss Torrijos," he said. "It's not something I want to do. It's something I'll try to avoid. But I'll do whatever it takes to stay alive. And by the way, if you have anything in your hand that could lead people to me, then as far as I'm concerned, it's worse than if you have a gun."

She turned. He still had the electric shaver in one hand, the gun in the other still pointed at her. There were still patches of beard on one side of his face.

"Who are you so afraid of?" she whispered.

He smiled sadly. "Pretty much everybody." He lowered the gun. "Get the phone."

She was shaking as she opened the car door and fumbled the cell phone out of her purse.

"Come on back inside." He stepped aside and let her precede him back into the storage unit. He set the shaver back on the bench.

"Give the phone to me." She handed it to him.

"Sit in the truck." She complied. He flipped the phone open. "Your friend's name is Howard, right?" He used his thumb on the phone's scroll buttons.

"Yes," Gabriella said.

Wolf held the phone up to her face. "This him on the speed dial?" She nodded. He hit the SEND button. She reached for the phone, but he shook his head and held it up to her ear. "Hands down," he said. "I'll tell you when the call's over." She put her hands back in her lap. She could hear the phone ringing. She heard someone pick up.

"Where you at, girl?" Howard's voice said. The relief washed over her like a cool breeze. She hadn't really thought Wolf was lying to her, but there was still that uncertain feeling that maybe something had gone wrong.

"I'm not sure, Howard," she said. "But I'm all right."

There was a pause. "He holding a gun on you?"

"Not right now."

"Not right . . . okay. Okay. You just stay calm, Gabriella. The FBI's on it. That boy's face is gonna be all over the news after tonight. I got a real good shot of him. CNN's even picking it up. By 7:00 P.M., more people're gonna recognize him than the president."

She looked at Wolf. The loss of the beard had completely changed his looks. It would be hard, she thought, to give a description of him. The man she saw now looked completely unremarkable. "I don't know about that." A thought occurred to her. "Who's got the story?"

"Brian."

"Shit."

"Yeah, I know. And he's following the idea that your buddy there was the kidnapper's accomplice."

"That's moronic."

"That's the Beav . . . wait. What do you think he's going to do if he finds out that's what's going out on the news?"

"I don't know."

A pause. "Put him on."

"What?"

"Put the boy on the phone."

She looked up. Wolf's face was impassive. "Howard wants to talk to you," she said.

The expression didn't change. Wolf put the phone to his ear. "Yeah?" He listened for a moment, then closed the phone.

"What'd he say?" Gaby asked.

Wolf shrugged. "It started off with 'Listen, asshole, if you hurt one hair on her head . . . ; I could figure out the rest." He stuck the phone in his pocket. "He's kind of old for you, isn't he?"

"What? Oh. No. He's a friend. He looks out for me."

"Whatever. We need to move."

"Where are we going?"

"Someplace safe to drop you off."

"What about my story?"

"What about it?" He turned away and picked up the shaver.

"Look, there's something you need to know. The story's going out that you and the kidnapper were in it together. That you killed him because you had a falling-out. Maybe jealousy over one of those little boys."

Wolf turned back toward her. The look in his eyes made her recoil. There was nothing nondescript or unremarkable about him now. "What?"

"The reporter who's got the story now has that theory. I don't know if the FBI gave it to him or what, but that's how they're going to play it. And considering that you did kidnap me—"

"*Damn* it!" He slammed the shaver down on the workbench.

"There's one way to fix this, Mr. Wolf," Gaby said, "and that's to tell me the truth. All of it. Who you are. Why you're running. Who you're afraid of."

He didn't say anything. He picked the shaver back up and turned it on. It only took a few moments to eradicate the last few patches of beard. He turned back to the workbench and splashed some water from the bucket on his face. She watched him, barely daring to breathe while he made up his mind. Finally he spoke.

"Okay," he said. "But it's going to take some time. And I'm not going to do it here. Help me finish loading the truck."

CHAPTER TWENTY-TWO

THE COFFEE TABLE WAS PILED HIGH with stacks of cash, mostly fifties and hundreds. Clay finished the count and nodded with satisfaction. "Not a bad week," he said. He picked a loosely rolled joint up off the table and lit it.

"We can do better," Johnny Trent said.

"Man," Clay said, his voice strained from holding in the smoke, "why're you so wired up? You act like you're some corporate suit, always thinkin' about gettin' more."

Johnny took the joint, gave it a long pull. "So?" he said.

"You never used to be like this, dude. You used to know how to let your hair down. Kick back. Have some fun."

Johnny didn't answer. He passed the joint back and picked up the TV remote. He flicked a button and the fifty-five-inch plasma TV across the room came alive.

"Hey, I got *The Hills Have Eyes* on DVD," Clay said. "Unrated version. It's supposed to be kick-ass."

"Whatever," Johnny said.

"Now see, this is what I was talking about," Clay said. "We're talking major cranial damage in fuckin' wide-screen with surround fuckin' sound and you can't work up more than a—"

"Shut up," Johnny said. The phone was ringing.

"Hey," Clay whined, "What the—"

"I said shut. The fuck. Up." Clay subsided back into his seat, looking sulky. He took a long hit off the joint as Johnny picked up the phone. "Yeah." There was a pause. "Long time no see." Another pause. "What? Why?" Still holding the receiver to his ear, he picked up the remote and pressed a button. "Holy shit," he said.

Clay looked up from where he was rolling another joint. "What?"

"That guy," Johnny said. "On the screen."

Clay squinted. "Who? Where?"

"*There,* goddammit!" Johnny yelled. He pointed at the image frozen on the screen as the reporter's voice described the man who had helped kidnap two boys, killed his partner, then shot it out with the cops before kidnapping a reporter and making his getaway.

Clay's brow wrinkled. "What about him?"

Johnny was speaking into the phone. "That's him, isn't it?"

"Who?" Clay said.

"Will you pipe the fuck down?" Johnny snapped. He spoke into the phone again. "Yeah. So where is this place? Uh-huh. Okay. Thanks. We'll remember you. The usual." He snapped the phone shut.

"Mind telling me what's going on?" Clay said.

Johnny turned to him. His eyes were bright with excitement. A spot of color stood out high on each cheek. "Call the boys," he said. "Get three . . . no, five of your best soldiers. We're taking a trip."

"What? Where? Why?"

"That was a friend of ours," Johnny said. "A pretty highly placed friend. We found Axel."

"Axel? Wait . . . Axel McCabe? The guy who shot you?"

"Yeah. Or at least we know where he was earlier today."

"Whoa," Clay said. "You sure?"

"Didn't you see that guy?"

"The guy on TV? What about him?"

Johnny closed his eyes and counted to five. "That was Axel McCabe, dumb-ass."

"What? That guy? He didn't look like—"

"Trust me. It was. I have it straight from the horse's mouth."

"Whoa," Clay said again.

"Clay," Johnny said, his patience near the snapping point. "We need to get moving."

"Where are we going?"

"North Carolina," Johnny said. "A little dipshit town called Pine Lake."

THEY HAD rented a room in a Motel 6 off the interstate. Earlier, they'd stopped by a Wal-Mart. Gaby had gone in and used some of the wad of cash Wolf had given her to buy a cheap cassette recorder and half a dozen tapes. She was surprised to find him still there when she came out. She had been convinced he'd run.

He sat across from her now, looking at the closed curtain as if he could stare through it and into the parking lot beyond the window if he just kept his gaze steady enough. He didn't speak as she set up the recorder. Finally, she looked up. "Whenever you're ready," she said softly. He looked at her and nodded. She hit the record and play buttons.

"My name is Anthony Wolf," he began.

PART TWO

Soldier

CHAPTER TWENTY-THREE

BLOOD LOOKS DARK IN THE WASH OF NEON. It looked like chocolate syrup on Khandi's lips as she sagged against the cinder-block wall, under the sign that advertised the Leopard Lounge to the horny soldiers and lonely businessmen passing by on the main drag.

Khandi wasn't her real name. It took me a moment to recall that it was actually Amber. Amber's a perfectly good stripper name, but the club already had an Ambyr, so Nathan Trent, the club's owner, had casually decided that she would be Khandi. Before long, her real name was nearly forgotten.

She was young, but more important, she looked young. Some girls went for the classic stripper look: absurdly large, clearly enhanced breasts over a flat belly and slender hips. No woman born of Nature really looked like that, but reality wasn't the business we were in. Amber/Khandi, on the other hand, had the slim body of a preteen and a face to match, and she was either smart enough or afraid enough of the plastic surgeon's knife to play the hand she had been dealt. And it worked. There was a certain audience out there who I couldn't help but think of as guys who'd be

pedophiles if they'd only had the nerve. They were there most
nights when Khandi was working, looking up as she gyrated on
the runway, jaws slack, dollar bills clutched in their hands. She
was a good earner. When she cashed out her "stage fee" to the
club, she wasn't always the top, but often enough so Trent
noticed. She wasn't going to keep earning long, though, if her
boyfriend kept smashing her against the wall like that.

His given name was Frank, but only Amber called him that.
Everybody else, including his fellows in the Brotherhood, called
him Furry. I'd always thought it was for the fur-trimmed denim
vest he wore everywhere, but then I saw him at a club-sponsored
"luau" at a local lake, where the Trents showed their appreciation
to "loyal customers" by charging them a hundred dollars a pop to
drink keg beer and "hang out" with "the ladies of the Leopard."
The "ladies" bitched and moaned, because they'd be getting the
same old ogling and lame attempts at conversation without getting the bills stuffed in their lingerie, but Clay Trent had let it be
known that attendance was mandatory, and none of the girls
wanted to cross Clay. Clay also hadn't wanted the girls' boyfriends
there, but Furry was too big and too dangerous to challenge for
small stakes, so Clay had let that one slide. Until Furry had gotten
shitfaced and stripped off his denim vest, T-shirt, and pants in order to jump into the lake. "Jesus," one girl had remarked, "Winnie
the goddamn Pooh wasn't that furry."

Winnie the goddamn Pooh also probably wouldn't have his
girlfriend jacked up against the wall, pinned with one ham-sized
hand around her throat with her feet dangling in the air. Her hands
looked tiny as they clawed at his tree-trunk wrist. Her eyes were
locked on his face. From my angle, I couldn't see his expression, but

her despairing look didn't indicate that I'd find much room for compromise there.

I sighed. I'd just worked a double shift, 11:00 A.M. till three in the morning, including cleanup and cashing out the bar. I was tired and definitely not in the mood to be fucking around with a drunk asshole like Furry. On the other hand, some things you just don't walk away from. I walked toward them. As I got closer, I could hear Furry's low growl. If grizzlies could talk, they'd sound like Furry.

"Goddamn cunt," he rumbled. "Think I'm payin' for this rest o' my goddamn life?" He smacked her against the wall again, then let go. She crumpled to a heap in the gravel.

She looked up at him, a pleading look in her eyes. "Please, Frank," she croaked, "don't' . . ." She crossed her arms over her belly, trying to curl and protect herself.

"Move your hands, bitch," Furry snarled down at her. She shook her head desperately. *"Move your goddamn hands!"* he shouted down at her.

"No. Frank. No. Please. It's your baby, Frank, I swear it . . ."

"Not for goddamn long it ain't. Now I can kick that little shit out of you, or"—he reached into his vest and flicked open a butterfly knife—"I can cut it out. Your choice, bitch."

"Please!" she screamed, even as she slowly drew her arms away from her abdomen. It was as if she had to drag them away.

I had noticed a little thickening around her midriff. I had thought maybe she'd been putting on a little weight. Now I knew. Amber/Khandi was pregnant, and Furry was displeased enough to try an impromptu abortion. I could feel blood pounding in my own temples. I felt my breathing quicken. I thought back to a summer day on a barren sandy field in North Carolina, where a grinning black man in desert camo was methodically kicking the shit out of me.

"Mad now, boy?" he taunted, each time I crashed to the ground. *"That's why you gonna lose. That's why you always lose. You get mad, you lose. Get icy, boy. Get icy." Then he swept my legs out from under me, cutting off my mad-bull charge, my own weight smashing me to the ground again.*

I took a deep breath and shoved the anger back down. *Ice,* I thought. *Think of ice.* I thought of glaciers. I thought of mountainsides covered in snow.

"Hey," I said as calmly as I could. "Cut it out."

He turned, a look of dumb shock on his face. The shock turned to purple rage when he saw it was me. "Get lost, punk," he spat as he turned back to his work. He drew back one huge booted foot to smash Amber/Khandi in the belly and destroy whatever it was she carried inside her.

Ice, I thought. I reached out with my right foot and hooked it against his drawn-back ankle. *Ice,* I whispered to myself as I pulled my leg back and up, throwing him off balance. *Ice,* I thought as he fell to the ground.

I stepped back, dropping into a guard position. He was slowly rising to his knees. I checked his eyes. There was madness there. So be it.

Ice, I thought as I pulled one knee up, pivoted on the standing leg, and kicked him as hard as I could in the face. I felt the cheekbone and probably the orbit of one eye crunch under my heel. Furry dropped like a slaughtered cow. Amber/Khandi screamed as if she were the one who'd been kicked.

I stepped back, waiting to see if he'd try to get up again. He didn't. I let the cold pass through me and took a deep breath before turning to the girl. She was sitting huddled against the wall, her knees drawn up to her chest. I could see the whites of her eyes.

"It's okay," I said. "He's down."

She staggered to her feet and stumbled over to the mound of fallen biker lying on the gravel. "Frank?" she quavered. "Frank?" She looked up at me, panic in her eyes. "You killed him," she said. "You killed him, you son of a bitch!"

I sighed. Two minutes ago he was ready to gut her; now she was weeping over his limp body. I felt very tired again. Suddenly there were bright lights shining on me, a white spotlight with flashes of red and blue that reflected off the wall. *"Police!"* a voice shouted. *"Don't move!"* I put my hands up. Looked like the night wasn't over yet.

CHAPTER TWENTY-FOUR

TWO HOURS LATER, I WAS SITTING in a brightly lit room, cuffed to a bench while a bored desk officer tapped away at a computer. I had my eyes closed and my head back against the cinder-block wall, but the fluorescent lights were bright enough even through closed eyelids to keep me awake. The clackety-clack of the computer keyboard didn't help.

"Axel," a voice said. Tired as I was, it took a moment to register that that was my name on this assignment. That was the kind of mistake that could get me killed. I needed to get real sharp, real quick. I opened my eyes.

Johnny Trent was standing there, dressed in blue jeans and an Oakland Raiders jersey. He looked pissed.

"Get up," he said. I didn't answer, just raised my cuffed wrist as far as it would go. Johnny turned to the cop. "Uncuff him," he said. The cop looked like he was about to make an argument of it, but if there was one thing I had learned about Parham County, Kentucky, it was that not even the cops wanted to cross the Trents. The cop had a sour look on his fat face as he got slowly to his feet, shuffled over, and unlocked the cuff.

I stood up, rubbing my wrist. "Thanks," I told Johnny.

"Thank my uncle," he said. "If it was up to me, I'd still be in bed."

"Sorry," I said. "Wasn't how I wanted the evening to end up, either."

Johnny grunted. "Come on," he said. He turned to go.

"Wait a minute," the cop said. "I got to finish this report."

"You can finish it without him," Johnny snapped. "And write it up as self-defense."

"I still got to get a statement from the girl. And the victim, when the hospital'll let me—"

"They'll tell you the same thing," Johnny said. "Self-defense. Write it up." He started walking again. The cop looked like he was going to say something else, then shut his mouth. He looked at me with pure hatred. I looked back at him steadily. I didn't have a damn bit of sympathy for him. He and his whole department had put themselves in the pocket of the Trent family; they deserved any petty humiliations that they had to swallow, as far as I was concerned.

I followed Johnny out of the double doors of the police station into the parking lot. Johnny's big Chevy Suburban was parked crookedly across two spaces. He got into the driver's seat. I climbed into the passenger side. He didn't speak as he started the engine. It wasn't until we pulled out of the parking lot that Johnny spoke. "Tell me what happened" was all he said.

I told him, just as it had gone down. I didn't know if he'd talked to the girl, or if what she said would back me or Furry. When I was finished, he didn't speak for a moment. Then: "Your bike at the club?"

"Yeah." Well, at least he didn't shoot me. We drove in silence to the club. The sky was starting to redden like a burning coal as we pulled into the parking lot. I thought of the old rhyme. *Red sky at morning, sailor take warning.* We were miles from any ocean, but it still felt like a bad omen. He pulled over next to my Harley. I was halfway out of the Suburban before he spoke again. "Come in at three thirty," he said. "My uncle'll want to talk to you."

"Okay," I said. I closed the door and watched him as he drove off. I got on the bike and drove to the tiny one-bedroom rental I called home. I was bone weary, and time for work would come all too fast, but I needed to call in.

The cramped bedroom was depressing in the grayish light of early morning. I pulled the cell phone out of the shoe box in the closet where I kept it and dialed a number I knew by heart.

The phone rang once and a voice answered. "Steadman."

"You're up early."

"Always. Any news?"

I told him what had happened.

"Hmm," he said. "You think you're in trouble?"

"I don't know," I admitted. "Furry's a full brother, but the Trents don't tend to take kindly to anyone messing with a good earner."

"We can pull you out."

I thought it over. "No," I said finally. "I can handle it."

"Your call, Tony."

"I know," I said. "I'll be fine."

"Anything else?"

"How's Kendra?"

"Worried sick about you."

"Yeah, well, tell her . . ." I stopped.

"Yeah," he said, "I will. You take care."

"Always," I said and broke the connection. I pulled the blinds shut against the morning light and took off my boots. I lay down on the narrow bed and stared at the ceiling. My gut was knotted in apprehension. Tired as I was, I wondered if I'd be able to sleep. I didn't wonder long.

IT'S STRANGE. When I'm back in the real world, my dreams are fairly linear. There's a story. A beginning, a middle, and an end. When I'm on the job, however, all I can get back out of sleep is fragments. Pictures that flash by like bits of programs scanned by a channel surfer on crank. I saw the lights of the club where I'd been working the last four months, looking for a way into the Trent organization. I saw a flash of leg on the stage, a glimpse of blond hair . . .

Flash.

I was sitting across the table from my wife. She was wearing a leather jacket I'd bought her, laughing at some joke.

Flash.

I was climbing an almost vertical slope, hands and booted feet clawing for purchase in the soft earth. I'd gain a few feet, slide back a foot, then start again. My breath burned in my lungs. I looked up, lost my grip, and started to slide. I scrambled frantically to stabilize myself before I looked back up. Kendra was standing at the top of the slope. She was dressed in the same gym shorts and T-shirt as I was, but her ball cap had the word INSTRUC-TOR written across it. She ostentatiously checked her watch. "Sometime today," she drawled. I scrambled forward another foot or so, enough to lock a hand around her ankle and yank. She yelped and threw herself backward, narrowly avoiding falling off but crashing to her ass. I hauled myself over the lip of the slope; the move brought me over on top of her. For a second we were looking into each other's eyes. She had great eyes. She looked pissed for a moment; then she grinned. "Not bad," she said. Then she punched me. It wasn't a hard blow, but it was right on one of the nerve centers she was always telling us about in personal combat training. It hurt so bad I rolled off her, gasping with pain. She sprang to her feet, still grinning down at me. There was a sound of thunder.

Flash.

CHAPTER TWENTY-FIVE

Y EYES OPENED. I WAS STARING at a light brown water stain on the ceiling. There was the sound of surf in my ears, and I heard the thunder again. I shook my head. I realized that the sound I was hearing wasn't the ocean but the noise of pouring rain on the house's tin roof. I looked over at the clock. Three o'clock. Shit. I wouldn't even have time to shower. I needed to get up or I'd be late for my meeting with Trent, but still I lay there. The dreams of my wife were so real they made me ache with wanting to see her. Even the memory of her slugging me made my throat tighten up. That had been the first day we started noticing one another.

After a few minutes, I sat up. I changed my shirt and socks, splashed water on my face, and looked out the window. It was still raining. That would have to do for a shower.

By the time I got to the club, it had cleared off a little, the heavy thunderheads having dropped their load and moved on, leaving a few wispy gray scraps scudding before the wind. I had gotten a pretty good soaking, but I'd live. I had an extra shirt and bow tie behind the bar, and the black pants would be clammy for a while but wouldn't show the damp. My Harley and one of the Trents' black Suburbans were the only vehicles in the lot. I entered the club, taking a moment to let my eyes get accustomed to the gloom. The place would be lit up like the starships from *Close Encounters* later, but right now, the only lights were the dim ones behind the bar.

I saw a door open on the other side of the room. Nathan Trent was standing there. The president of the Brotherhood was wearing one of the expensive suits he'd only recently begun to favor over biker leathers. He still wore his hair long, but he'd cut the ZZ Top beard back to a more respectable length. He waved me over, turning to let me follow him into his office. It was cramped, with a simple wooden desk, a single rickety chair, and a gray metal file cabinet as the only furnishings. The walls sported tattered posters from "special appearances" by various porn actresses who used fuck films as promotion to hype their major source of income: dancing on the "gentlemen's club" circuit. Trent sat down behind the desk. He took a cigarette out of the pack on the desk and lit it. He didn't say anything at first, just looked at me. Finally he spoke.

"Heard you and Furry had a little trouble last night."

I just nodded.

"Tell me."

Just as with Johnny, I had no idea how much or how little Trent knew. I told it to him straight.

CHAPTER TWENTY-SIX

SO WHY'D YOU DO IT?" he asked when I finished, looking at me through the curl of smoke. "You been fucking her yourself?"

"No," I said. "She's a good kid. Works hard. Doesn't cause any trouble, and she packs 'em in when she's working. I make a lot of tips when Khandi's on." I looked him in the eye. "The club does better, too. She gets her face fucked up or gets cut, well, she can't work. There's that much less for all of us."

Trent's eyes narrowed. He was trying to figure out if I was bull-shitting him. He tipped his chair back and stared at the ceiling for a moment.

"Furry's always liked being one of the Brotherhood," he said, as if to himself. "He likes drinking, getting laid, kicking ass." He grimaced. "Sometimes all at the same time." He sat forward and looked at me. "But he's never seen the big picture, McCabe. He doesn't contribute to the greater good. He doesn't have any commitment to something bigger than himself."

I tried to keep my face expressionless. Trent headed a biker gang, not the U.S. Marines. But I didn't think telling him he was full of shit would be too smart at that moment. "I guess" was all I said. "I don't know him that well."

"I've been keeping an eye on you, McCabe," he said. "You're a good employee. You get here early, you stay late when needed. You don't show up drunk or fucked up. Things get slow, when other bartenders would be leaning against the bar bullshitting with the ladies, you're looking for something to do, even if it's just wiping down the bar. I like that."

I shrugged. "I like to stay busy," I said.

"That," he said, "and your cash box always balances. To the cent. Some fellows come in here, they see how things are done, they start thinking they've figured out slick little ways to skim off some green."

"Yeah," I said. "I saw a few of those."

"And you never tried any."

"I'm making good money already. Plus, if I've got money in my pocket, I like to feel like I earned it."

"Good," he said. He smiled nastily. "Because I've figured those little tricks out, too."

"And I figured you might have," I said. "That's the other reason."

He laughed out loud for the first time. "That's honest. I like that." I didn't reply.

"You learn to fight like that in the army?" he asked. The abrupt change of pace was meant to throw me off. I didn't let it.

"I don't remember ever telling you I was in the army," I said calmly. "Or anyone else, either."

"I did a little background check," he said. "I like to know who's working for me."

I felt a twist in my gut. I'd prepared a good cover, with good backup, the best the FBI's resources could give me. There was even a file for Axel McCabe in the military records repository in St. Louis if anyone had thought to check. Still, no cover is perfect. For one thing, if anyone ran my fingerprints, "Private Axel McCabe" would have the same prints as Staff Sgt. Anthony Wolf. I didn't think Trent had the wherewithal to do that, but if there was any other flaw, if I'd overlooked anything, I was dead.

"Well," I said, "I knew how to fight before I went in. They just taught me to do it better."

"You like being a soldier?"

"It was all right."

"Why'd you leave?"

"My hitch was up. It was time to move on."

Trent stood up. He reached into his desk, took out a set of keys, and tossed them to me. I caught them one-handed.

"I've got a job for you," he said. He reached into the same drawer and took out a business card. He handed it across the desk. It was the address of a women's clinic in Louisville.

"I need you to give Khandi a ride there," he said. "Take my Suburban." He gestured to the door. "She should be here by now."

I walked out and looked again at the card. I had a bad feeling about this.

CHAPTER TWENTY-SEVEN

AMBER/KHANDI WAS WAITING FOR ME in the darkened club, sitting at a table in the shadows. She was dressed in ragged jeans, sneakers, and a hooded sweatshirt that looked two sizes too big for her. It was too warm for the hoodie, but the way she was hunkered down inside it with the hood pulled over her head, I guessed she was willing to sacrifice some comfort for whatever small feeling of security she could get. Without her stage makeup on, she looked even younger. She seemed surprised to see me.

"I'm supposed to give you a ride," I said. She just nodded and stood up. I let her go first. She walked with her head down, her arms folded across her chest.

She didn't speak for the first few miles. I didn't, either; I didn't have any conversation starters for a situation like this. Finally, at a stop sign at the outskirts of town, she spoke up in a small voice. "Thanks," she said. She cleared her throat and spoke a little louder. "Thanks for helping me out last night."

"No problem," I answered.

She didn't speak for a few more miles. Then: "He's really not a bad guy."

"You mean Furry?" I said. She nodded. There was a look of pathetic defiance on her face, as if she were daring me to contradict her. I could see how it would play out if I did, if I pointed out that this not-so-bad guy was ready to gut her the night before and kill her unborn child. She'd deny he really meant it, and I'd be the one she'd end up getting mad at. I wasn't up to that dance right then, so I just grunted noncommittally. Grunting was more in character anyway. She looked disappointed.

A few more miles rolled by before she spoke again. "You know where we're going, right?"

"Yeah," I said.

"You don't look happy about it," she said.

I shrugged. "Not like it's any of my business." Then I surprised myself. "You know," I said, "you don't have to do this if you don't want to."

She looked out the window and gnawed at her thumbnail before turning back to me. "You think Frank's making me do this? Or Mr. Trent?" I didn't answer. I was too busy cursing myself. It wasn't something McCabe would say, and it was damn sure not calculated to score brownie points with the boss if I talked one of the Leopard's best dancers into taking herself off the stage. I looked over at her. She was slumped in her seat, looking at her shoes. She muttered something I couldn't catch. She caught me looking and said it again, louder. "It was my idea," she said. "I just asked Mr. Trent for a place to go."

"Okay," I said.

"I mean," she went on, "can you see me as a mom? Fucked up as I am?" There was a shocking lack of bitterness in her voice. She sounded as if her fucked-upness was as much a given as her height

or her hair color. "And Furry?" she went on in the same reason-
able tone. "I don't think he'd be much of a father, even if he did
stick around, which he ain't gonna do." She shook her head.
"Plus, only job I can make any money at is shakin' my ass, and I
can't take nine months off from that. I got bills to pay."

"You ain't got to convince me, Amber."

She looked at me, then laughed. "You're right," she said, her
voice bright and cruel. "Why am I tryin' to justify myself to the
damn driver?" I turned my eyes back to the road without answering.
"I'm sorry," she said, her voice now small and childlike again. "That
was mean." I shrugged. We spent the rest of the trip in silence.

The Sanger Women's Health Clinic was a one-story cinder-
block building in a part of town dominated by pawnshops and
"Speedy check cashing" stores. The parking lot off to one side was
an obstacle course of broken pavement. A couple of young men
slouched at the street corner eyed the Suburban. I gave them a
hard look back, and they quickly averted their eyes. Still, I didn't
give the car much chance if I didn't check on it frequently.

Despite the shabby look of the outside, the inside of the clinic
was brightly lit and clean, if Spartan. At the desk, a middle-aged
black woman in a blue smock looked at me over her spectacles as
Amber filled out the forms. "You the boyfriend?" she said in a
voice that ranked that particular species somewhere below the
wood tick on the evolutionary scale.

I shook my head. "No," I said. "Just . . ." *Just the driver,* I was going to say, but I amended it at the last minute. "Just a friend."
Amber shot me a look I couldn't read.

"Will you stick around to give her a ride home?" the lady asked.
I nodded.

"Okay," she said. "You can wait in there." She gestured toward a small waiting room with a row of brightly colored hard plastic chairs bolted to the wall. Amber had disappeared.

I took a seat, leaned back, and closed my eyes. A long time ago when I wore a chocolate chip camo suit to work every day and more than a few nights, I learned to grab sleep anywhere, anytime you got the chance, because you never knew when you were going to get it again. I'd gotten pretty good at that. This time, however, sleep wouldn't come when I called. After a while I got up and went to the door. I glanced back and caught the receptionist's sharp eyes on me. "Just going out to smoke a cigarette," I said.

"Uh-huh," she said.

I stepped out and looked at the Suburban. Still there, but so were the kids on the corner, and this time they had friends. I ambled over to the big car, more to show that I was watching than anything else. As I passed by, I glanced in the rear cargo compartment. I saw something there that gave me an idea. I opened the rear driver's side door and climbed in. When I climbed out, I was holding a leather jacket with the symbol and colors of the Brotherhood stitched to the back. I wasn't a member, and getting caught flying the colors would get my ass kicked if any of the brothers saw me, but I figured that was a long shot here. I walked back toward the clinic, shrugging the jacket onto my shoulders and hoping they wouldn't notice it was too big for me. The jacket was probably Nathan Trent's; he only wore it on ceremonial occasions now. When I reached the door I looked back. The watchers on the curb had vanished. I smiled. Nobody wanted to fuck with any vehicle belonging to the Brotherhood, even this far from their usual stomping grounds.

The lady behind the desk looked surprised to see me come back in. Then her face hardened again as she saw the jacket. It just wasn't going to be my day to make new friends. This time, when I slumped into the chair, I did fall asleep.

I came to when Amber touched my shoulder. She barely laid her hand on me when I was on my feet. She shrank back, looking startled. "Hey," she said.

"Hey," I replied. I looked her over. Her face was pale and her eyes were red, as if she'd been crying. She clutched a wad of papers in one hand.

"You ready to go?" I said. She just nodded.

"Will you be able to stay with her tonight?" a voice said. I turned. A short, broad woman in a white lab coat was standing there. She had a stethoscope looped around her neck.

I looked at Amber. "I guess," I mumbled.

"In case there are any complications," the doctor said. "Any unusual blood loss. Things like that. I like to know somebody's there to keep an eye on her."

"Okay," I said. The doctor nodded abruptly and walked away.

CHAPTER TWENTY-EIGHT

YOU DON'T HAVE TO STAY WITH ME," Amber said as we walked to the car. "I'll be okay."

"I said I'd stay," I answered. "It's not a problem."

She nodded, her eyes still downcast. "I can't do nothin' tonight," she said. "I'm sore. But I could give you a blow job in the mornin', maybe."

I gritted my teeth. It had probably been so long since anyone had done anything for her without expecting something in return that she'd forgotten there was such a thing. "You don't owe me anything, Amber," I said. Then, more in character, I said, "I'm just doin' my job."

"What's the matter?" she said. "You afraid of Furry?"

"You ask that after last night?"

She opened the passenger door and got in. "I'm ugly, is that it?"

"No," I said as I got into the driver's seat. "You're not ugly."

That bright cruel smile was back again. "You're a faggot, is that it? Well, close your eyes and think of Brad Pitt or something."

I was getting fed up with her yanking me around. "Maybe I don't like the idea of taking Furry's sloppy seconds." The minute the words were out of my mouth, I regretted them. A look of shock crossed her face, exactly like that of a child who's just fallen on its ass and is too stunned at first to cry. Then her face crumpled, she buried her face in her hands, and she started bawling again. I felt like a complete shit. I tried to console myself with the fact that Axel McCabe was supposed to be a mean bastard. When you looked at it that way, it was the right thing to say. It just didn't make me feel any better.

After a while, she ran out of tears, but she didn't speak again until we reached home and I pulled up in the dirt driveway of the single-wide trailer where she lived. "Don't get out," she said. "I don't want you here."

I stared straight ahead as she got out. "Hey," I said as she started to close the door. She stopped and looked at me, her face blank and dead. "You want me to call somebody else?" She just shook her head and slammed the door. It was starting to rain again.

———

"HEAR YOU turned Khandi down," Johnny Trent said. He was sitting at the bar, drinking a Heineken. Another member of the Brotherhood sat at his right, a bearded guy named Florida Bob. He was drinking rum, straight up. It was an hour after closing, and I was finishing up with the cleaning.

I stopped wiping down the bar. "Where'd you hear that?"

"Around." He smiled nastily. "Your loss, man," he said. "She's good. I mean, really good." I must have looked surprised, because his smile got wider and meaner. "How you think she got a job here?"

I went back to cleaning. "I thought your uncle did all the hiring."

"Sure," said Johnny. "But he's always willing to share the

wealth. Right, Bob?" Florida Bob just nodded and stared into his glass.

Johnny took a rolled-up plastic bag out of his jacket pocket. "Feel like a little toot?" There was an undertone in his voice, almost challenging. Without waiting for my response, he took a plastic change tray from behind the bar and shook a pile of the white powder out. Florida Bob was looking more interested. Johnny took out a razor blade and chopped the coke into six neat lines. "Get a bill from the register," he ordered. I handed him a twenty. He rolled it into a tight tube and handed it to me. "After you," he said.

No one's ever come up with a real solution to one of the biggest problems of working undercover: how to pass among people who do illegal things without doing those same things yourself. In training, you're told to "simulate" drug use, but the trainers weren't all that helpful when it came to exactly how you're supposed to do that convincingly with a pair of experienced users sitting two feet away. Eventually, you come to realize that "simulating" drug use is just what you tell your bosses and the jury. If I tried that trick in front of these two, I didn't have much chance of seeing the dawn.

I didn't know Johnny Trent then as well as I got to know him later, but I knew of his reputation. Two years before, the rumor went, one of the Brotherhood had gotten busted with at least three pounds of high-quality coke in Georgia. Looking at serious federal time for trafficking, the guy was reported to be warming up to the idea of cooperating with the Feds. The next time the guy's mother visited him in jail, however, she had her hand wrapped in a heavy bandage. When the guy asked what was wrong, she didn't speak, just unwrapped the hand to show where her ring and pinky fingers had been. "Johnny" was all she said. At least that was the rumor. She told the people at the hospital she'd lost the fingers trying to fix a stuck lawn mower. Whatever really happened, the guy apparently decided that hard federal time looked like the lesser of two evils. Long story short, I didn't think much of my chances if Johnny Trent thought I was "simulating."

I took the bill and hoovered up first one line, then the other. It was good coke. It shot through me like a white jolt of electric light. I shoved the tray over to Florida Bob and handed him the bill. "Thanks," I said to Johnny, looking him in the eye.

He seemed to relax slightly. I'd passed the test. "You feel like makin' a little extra cash," he said, "I got some work for you."

"Everyone needs cash," I said noncommittally.

He bent down and sucked up the coke slowly. When he was through, he threw the twenty on the bar. "When you get done here," he said, "Bob'll tell you what to do." He got up and walked out. I looked at Bob. He grinned, showing off his missing teeth.

CHAPTER TWENTY-NINE

I FINISHED UP AND MET FLORIDA BOB in the parking lot. He was standing by a battered Ford pickup. As I walked up, he opened the door and reached behind the seat. He pulled out a stubby little machine gun. "You ever use one of these?" he said.

I took it from him. It was a Heckler and Koch MP5. I worked the bolt and checked the selector. As I suspected, it was the full-auto version. "Nice," I said.

"I guess you have used one before, then," he said. He reached out for the weapon. I handed it back to him. The message struck me loud and clear. They wanted to know how much I knew about the hardware, but they didn't trust me with it. Not yet.

"Once or twice," I said. I felt something in my right leg, like a series of electrical shocks. Some instinct made me fight the urge to look down. I realized after a moment that the toe of my right boot was tapping against the pavement. It was a perfectly normal reaction, but it was one that could get me killed. If Florida Bob reported back that I was acting nervous on this run, the least disastrous outcome I could expect was that I'd fail to get inside the Trent organization.

Bob didn't seem to notice the foot tapping before I choked it to a stop. "We're like the Boy Scouts, man." He grinned. "Always prepared."

"Uh-huh."

"Naw, man," he said. "Ain't nothin' serious. But it pays to be careful, right?"

"Right," I said. "Especially at three in the morning."

"Hey," he said, "we ain't workin' banker's hours. But I'll bet we have more fun than bankers." I forced out a laugh and got in the truck.

We didn't talk as we drove; what Bob had saved by not getting the dings and dents in the truck fixed had apparently gone into the sound system, which he kept cranked up to a level that sounded like Molly Hatchet was playing at full concert volume in the truck bed.

I'm travelin' down the road and I'm flirtin' with disaster . . .

I was seeing omens everywhere those days, but that seemed particularly ominous.

We drove out of town and into the sticks. After a while, we got off the hard road and onto a rutted gravel track that bounced us around in the truck. Finally, the road widened into a clearing with a beat-up trailer and shed at the far end. Bob killed the engine and got out. I followed. Before we got to the door, it opened. A guy with long hair and a mustache stood there. Bob waved. "What up, Eugene?"

Eugene waved back weakly and stepped aside. Inside, the trailer was a mess, with food-caked dishes piled in the sink and a coffee table whose surface was entirely taken up with mostly empty beer bottles. On the couch behind the table were two duffel bags. Bob walked over, picked up one, and gestured at the other. I picked it up. It was heavy.

"Pleasure doin' business with you, Eugene," Bob said as he walked to the door. "You keep it between the ditches, now."

"Ah," Eugene spoke up. "What about . . ."

Bob stopped and looked expressionlessly at him. "Yeah?"

Eugene looked down. "I guess Johnny'll settle up later."

"Yeah," Bob said. "Count on it."

We walked to the truck and tossed the duffels into the back of the king cab. Bob looked at me shrewdly as we got in. "Don't you want to know what's in the bags?" he said.

I shrugged. "Figure if anyone wants me to know they'll tell me." He just grinned and started the engine.

On the way back we didn't talk to the sound of the Marshall Tucker Band.

CHAPTER THIRTY

I MADE ANOTHER HALF DOZEN or so runs like that, to various places. I rode with different members of the club: Stoney, Fergie, Little Joe, Cherokee Phil. I never asked what was in the bags that we picked up: duffel bags, gym bags, old suitcases. I was just a grunt, going where I was told, doing the jobs they gave me to do. I reported those back to Steadman as often as I could, but the intel I was getting really wasn't worth much. Steadman would occasionally press me to ask more questions. I put him off. There was a rhythm to this kind of undercover work. You had to wait for the right time, not push too hard, develop a feel for when to get closer and when to back off. It was almost like seduction.

Once in a while I got to talk to my wife. It always left me feeling off-kilter and disconnected. She grounded me too much in being Tony Wolf—the me I couldn't afford to be right then. I tried to avoid people after those conversations until I could get my head back in Axel McCabe's skull.

All in all, it was a very weird six months.

After a few runs, I started getting invited to parties "hosted" by the Brotherhood. There was plenty of booze and drugs around, but the things were usually so crowded, dark, and chaotic that I could get away with only partaking slightly. It wasn't any sense of propriety; I just didn't want to get fucked up and make a mistake that could get me killed. My old pal Furry attended a few of those, with Amber back on his big hairy arm. I avoided them as best I could, but I got more than a couple of hard looks from both of them. Once or twice, I also noticed Johnny or Nathan Trent staring at me from across the room. I was being sized up, I could tell, which was another reason to keep my head straight.

Early one morning, as I was closing up, Clay Trent came out of the back office. He was stoned out of his gourd, as usual. His clothes reeked, his eyes were glassy, and he had a big stupid grin on his face.

"Uncle Nathan wants to see you," he said.

"Be right there," I promised as I moved beers from a pallet into one of the big coolers.

"Now," Clay said flatly.

I didn't argue. I'd seen Clay go from merry to psychotically vicious in a flash.

Back in the office, Nathan was again behind the desk. His nephew Johnny stood to one side, arms crossed. He looked serious. Clay took up a position on the other side, crossing his arms like his cousin. It looked vaguely ridiculous, but my stomach knotted with apprehension anyway. They all looked at me for what seemed like hours. Then Nathan spoke.

"Some of the brothers have talked it over, McCabe. I hope you realize the honor you're being offered here."

"What's that?" I replied.

Clay spoke next. "You're being offered the chance to join the Brotherhood."

I kept my face expressionless and was still for a moment, then nodded. "Thanks."

Clay looked upset. He started to say something, but Nathan cut him off with a laugh. "You just don't get very worked up about anything, do you, McCabe? You're like the great stone face."

"Just the way I am, I guess."

"Well, it means you keep your mouth shut. That's good." He wrote an address on the back of one of the club's business cards and shoved it across the desk at me. "Be at this address, midnight Sunday," he said. "We'll have your colors ready for you."

I took the card. "That's it?"

Johnny spoke up. "Oh, there's a ceremony," he said. "Wouldn't be right if there wasn't a ceremony." The way he said it made me uneasy, but there was no going back now. This was what I was there for.

I nodded. "I need to finish closing," I said.

Nathan waved. "See you Sunday night."

CHAPTER THIRTY-ONE

I FINISHED CLOSING AND DROVE HOME, where I pulled out the cell phone and called Steadman. "I'm in," I said.

"Good news," he replied. "I thought you were just going to be an errand boy for good."

I told him about the upcoming "ceremony," and his voice grew concerned. "I don't like the sound of this, either. I want you wearing a wire. And we'll have backup handy."

It was an attractive idea, but I told him no. "I can handle it. If they think I'm being tailed or if they find a wire on me, I'm toast, backup or no backup. And I've worked too hard getting here to blow it."

"I still don't like it."

"If they wanted to kill me, they'd have just done it. Worst I'll probably get is beaten in. And I can handle that. Just don't tell Kendra."

"Yeah. Okay. I mean, I won't." He paused. "Be careful, Tony."

"I always am." He didn't answer, so I broke the connection.

I went through the next day trying not to think about what lay ahead. Initiation ceremonies for groups like the Brotherhood usually involve something unpleasant. A lot require the new initiate to be "beaten in"—subjected to a beating by the entire club, usually for a specified limited time period. Knowing you're going to get the shit beaten out of you at midnight—if you're lucky—tends to throw a cloud over the whole day.

Finally, eleven thirty rolled around. I followed the directions I'd been given. It was a place I'd never been to before, a crumbling brick warehouse that looked a hundred years old. There were large loading dock doors and a smaller door off to one side. I knocked on that one.

Clay answered. He had a beer in his hand and a joint dangling from one side of his mouth. He had that loopy grin on his face that generally meant some kind of fun was in the making. Only problem was, fun for Clay usually wasn't all that much fun for everyone else in the room. "C'mon in." He motioned me through the vestibule, past the old office space. It opened into a large high-ceilinged room. The only illumination came from candles stuck in bottles. There were at least a dozen bikers in the middle of the space, standing around in a circle. They didn't look at me, just stood there with their arms crossed. In the gloom I picked out Johnny Trent, Florida Bob, Stoney . . . and Furry.

Oh, shit, I thought.

Nathan Trent's voice came out of the gloom. "Stand in the circle."

Two of the bikers stood apart to let me pass. I took a deep breath and stepped into the circle. It closed behind me. I turned around, looking into the expressionless faces that surrounded me.

I finished up facing toward Furry. Whatever else was going to happen, I didn't want that bastard behind me.

"Do you wish to join our Brotherhood?" Nathan Trent spoke up.

"Yeah" was all I could choke out.

"To be our brother," Nathan said, "you must be reborn. And in every birth, there is blood. Blood and pain."

CHAPTER THIRTY-TWO

THE FIRST BLOW HIT ME SQUARE between the kidneys. Pain exploded through my whole midsection. I heard the breath go out of me, and my back arched involuntarily. Furry stepped forward and smashed a big fist into my stomach. I dropped to my knees, doubled over and retching. Someone kicked me in the side, and I went over. I curled into a ball and covered my head with my hands. I lost track of how many times they punched and kicked me. I couldn't think. My mind had shut down, except for the parts that registered pain. I twisted and turned like a worm on a griddle, trying to get away even as what was left of my brain was telling me it was useless. The only sounds were the thuds and cracks of fists and boots hitting me, the grunts of effort made by the people hitting me, and my own grunts of pain. Then someone yelled, "Hey!" someone else hollered, "No!" and the blows stopped. I uncurled just enough to look up with one eye. The bikers were backing away. There was a look of shock and confusion on Florida Bob's face. I shifted a bit to see where he was looking.

Furry was standing over me, his face mottled with rage.

Something glinted in his right hand. It only took me a split second to register the knife.

"Son of a bitch," he growled, reached down and grabbed a handful of my hair. I cried out as he yanked me upright, drawing the knife back for a slash across my unprotected throat.

Training took over. I got my legs under me and drove my body straight up and in, getting inside the range of the slash. I slammed the heel of my hand into Furry's lower jaw with every ounce of force my legs and arms could provide. The blow connected solidly, snapping Furry's head back. He went over backward, the knife dropping from his hand. His head hit first with a crack that I could hear over the shouts of the others in the room. His body began to jerk, the tree-trunk legs twitching spastically. I felt something warm and wet against the skin of my arm. I looked down. I couldn't identify it at first. It was soft and squishy and pink under the thin coating of blood that held it to the flesh of my forearm. With a gasp of disgust, I peeled Furry's severed tongue away and threw it down onto his spasming body. He'd obviously had his tongue between his teeth when I hit him. Furry's body continued its dance for a few more moments, and then he lay still. I didn't have to check to confirm he was dead. That blow was meant to crush vertebrae, and smashing the unprotected back of Furry's head against the concrete floor was probably fatal on its own.

The room fell silent. I looked off into the shadows where I'd heard Trent's voice. "He wasn't supposed to have that knife, I guess."

There was a pause. "No" was the only reply.

"Shit," another voice said. "What the fuck?" said a third.

Florida Bob came over and crouched by the body. "He ain't breathing," he said.

"Probably not," I replied.

"Fuck," Stoney breathed. "You kilt him."

"Yeah," I said.

Johnny Trent spoke up. "It was his own fault," he said. "He pulled a knife. On a prospect going through his rebirth. He broke the law. Our law. And he paid the price." There was something strange in his voice. He was using the same pompous tone as Nathan had when discussing "rebirth," but there was an exaggerated quality to it, as if he were mocking it. I looked at him. There was a slight smile on his lips. It looked like satisfaction. I began to get the suspicion that the son of a bitch had been behind the whole thing.

"So what the fuck do we do now?" Florida Bob said.

"I dunno, Bob." Clay spoke up. His voice was heavy with sarcasm. "Why don't we call the cops and let them sort it out?"

Nathan took charge. "Johnny, Clay," he said, "you stay here with me. We'll deal with this. The rest of you haul ass. Back to the clubhouse. You, too, McCabe." He finally stepped into the light. He also had a smile on his face I didn't like. "You've got a party to go to."

CHAPTER THIRTY-THREE

I DON'T FEEL MUCH LIKE PARTYING right now," I said.

"Did I ask what the fuck you felt like doing, McCabe? It's your initiation party. You don't show up, the associates and the pussy are gonna wonder what happened. Just go. Act natural."

We stared at each other. "That's. An. Order," he said finally.

"Yeah," I said. "Okay."

It was a short ride to the old run-down house in the woods that the club owned and used for parties, but it seemed to take forever. I was still wired from what had just happened, elated and sick at the same time, like the comedown off a long meth jag. I was also wondering what the hell the Trents were up to. For all I knew they were setting me up to take the fall for Furry's death. I wondered if I'd show up at the clubhouse and run into a wall of cop cars. I wondered how the hell I was going to explain this to Steadman. I knew he'd try to pull me out. There wasn't any SOP for this, but the FBI's Office of Professional Responsibility would sure as hell want an investigation into the killing of a subject by an undercover investigator. The whole operation was probably blown. I couldn't face that happening. I was so close to getting inside. It would only be a few steps more toward taking down the whole lot of them. There was the methamphetamine manufacture and distribution, of course. That was bad enough. But I remembered some of the images I'd seen on DVDs and computers we'd seized in the past two years. Children as young as ten, boys and girls, always paired with older men, sometimes women, sometimes both. I remember looking into the eyes of a girl being taken from behind on-screen by a fat balding guy covered in jail tattoos. The cameraman, either sadistic or clueless, had zoomed in to capture her face. Her eyes were dead, like doll's eyes, like the eyes of a mannequin. Anything human had fled from her long ago. According to the crudely lettered credits on the DVD box, she was eleven years old.

No. This wasn't going to end until I decided to end it.

When I got there, the party was in full swing. Every light in the old house was blazing, and music blared from the windows. There was a line of bikes parked outside, and a couple of others roaring up and down the road aimlessly. One of the riders was dressed in his vest and boots, nothng else. I hoped he would remember to keep his bare legs away from the hot exhaust pipe. It sounded like there were at least three stereos competing. The few residents left in that neighborhood knew better than to complain.

A shout went up as I walked through the door. Someone shoved a beer into one of my hands and offered me a joint for the other one. A few of the "associates," hopeful new guys who hadn't been made full brothers yet, pounded me on the back and offered congratulations. I acknowledged them with single words of thanks. No one thought it strange. Axel McCabe was known as a closemouthed guy. Before long, people stopped noticing me altogether. Even though it was supposed to be my party, it was really just an excuse for everyone to get high. That suited me fine. I leaned against the kitchen counter and let the party ebb and flow around me.

After about a half hour of that, one of the dancers from the club zigzagged her way across the room to me. She was a bleached blonde who went by the stage name of Fiona. I had no idea what her real name was. She was so drunk, I wondered if she even knew.

"Hey," she slurred. Then she put her arms around my neck and kissed me. It was a sloppy, clumsy kiss that left spit smeared around my mouth. She looked up, practically hanging by her arms crossed behind my neck, her eyelids at half mast over her pale blue eyes. "Congrat'lations," she slurred. Her breath was stale with beer and cigarette smoke. Her silicone implants were digging holes in my chest. "Al'ys knew you'd make it."

"Thanks," I said.

"Y'don' say much," she mumbled. "I like that."

I looked over her shoulder. Guys were elbowing one another and grinning. One of them gave me a thumbs-up.

I looked back down at her. "You got a car?" I asked.

She grinned. "Y'don' waste time, either," she said. She gave a little bump with her hips that brought her crotch into contact with mine. Despite myself, I was getting hard. She did it again. "I like that more."

"Come on," I said. "Let's find someplace where we can be alone."

"Awright," she drawled. She shifted around beside me and put an arm around my waist.

As we walked out, one of the guys standing by the door had a disappointed look on his face. "You ain't sharin'?"

"Maybe next time," I said. I half walked, half carried her to a beat-up Toyota Camry parked out by the street. She was fumbling her keys from her pocket when I took them away from her. "I'll drive," I said. "You rest up. You're going to need all your strength."

She giggled. "I'll be wantin' more when you're dead on th' bed, cowboy."

By the time we got to my house, she was out cold.

CHAPTER THIRTY-FOUR

I OPENED THE DOOR, then went back to the car to bring her back in. I struggled a little with her dead weight but finally got her inside and dumped her on the bed. I arranged her in the recovery position, on her side so she wouldn't choke to death if she threw up. I thought of undressing her to make it seem as if we really had had sex, but I was just too damn tired. I went out and lay on the living room couch. Tired and wiped out as I was, sleep wouldn't come. I kept feeling the sensation of Furry's severed tongue on my arm. I was shaken and sick. I wanted more than anything else in the world right then to talk to my wife, to be with her, to know there was one sane thing left in the world. It wasn't a good idea, not with someone in the house who could wake up and hear me. Still . . . I looked at the bedroom door. I could hear Fiona snoring. I got up and crept as quietly as I could into the room. Moving as slowly and carefully as a cat burglar, I took the cell phone out of its hiding place. Fiona didn't stir as I tiptoed back out. I took the phone out on my front stoop.

The sky was beginning to get light in the east. I checked the time. It was almost dawn. I looked at the phone, then opened it and dialed. It rang three or four times; then a sleepy voice answered. "H'lo?"

I closed my eyes. It was so good to hear her voice. "Hey," I said.

Kendra's voice suddenly was a lot more alert. "Tony?" she said. "What's wrong? Are you okay?"

There was a sudden flare of headlights at the end of the street. Shit.

"Yeah," I said. "I'm okay. Sorry to wake you." She started to say something, but the headlights were getting closer. "I've got to go," I said. "Sorry." I snapped the phone shut. There was no time to raise up and stick it in my pocket. I shoved it under my leg.

The black Suburban pulled up, and Johnny Trent got out. He raised a hand in greeting. I waved back. He came over to where I was sitting. I slid over a bit to let him sit next to me.

"Heard you left with Fiona," he said.

"Yeah," I replied.

"Good choice," he said. "She's a real screamer when she gets going."

I didn't answer.

"We took care of Furry," he said. "Took him and his bike to the overpass on Highway 9. Shoved 'em both over. Furry was drunk and cranked enough that the ME'll rule it a drunk driving accident."

"I feel pretty ungrateful asking this," I said, "but why?"

"What do you mean, why?"

"Furry was a full member," I said. "I'm just the new guy. Why take me off the hook for what happened?"

Johnny gave me a hard look. "Are you questioning my judgment?"

"No," I said. "I'm just kind of confused."

He took a pack of cigarettes out, put one between his lips, lit it. He didn't offer me one. He took a long drag, not looking at me. He was obviously contemplating whether or not he should bother explaining himself to me. Finally, he spoke.

"Furry was getting to be a problem," he said. "Didn't much like following orders anymore. Kept thinking he was running things. Pulling a knife on you during your initiation was the final straw. I was going to have to do something about that anyway. You just saved me the trouble." He looked at me. "But keep this in mind, McCabe. You owe me a lot more than I owe you. You're not going to cause me the same type of problems. Are you?"

I shook my head. "No," I said. "I get it now. Thanks." The tone in my voice was submissive enough, I guess, to reassure him that he was still the alpha male.

Johnny stood up. "Good," he said as he started walking toward the car. He stopped halfway there and turned back. "Take tonight off," he said.

"Thanks." I watched him get in the car and drive away.

He was right. I owed him. And that meant he had me. The more I thought about it, the more I realized that if I told Steadman about killing Furry, he'd pull the plug, yank me out just as I was working my way in. I knew that if I told Kendra, her sense of duty would force her to tell Steadman, and again he'd pull the plug. The rational part of me knew that I should let him. This whole op had gone sideways. But I couldn't let it go. I kept seeing the dead eyes of the girl in the video. I knew that people like the Trents were behind that video and others like it, to say nothing of the lives their meth business was destroying. If I could take this network down, it would all be worth it. That's what I told myself. Steadman didn't have to know. He'd probably prefer not to, just as your average Special Agent in Charge didn't really want to know that his undercover people weren't actually "simulating" drug use.

Suddenly I felt weary, the kind of tiredness that seems to make your very bones cold. The last remnants of the night's adrenaline bled away. My head hurt. I stood up and stumbled inside, barely making it to the couch before I collapsed.

CHAPTER THIRTY-FIVE

THE SOUND OF GLASSES RATTLING in the cupboard woke me. I sat up, rubbing my eyes. Fiona was in my kitchen, rummaging around. She stuck her head around the door. Her hair stood out from the sides of her head like straw and her eyes were bloodshot. "You got any aspirin?" she said, her voice a strangled croak.

"Medicine cabinet," I said. "In the bathroom." I gestured in the general direction and realized I still had the cell phone in my hand. She didn't notice, just grunted her understanding and bent to the sink, bending down to drink from the faucet, oblivious to the glass still in her hand. I stuck the cell phone in my pocket, went into the bathroom, and started searching the medicine cabinet. I was interrupted by Fiona, who came running in, fell to her knees in front of the commode, and began throwing up. I looked away as she emptied her stomach of last night's alcohol and, if the sound was any indication, most of her stomach lining. When she reached a pause, I leaned over and brushed a few hanging strands of blond hair behind her ear. I poured her a glass of water from the tap and wet a washcloth. "Here," I said, handing her the water and the cloth. "Wipe your mouth and rinse the taste out."

"Thanks," she whispered. Then she was off to the races again. I left the bathroom.

I was sitting on the couch when she came out, pale and shaking. She couldn't have been more than twenty-five, but I suddenly got a glimpse of how she'd look when she was old.

"Oh, fuck," she groaned, flopping down on the couch next to me. She leaned over, putting her head on her knees. She looked up after a few seconds. "Did we . . ."

I shook my head. "Both too fucked up, I guess."

"Oh, fuck," she said again. She put her head back on her knees. "Sorry," she said, her voice muffled.

"S'okay," I said. "Bad luck."

She muttered something I couldn't understand. I thought I caught the name Johnny.

"What?" I said. "What about Johnny?"

She sat up and smiled wanly at me. "Nothing, baby," she said.

"No," I said. "Tell me."

She bit her lip and looked away. "It's nothing."

I grabbed her wrist. "Ow," she complained. "You're hurting me."

"What about Johnny?" I said.

She looked down at the floor. "Let go of my wrist first."

I turned her loose. She still wouldn't look at me. I waited.

Finally, she said, "Johnny told me to show you a good time tonight."

I sat back. "You mean this was Johnny Trent's idea."

She put a hand on my knee. "Oh, no, baby," she said. "I already thought you were cute. I said that to a couple of the other girls. So Johnny told me that I should go with you on your initiation night. That's all."

"Was it a suggestion or an order?"

"Sweetie, don't be like that." Her hand moved higher, to the inside of my thigh. She began moving the hand in slow circles. "I wanted to be with you. I still do." She leaned over and kissed me on the ear. "Hey, Axel," she whispered, "can I use your shower? Maybe if I get cleaned up a little, I'll feel more like . . . you know."

"I just want to know if this was your idea or Johnny's," I said.

She took her hand off my leg. She looked away from me for a long moment. When she spoke next, her voice had lost the flirtatiousness. "It's not that simple."

"Explain it to me."

She looked back at me, her face as bleak as an arctic horizon. It was the first time I noticed how blue her eyes were. "Axel, when Johnny Trent suggests I do something, it's damn sure an order. And I do it, okay? Because I've seen what happens to people who don't do what he says. It's just that this time, I was happy, because he was telling me to do something I wanted to do anyway."

I didn't know how to respond to that. "Towels are in the cabinet next to the sink," I said.

She stood up and smiled. "Thanks," she said.

As the shower ran, I got up and paced the living room. Johnny Trent had aimed Fiona at me for a reason. Was she a reward? Was one of the girls from the club standard issue for new members? Or was he recruiting her to spy on me, figure out what was going on in my head? If so, I'd be crazy to play along. Plus, there was the fact that I was already married. On the other hand, if I refused her, he'd be suspicious. He'd either lock me out of where I needed to be or find some other way to spy on me, something I couldn't see coming.

The shower cut off. I stopped pacing. Before long she appeared in the doorway, dressed only in a towel. She had scrubbed off the caked-on makeup and the too-bright lipstick. Her hair was wet and hung straight to the small of her back. For the first time since I'd met her, I could see the pretty girl beneath the mask.

"I'm feeling a lot better," she said softly as she let the towel fall. I didn't move. She walked across to me, put her arms around me, and kissed me. Her lips were soft and sweet, and she moaned low in her throat as my own arms went around her. I broke the kiss and lay my head on her shoulder.

"What's the matter, baby?" she whispered in my ear.

"I'm pretty wiped out," I said. "It was a long night."

She took me by the hand. "Come on," she said, "let me tuck you in." She led me to the bedroom and drew me down onto the mattress with her. As I lay there wondering what to do, she unlaced my boots and pulled them off. The socks were next. She wrinkled her nose, balled them up, and tossed them out the door. Then she did something that surprised me. She slid up and snuggled onto my shoulder. "Sleep, baby," she said. "I'll be here when you wake up." I didn't think it would be possible to fall asleep with a naked girl tucked under my arm. I underestimated how tired I still was.

CHAPTER THIRTY-SIX

I AWOKE SLOWLY OUT OF THE DEEPEST SLEEP I'd had for a long time. Suddenly I realized that something felt very, very good. My eyes snapped open.

Fiona, still naked, was kneeling between my legs. She'd unzipped my jeans and taken me into her mouth. She moved her lips slowly up and down, her eyes on my face. I groaned in mingled pleasure and despair. She slowly slid me out of her mouth and smiled up at me, her hand moving slowly where her lips had just been. "Hey, sleepyhead," she whispered before plunging back down on me.

"Oh, shit," I grunted as she moved faster. This is not good, one part of me insisted. Like hell it's not, answered another. Then both voices were drowned in the rising tide of pleasure. I heard my own voice crying out, felt as well as heard Fiona's answering moan. Then she took me out of her mouth and slid her body up over mine. I slipped into her easily. "Oh, God," she groaned, then leaned over to kiss me as she began riding me, hard and fast. She threw her head back, her eyes closed tight, moaning and gasping. All I could do was hang on, the pleasure ratcheting higher and higher, taking me to the breaking point . . . then everything in my head exploded.

When I came back to my senses, Fiona was getting up. She darted to the bathroom. I heard the water running.

Shit. Shit. Shit.

Fiona came back in, still smiling. "That was fun," she said as she snuggled back into my arms.

"Ah . . . thanks," I said.

"Anytime, stud," she whispered. "And I do mean anytime." The line sounded rehearsed, like something she'd seen in a movie. I felt my paranoia rising. She didn't notice my tension, or if she did, she chose not to say anything. She kissed me on the chin and popped up out of the bed again. "I'd love to stay and do it again, baby," she said, "but I gotta go to work." I stole a glance at the clock. Two thirty. I remembered I had the night off. That was good. I didn't think I could deal with the idea of watching Fiona onstage shaking her ass for strangers all night after what had just happened. Something occurred to me.

"Hey," I said. She stopped putting her clothes back on and looked at me. "What the hell's your real name, anyway?"

She looked surprised, then lowered her eyes shyly. "Why do you want to know?"

"I just think it would be a good time to find out," I said. "All things considered."

She laughed. "My birth certificate name is Susan," she said.

"Look, Susan—"

She interrupted me. "I like being Fiona. Susan's boring." She bent down and kissed me again. "See you later, alligator," she said.

Oh, God. I thought. *Kill me now.*

I WANTED to go back to sleep and try to forget what had just happened, but I knew Steadman was probably climbing the walls wanting to know if I'd made it all right. I pulled out the cell phone and dialed.

"Glad you called" were the first words he said. "I was getting ready to send in the National Guard." He paused. "You okay?"

Hell, no, I wanted to say, *I just got the hell beaten out of me, killed a man, and cheated on my wife.* "I'm fine," I said. "A little bruised and banged up, but I'll make it."

"Tony," he said, his voice guarded, "we picked up a report from the local cops. Last night, a Brotherhood member named Frank Coleman, aka Furry, was found dead. Apparent cycle crash."

"Huh," I said.

"I seem to recall that was the guy you'd had some trouble with."

"Yeah."

A long pause. "Anything you want to tell me, Tony?"

Glad you put it that way, I thought. "No," I said. It wasn't a lie. I really didn't have anything I wanted to tell him.

TER THIRTY SEVEN

CHAPTER THIRTY-SEVEN

I DON'T KNOW HOW MUCH FIONA TOLD HIM, but Johnny Trent seemed to relax his vigilance a little after that. In the weeks after my initiation, he began to trust me with more sensitive errands. I was allowed to go solo, without a chaperone. Sometimes another member would come along, but only if there was some need for extra muscle. Mostly I made pickups from meth labs, divided the product up, and delivered it to various dealers and clubs. I moved large parcels of cash to and from various places, with the money mostly ending up flowing one way, to Johnny or Nathan Trent. I got a pretty good idea of the layout of the drug distribution network. My "other duties" had cut back my hours at the club, but Johnny or Clay always made sure I had money in my pocket.

I GAVE Steadman regular, terse reports. If he thought something was wrong, he didn't let on. I tried not to talk to Kendra. I knew she'd figure out if I was hiding something. I never had been able to lie to her. I could tell Steadman was getting antsy, wanting to put together the kind of massive, multisite raid that would get

him onto the evening news, standing with the U.S. attorney behind a table piled high with seized drugs, cash, and weapons. I
put him off. I wanted into the Trents' other business. The tapes
and DVDs that went out by mail. The ones that went to "special
collectors."

I got my first glimpse one day when Johnny Trent came up to
the bar. "Axel," he said, "I'm about to cut you in on the easiest
money you ever made."

"Okay," I said.

"How'd you like to be in pictures?"

I played it dumb. "What?"

"I hope you don't mind, but Fiona and I were talking. She said
you have the, ah, kind of talent we might be looking for." He
grinned. "I think she just wants another shot at you." Fiona had
hung around for a while, intimating she'd like to "get together"
again, but I'd been putting her off. Her flirtation had turned to
puzzlement, then irritation when I failed to pick up on her offer.

"Sorry, boss," I said. "I'm still not getting you here."

"We've got a little sideline going," Johnny said. "We figured,
we've got all these bitches around that guys want to drool over.
They go home every night after the club closes and pull their puds
thinking about Fiona or Ambyr or whoever. Well, why not take
that and run with it?" I didn't say anything, and he snorted with
exasperation. "I'm talking video, my man. I'm talking a-dult en-
ter-tainment." He spaced the syllables out as if he were talking to
an idiot child.

"You mean fuck films?"

"Now you're getting it, brother," he said. "And the key word
there is 'fuck.' You ever thought of being a movie star?"

"Shit," I said. "Me? Fucking on camera?"

"Hey, from what Fiona says, you've got, ah, star quality."

"Fiona talks too goddamn much," I snarled.

"Hah," he said. "That's a bitch for you."

"Yeah, well, I don't like it."

"Ah. That's why you've been brushing her off?"

"That's my business, ain't it?" I snapped.

He held up his hands. "Hey, easy, brother," he said. He was chuckling. "Guess you like to keep things private. That's cool." He leaned over the bar and whispered conspiratorially. "Ever change your mind, though, some of that shit'll blow your mind. I'm talking two, three bitches at once, girl on girl, all kinds of wild-ass shit."

I realized I was probably squandering an opportunity, but I didn't think I'd be able to explain away my image in a fuck film to the Bureau when this was over. As Johnny was walking away, I tried a different line of attack. "Hey, Johnny," I called.

He turned back. "Yeah?"

"Sorry for jumping on you like that, brother," I said as humbly as I could.

"No problem." He smiled. "I should have figured. Closemouthed guy like you wouldn't be into flashing his cock on-screen."

"No," I agreed. "But, hey . . ." I hesitated.

"Yeah?"

"Pretty good money in that?" I asked as casually as I could. "Not on camera. I mean making 'em."

Johnny's smile faded. He studied me for a minute, and I felt my heart trying to climb into my throat.

"You know, Axel," he said. All the good-buddy tone was gone.

"I keep underestimating you. You hardly say shit, and so I make the mistake of thinking you're a dumb-ass. But you're not, are you?"

"Don't guess so," I said.

"A lot of brothers would have gone right for the pussy. You're thinking about where the money is."

I tried to keep my voice steady. "You got enough money, pussy'll find you, right?"

"Right." He turned and walked out. I let out the breath I hadn't known I'd been holding and went back to work restocking the bar.

CHAPTER THIRTY-EIGHT

THE NEXT DAY, I WOKE UP to a knocking on the door. I pulled on a pair of jeans and answered it. It was Johnny Trent. "Get dressed," he said. "We've got someplace to go."

The Suburban was waiting outside. Johnny drove. We didn't talk. I tried to keep still, to keep from tapping my fingers on the armrest or my boots on the floorboard. It was torture, like being wrapped in a wet blanket, but I had to appear relaxed.

I was surprised by where we ended up, a nice suburban home on a nice suburban street. The place had a big, well-tended yard out front, complete with a large dog. Johnny pulled the Suburban up behind a new-looking Lexus parked in front of the garage. The dog, a mutt of indeterminate gender, raised its head, blinked, thumped its tail, and went back to sleep. Some watchdog.

The woman who answered the door didn't seem at all taken aback by the spectacle of two leather-clad bikers on her nice middle-class street. "Johnny," she smiled, "this is a nice surprise. Come on in." She was in her late forties, tastefully dressed, every hair in place.

We followed her into the living room. I looked around. The place was gorgeous, with a high, beamed ceiling and skylights to let the afternoon sun in. Below the heavy oak beams, the room was spotless, furnished in standard middle-class style. I thought I recognized a Thomas Kinkade painting over the leather sofa, a small ivy-covered cottage with yellow light spilling out onto the ground in front of it.

The woman held out her hand to me, still smiling. "I'm Linda Spelling," she said.

I took it, feeling a little surreal. "Axel," I said. "Axel McCabe."

"So nice to meet you, Axel," she said. The smile was beginning to unnerve me. There was something unnatural about it, something Stepford Wife-ish. For a moment, I had the insane thought that she might be some kind of robot.

"Charles is in the computer room," she said. "I'll tell him you're here."

"Give him this," Johnny said, holding out a small foil-wrapped package.

Linda Spelling's smile grew a half inch wider. "Oh, good," she said brightly. "Charles was almost out of his medicine. He'll be so grateful." She walked out. We sat down.

"Nice place," I said. Johnny just grunted.

In a moment, a man came in. He was as well dressed and groomed as his wife, but he had none of her self-possession. He was skinny, almost cadaverous, with sunken cheeks and a yellowish complexion. His long, skinny fingers twitched and tapped against one another nervously. He didn't seem to want to meet our eyes. "Hi, Johnny," he said in a hoarse, hollow voice.

Johnny nodded. "Chuck," he said. He pointed at me. "This is

Axel McCabe. He'll be helping me out with this end of the business from now on."

I stood up and shook hands with him. He kept his eyes downcast, like a whipped dog's. He mumbled some unintelligible pleasantry.

"Why don't you show Axel the operation?" Johnny said.

Without speaking, Spelling turned and walked back out the door he'd come through. I looked over at Johnny, shrugged, and followed him.

We entered a room that looked as if it had started life as a spare bedroom. Now, however, it looked more like a computer nerd's vision of heaven. There was a rack of computer equipment I couldn't identify along one wall and a big computer desk along the wall adjacent, dominated by a huge monitor and a couple more tower cases. Words were scrolling across the monitor at a blistering clip. Fans whirred softly. Spelling was muttering something about commerce servers and affiliate networks.

"Hang on." I stopped him. "Slow down. Exactly what're you doing here?"

He shuffled over to the big leather office chair in front of the monitor and pulled out the keyboard. He typed a few lines, then hit a key. The words scrolling across the screen were replaced with a brightly colored Web site. "YoungPassion.com" was written in letters striped to look like candy canes.

"Okay," I said. "Porn sites. I get it." Spelling didn't seem to hear me. He scrolled down, his eyes fixed on the screen. I had to look away from what I saw there. My heart was pounding like a drum in my chest. This was it. This was the center of what I'd been looking for. I tried to keep Spelling talking. "So how does this work?" I asked.

"Orders come in," he mumbled. "Product goes out. Simple."

"Product? Like what?"

"Lots of people download the product. If they've got a fast enough connection. We ship DVDs to people who want them." He worked the mouse. Another Web site popped up, this one called LolitaLuv.net He scrolled down for another moment, then shut it down. My skin stopped crawling.

"So where does all this, ah, product, come from?"

He shrugged. His attention had wandered from the screen and was now fixed upon the foil-wrapped package lying on the computer desk. He licked his lips.

"Chuck," I said. "I asked you a question."

He looked at me for the first time. His eyes took a few seconds to focus. "I don't know," he said. "I don't make it. I just run the computers. Johnny brings me the files. I load them."

"What about the DVDs?" I said.

He gestured vaguely out the door. "Burner's in the other room. I try to keep up." He was fixated on the package again. "I need to take my medicine," he said. He picked up a manila envelope that lay on the desk next to the monitor and handed it to me. "Here's the list Johnny wanted," he said.

"Okay, Chuck," I said. "Go take your medicine."

He shuffled to the door. He stopped and turned back. "Will you be dropping off my medicine from now on?" he said.

"Probably. What difference does it make?"

He looked quickly in the direction of the living room. "Johnny . . . my wife . . ." He shook his head as if he'd said too much. "You seem nicer than he is."

"Don't let that fool you," I said. "Business isn't going to

change." Hopefully, he was going to find out soon just how big a lie that was.

"I don't mind the business," he said. "But Johnny . . ." He stopped again. "I need my medicine." He walked out, leaving me alone. I wanted more than anything else to walk over and smash every one of those computers, to rip YoungPassion.com and LolitaLuv.net right the fuck out of the World Wide Web. *Soon,* I told myself. *Soon this shit will all be over.*

I looked at the envelope. It was just closed with the little brass clasp, not sealed in any way. Carefully, I pried the clasp open and shook out the papers inside. It was a spreadsheet, divided into several columns. The first column was names, the second addresses. The third column was a list of sixteen-digit numbers, followed by a date. Probably credit cards. The last column contained a mix of letters and numbers. I didn't know what those meant for sure, but since this was obviously the customer list, I suspected that those were codes designating various "products."

I walked back out into the living room. I stopped dead in the doorway.

Johnny was seated in a leather recliner, kicked back and drinking a beer. Linda Spelling was seated on the couch across from him. She had her hands behind her head. She was naked from the waist up. She still had the same fixed smile, but there were tears running down her face, leaving tracks through her makeup.

"Sorry," I choked out. "Didn't know you were busy."

Johnny got up. "I'm not," he said. He grinned at Linda. "I was just bored. You got the list?"

"Yeah," I said, trying not to look at the humiliated woman on the couch.

"Okay, then," he said. "Let's motor." He walked over to where Linda sat on the couch and chucked her under the chin in a parody of fondness. "Gettin' a little saggy there, Linda," he said, a cruel smile on his face. "Might ought to consider getting a boob job." He turned away, then turned back. "By the way," he said, "just because Axel here's going to be making this run from time to time, don't think I won't know if you try to fuck me over. And if I even think that, if I have even the slightest motherfucking suspicion that you're trying to cheat me or that Chuck in there's slacking off, it won't be me or Axel here paying a visit. It'll be Clay. And I don't think you ever want to see him again. Isn't that right?"

"Yes, Johnny," she whispered. The smile was still plastered across her face, but her eyes were filled with horror.

Johnny smiled again, turned, and walked out, with me behind him.

CHAPTER THIRTY-NINE

"WHAT THE FUCK WAS THAT ALL ABOUT?" I asked when we got in the car.

He laughed. "A little fun is all." He started the car. "Chuckles in there got in a little over his head. He was into me for a couple of grand. He likes his black tar heroin a little bit more than he likes paying for it. So I took Clay and went out to see him. After I worked on him a little while," he grinned, "and Clay started, ah, working on Linda, he let slip about his little sideline. So we made a deal."

"He cut you in."

"I like to think of myself as a silent partner," Johnny said. "He was just selling stuff he'd copped from other sites. I figured, what the hell, I had a ready-made pool of talent, right at my fingertips, you might say."

"Most of your talent's a little old for the sites I saw."

"Ah," Johnny said. The smile faded. "He showed you those sites, huh?"

"Yeah."

"You got a problem with it?"

I shrugged. "Money's money."

The answer seemed to satisfy him. "Damn right. That part of the business was only a few pictures here and there at first. But I noticed those were the ones most in demand. You got to give the customers what they want. Especially when they're willing to pay more for the, ah, more extreme stuff."

"How much money we talking about here?" He didn't answer at first. "Hey," I said, "You want me to be in on this part of the business, I'm in. But I ought to know everything that's going on."

He considered that for a moment, then nodded. "Usually around ten thousand."

"A month?"

He laughed. "A week."

"Holy shit."

"Exactly."

We drove in silence for a few minutes. "So what's in the envelope?" I asked casually.

He hesitated again, then said, "Insurance. It's a list of customers. Names, addresses, all the information I need. Every now and then, you'd be surprised at who you find looking at pictures of naked little girls. I get in a jam, maybe some of those people might be happy to get me out of it, so long as their little private hobby stays private."

"Find anything good?"

"Oh yeah. I've got a couple of get-out-of-jail-free cards."

"Like what? Cops?"

"Better than cops, McCabe."

"Better?"

"Let's just say, a lot more juice than the local yokels. And that's all I'll say for now."

I pushed a little. "What, you mean, like, Feds?"

He looked startled, and I knew I'd hit home. Then his voice turned cold. "MCabe," he said, "what part of 'all I'll say for now' do you not fucking understand?"

"Okay, okay," I said. "Sorry, boss."

That "boss" always did it. Johnny liked to be acknowledged as top dog. We drove the rest of the way in silence, while I mulled over the implications. When we got back to my house, Johnny turned to me as I was getting out of the truck. "One more thing," he said. "This end of the operation is mine. Mine alone. Get it?"

That was another thing to think hard about. Johnny's uncle Nathan, the theoretical leader of the Brotherhood, wasn't being cut in on this. Did he even know about it? Curiouser and curioser. I didn't mention any of this to Johnny. I just nodded and walked into the house.

WHEN I was sure Johnny was gone, I called Steadman. I told him about the visit to the Spelling household. When I got to the part about the mailing list, he stopped me.

"Who's got that list now?" he asked.

"Johnny," I said. "I didn't get a chance to make a copy."

"Can you get it?"

"I can try. But we've got what we need. We can move now on the Trents. The whole operation. I've got all the pieces in place."

"Not yet," he said. "That list changes everything. This may have just gotten politically explosive."

"Political?" I couldn't believe what I was hearing. "Jesus Christ, Steadman, these are children being used in those movies. Anyone who's on that list—"

"We don't know who's on that list," he said. "Or what their involvement is. We need to be careful here, Tony."

"You're bullshitting me. Tell me you're bullshitting me."

"Get the list, Tony," he said. "Get me a copy. I need to know who we're dealing with."

"Who cares!?" I yelled. "If they're on that list, they're dirty. They deserve to get taken down."

There was silence on the other end. Then: "There are other ways to use that information than just taking people down."

Then it dawned on me. "Holy shit," I said. "You want to use it as leverage."

"Like I said. We need to know who's who. Get a copy of the list." He broke the connection.

CHAPTER FORTY

I HELD THE PHONE AT ARM'S LENGTH and stared at it. I couldn't believe what I'd just heard. Steadman wanted to use that customer list for himself. Either that or he was afraid of who might be on it. I thought back to Johnny's reaction when I'd asked if anyone on the list was a Fed. Was Steadman afraid of who might be on it? Was Steadman worried *he* might be . . .

This was crazy. I sat down on the couch and put my head in my hands. I felt like I'd just fallen down the rabbit hole. Nothing made any sense. I had gotten into this op to shut the Trents and their operation down, not turn it into a bargaining chip. I had no idea who to trust anymore. Well, there was one person, but after what had happened with Fiona . . .

Screw it. I needed to talk to my wife. I flipped the phone open and dialed.

"Tony," she said as she picked up the phone. "My God . . . Are you okay?"

I closed my eyes. The sound of her voice was like a lifeline. "I'm okay," I said. "Better than I was a minute ago."

"What's wrong?"

I told her. I told her about Furry's death, the visit to the Spellings, my conversation with Steadman. I told her everything except what had happened with Fiona. She heard me out. She always did. When I was done, I felt limp and drained, as if all the air had been let out of me. But I felt better. Calmer. More centered. Until Kendra spoke up.

"We're getting you out of there," she said.

"No!" I blurted it out, almost panicking. I struggled, got myself under control. "You can't pull me out, anyway," I said. "It's not your operation. It's Steadman's."

"I'll go over his head. You're in trouble. This whole thing is about to go to hell in a big way."

"You can't do that," I said, hating the way I sounded.

"Tony, you're a wreck," she said. "I can hear it in your voice. This thing is destroying you. You're exhausted, you're paranoid, you're not thinking clearly. I mean, Jesus, *Steadman* being into kiddie porn? He's a fifteen-year veteran agent. He's a family man."

"I'll bet a lot of people on that list are."

"Will you listen to yourself?" she snapped. Then her voice softened. "I know what this means to you, Tony, but you're really starting to scare me."

"Okay, maybe not Steadman," I said. "But Johnny Trent all but told me that he's got someone on the inside. Someone he's blackmailing."

"He didn't say any such thing. You interpreted a look. And honestly, Tony, right now, I can't give that a whole lot of credit."

"Forget it, then," I said. "Forget I called."

"Right. Like I can do that. You don't talk to me for weeks, then you call me sounding like you've been up for days—"

She stopped. "Tony," she said softly, "you're not using, are you?"

I laughed bitterly. "No. I'm simulating. You know how that works."

"This is me, Tony," she said softly. "Not Professional Responsibility. I need to know what's going on with you. I need to know the truth."

I thought of the line from the movie. *You can't handle the truth.* "Look, I'm fine," I said.

"No," she said. "No, you're not." There were tears in her voice. "And it . . . and it breaks my heart that you'd tell me that. Let me help you, Tony. You want to hear me beg? I'll beg. Please. Let me get you out of there."

"Give me a couple more days," I said. "That's all I need."

"Now you're *bargaining* with me?" She was crying openly now. "This is so important to you? More important than me being scared out of my mind for you?"

"I'll call you in two days," I said and shut down the phone. I lay back on the couch and looked at the ceiling. I had just cut my own lifeline. And for what? Was it really worth all of this just to take the Trents down? I thought of Amber. I thought of the little girl I had seen in the movie. I thought of the Spellings, and Fiona, and even Furry. They weren't people as far as the Trents were concerned, they were raw material. Just meat for the grinder.

Yes, it was going to be worth it to destroy them. If my own people would let me.

I knew my time was short. I didn't realize just how short.

CHAPTER FORTY-ONE

THE NEXT DAY, I WAS SCHEDULED to work at the Leopard. When I got there, I was startled to see at least fifty bikes in the parking lot, along with half a dozen pickup trucks and SUVs. It looked like most of the Brotherhood was there. When I got inside, bikers were milling around, talking in low voices. A lot of them looked unhappy. I noticed Florida Bob sitting in the corner, staring into his glass of rum. I walked over and sat down.

"What the fuck?" I asked.

He looked up. "We got trouble."

"What kind?"

He took a swig. "Federal. I think."

I felt cold. "What do you mean, federal?"

"Johnny got word from somebody. Something big is coming down."

I tried to keep my voice from shaking. "FBI?"

Bob shrugged. "Who knows? But Nathan's bouncing off the walls. Him and Johnny are in the office with Clay." He gestured at the group of bikers. "Clay told everybody to be here."

At that moment, Nathan came out of the back office, followed by Johnny and Clay. The room fell silent. "Okay, brothers," he said. "We've got a problem. We're going to have to shut things down for a while." There was a momentary rumble of conversation; then he raised a hand. "We've got word that the Feds are planning to move on some of the labs. But when they get there"—he grinned— "there won't be anything for them to find." He gestured at Johnny and Clay. "They'll tell you where to go. Pack everything up. Product, equipment, cash, everything. Destroy what you can't carry. We'll move everything out of harm's way until this blows over. Then we'll start up again."

I raised a hand. Nathan looked annoyed. "What is it, Axel?"

"How do you know all this?" I asked as calmly as I could.

It was Johnny who answered. "Never mind that," he snapped. "I haven't got time to lay it all out for you. Just believe it." He started for the door. "Axel, Bob," he said, "you're with me." I didn't have any choice but to follow. At least he didn't give any sign of suspecting me.

We got into Johnny's Suburban. I sat in the front, with Bob taking the big backseat. He looked behind into the cargo compartment. "All right." He chuckled.

"What?" I said.

He lifted a stubby little machine gun up and showed it to me. "Heavy iron, man," he said.

"Hand up the pistols," Johnny ordered. "We'll only take the subs out if we need them." Bob complied. I took a Taurus automatic, Johnny his usual Glock 9. We laid them on the seat between us.

My apprehension deepened. "You expecting trouble?" I said.

"Just being careful," he said. He was trying to sound nonchalant, but I could hear the tension in his voice. "We're going to be transporting a lot of shit. A lot of product, a lot of cash. I don't want any punk-ass getting any bright ideas."

"I don't get it," I said, trying to draw Johnny out. "Where are we moving all this stuff to?"

"You'll see" was the only reply I got. Bob lay across the backseat and went to sleep.

OUR FIRST stop was Eugene's place. Johnny tucked his pistol in the back of his waistband when he got out. I did the same.

Eugene looked terrified when he answered the door. "Johnny, man," he whined, "what the fuck's going on?"

"Shut up," Johnny said. "You got the product bagged up?"

Eugene nodded and pointed at the usual brace of duffel bags on the couch. "But I got two cases of cold pills still stacked in the spare room."

"Flush 'em. Burn 'em. I don't care."

Eugene looked distraught. "Man, I paid a lot of money for that shit. And you still ain't paid me for the last . . ." The look on Johnny's face stopped him dead.

"Look, dude," Florida Bob spoke up, "the last thing you want to get caught with right now is a lot of fuckin' Sudafed. Or a lot of fuckin' cash. Get rid of it." Eugene still looked unhappy, but he nodded. We grabbed the duffels and threw them into the back of the Suburban.

We made a couple more stops. These were at the homes and clubs of distributors, and these duffels were filled with tightly rolled bundles of cash. Bob's admonition about getting caught with large amounts of green didn't seem to worry Johnny. Clearly he had some other hiding place planned.

My mind was racing. Obviously my suspicion was correct. Johnny had someone on the inside—but it was someone who knew only enough to be able to tell that a bust was coming. It wasn't anyone who knew the name of the guy on the inside, namely me. If that name had been dropped in Johnny's ear, I'd either be dead now or, more likely, praying for death while Johnny and Clay worked me over with a blowtorch and a cold chisel. I needed to get back in touch with Steadman to let him know about what I'd discovered, but there was no way to do that under Johnny's watchful eye.

The last place we visited was where it all went to hell.

CHAPTER FORTY-TWO

I T WAS ONE OF THE LABS way out in the sticks. There was an old rusted Quonset hut nestled in the woods beneath a stand of pines. The place was accessible only by a twisted dirt road so badly rutted that even the big Suburban bounced and rattled. Johnny's "cooker" at this lab was a squat, ugly Hispanic dude who lived in an old camper trailer on the premises with his wife and kid. The wife and kid didn't appear to speak any English, and the Hispanic dude didn't appear to want to speak any language. He mostly communicated with grunts, shrugs, and the surliest expression I'd ever seen anyone use on Johnny Trent without getting slugged in the mouth.

When we finally negotiated the rutted road, the Hispanic guy came out, wiping his hands on his jeans. I could smell the acrid chemical tang of methamphetamine cooking.

"What the fuck?!" Johnny yelled as he jumped out. "You're not done yet?!"

The Hispanic guy just shrugged and muttered something I couldn't catch.

"God *damn* it!" Johnny yelled. "You were supposed to have this batch finished fucking *yesterday!*"

The guy shrugged again. This time he didn't even bother to answer. Johnny went red in the face. He whipped the pistol out of his waistband and slammed the cooker across the face with it. The guy crumpled to the ground. I heard a scream and looked around, drawing my own gun. The man's wife, a plump woman in a shapeless flowered dress, stood in the trailer doorway. A little girl who looked to be about eleven or twelve clung to her leg, wide-eyed. She was dressed in blue jeans and a red top. She was barefoot.

Johnny was kicking the man on the ground, cursing. The man had curled into a ball, his arms covering his head. I looked over at Florida Bob. He had a sour look on his face, but he caught my eye and shrugged. *What are you gonna do?* his face said.

Suddenly, the little girl shouted something and left her mother's side, running toward her father on the ground. Her mother shrieked something in Spanish, but fear kept her rooted in the doorway. The girl reached her father on the ground before Johnny even noticed she was there. She threw herself across his prone body, shouting up at Johnny, her face streaked with tears. Johnny nearly leaped back in surprise. Then he growled deep in his throat, reached down, and grabbed a handful of the girl's thick black hair. She shrieked in agony as he used his grip on her hair to haul her free of where her father lay. "Maybe this little bitch can work off the money you're costing me!" Johnny screamed. "You like that idea, you greasy little fuck!?" He put the gun to her head. "Maybe we break her in on-screen, huh? Think that'll be a big seller?"

"Bob," I said over my shoulder. "We need to stop this."

"Ees not my yob, man," Bob cracked in a mock Mexican accent. The strain in his voice killed what little humor there was.

The man on the ground had gotten to his knees. For the first
time, his face registered fear. "Please," he said, "*por favor* . . ."

Johnny's grin was positively demonic. He ran the barrel of the
gun down the girl's cheek in an obscene parody of tenderness.
"See what happens to people who fuck around with me?" he almost crooned. "They get fucked back."

"Johnny," a voice said. I was amazed to realize it was mine. "Cut
it out."

He didn't look around. "Johnny," I said more loudly.

He turned slightly. "What is it, Axel?" he snapped.

"Let her go, man." I raised the gun.

He looked around at me with a look of amazement on his face,
as if I'd suddenly started speaking in tongues. When he saw the
gun pointed at him, the insanity in his face returned tenfold. He
started to raise his own weapon, and I shot him in the chest.

CHAPTER FORTY-THREE

H E STAGGERED SLIGHTLY, his eyes wide, his mouth gaping in shock. He didn't drop the gun. I shot him again. Now everyone was screaming. Johnny was howling in stunned rage and pain as he fell to his knees, the gun dropping from his hands. The mother and child were babbling something in Spanish that sounded like prayers. Even Florida Bob was yelling, "What the fuck—" I swiveled my weapon toward him. He hadn't even taken his own pistol out of his waistband. "Bob," I said, "get your hands in the air."

He looked as if he'd been poleaxed. *"Get your goddamn hands up!"* I yelled.

His hands shot skyward. "You shot him, man," Bob said in a voice filled with wonder. "You fucking shot Johnny Trent."

I could hear Johnny behind me, groaning. "Come here," I ordered Florida Bob. He walked over to me slowly. "Turn around," I said.

"Johnny's hurt, man," Bob said.

"I know that, Bob. I'm the one who shot him. Now *turn the fuck around!"* I shouted, my voice cracking with the strain. Bob turned around, and I snatched the pistol out of the back of his pants. Now I had a gun in each hand. "Get over there next to him," I ordered.

He complied, still shuffling like a sleepwalker. When he got to Johnny, he knelt down. "Johnny?" he said, his voice unsteady. "Hang on, brother. You're gonna be okay."

"My legs," Johnny moaned. "I can't feel my legs."

Bob looked up at me. "You gotta call a doctor, man," he said.

I looked over at the cooker. He had gotten up off the ground. He and his family were gathered in a tight knot by the camper. "Get out of here," I told them. They still looked shell-shocked. "*Vámonos,*" I yelled.

"Axel," Florida Bob said.

"Shut up," I snapped back. Keeping the pistols trained on Bob and Johnny, I walked over and scooped up Johnny's gun. I had to stick Bob's in my waistband to do it. Now I had all the guns except the ones in the truck. I looked at Johnny and Bob on the ground, then at the lab. I turned to the cooker. He was looking nervously at the Quonset hut where the lab was housed. "What's the matter?" I said, laughing a little hysterically. "Leave something on the stove?" He rattled something at me in rapid Spanish. All I caught was the word *fuego.*

"I don't give a fuck if the whole thing burns down," I snapped. I motioned with the gun. "Now get out of here." They finally seemed to get the message. They didn't even stop to get anything out of the trailer, just piled into an old Cadillac parked behind it. The cooker yelled something to me in Spanish as they drove past. It didn't sound like "thank you." I turned back to where Bob knelt by Johnny.

"You've got to get him a doctor, man," Bob insisted. "He's gonna die."

I stood over him. "Johnny," I said. "Tell me who your inside man is. Who's the Fed, Johnny?"

He coughed weakly. "Fuck you," he whispered. "Traitor."

"I'll get you a doctor if you tell me, Johnny. Otherwise I'll stand here and watch you bleed out."

"Holy fuck," Bob said. "You're . . . Axel, are you a goddamn cop?"

I ignored him. "Tell me, Johnny." But Johnny's eyes were closed. I could hear the rattle of his labored breathing, but he was either out or making a good show of it. I raised the gun and fired into the ground beside his head. The sharp report made Florida Bob flinch away. He tried to get up and fell on his ass. Johnny didn't move. Out of the corner of my eye, I caught a flash of light. I turned to look and saw a glow of flames coming from the cracked windows of the Quonset hut. Then there was a sudden loud thump and the air was full of flying metal and glass.

CHAPTER FORTY-FOUR

I GOT MY ARMS UP QUICKLY enough so that a sliver that would have sliced my face open slashed my forearm instead. Bob screamed again. I bolted for the truck, my arm streaming blood. As I slid behind the wheel and started the engine, I looked over. The Quonset hut was like a portal to hell, billowing flames and smoke from inside. The trees nearby were starting to catch. Bob was dragging Johnny away from the inferno. Something else inside the building went up, blowing the entire front of the building out in a rolling ball of flame. I hit the gas and tore out of there. I looked at the gash on my arm. It was flowing freely but not deep, and not spurting as it would be if I'd hit an artery. I knew I needed to get a bandage on it, but first I needed to get the hell out of there.

The truck bounced and rattled even worse going out as I gunned it down the road without regard to the ruts and gullies. A couple of times I was jolted so severely that I worried I'd snap the axle, but when I bounced onto the hard road, I was off. I needed to get away before Florida Bob brought the entire Brotherhood down on me. I didn't much favor my chances if Nathan or Clay

Trent got their hands on me. But first, I wanted to get to the Spellings. I wanted that list. I'd pile the entire computer rig into the back of the Suburban if I had to. Along the way I stopped and improvised a bandage out of an old T-shirt I found in the back of the truck. I also moved the two machine guns to the front seat.

I slowed down as I got near the Spelling residence. I didn't want to get stopped for speeding with blood all over the seats, not to mention a brace of submachine guns and . . .

I slowed even further and looked back. I couldn't see the two duffel bags full of cash in the cargo area, but I knew they were still there. I had no idea how much I was carrying, but it looked like a shitload. All of the liquid assets of the Brotherhood—and the Trents—were mobile right now, and I was carrying at least a high percentage of them.

I pulled into the Spellings' driveway. I tried to look as inconspicuous as possible as I walked to the door. It was no easy task in a leather jacket and boots, with one arm wrapped in a bloody rag.

I stopped and drew the pistol, moving slowly. The front door was slightly ajar. I nudged it with the barrel of the gun. There was no sound from inside. The only sound from outside was the muffled burr of a lawn mower engine from down the street. I slipped inside.

Chuck Spelling hung from a rope tied to one of the beams in the living room. His tongue protruded grotesquely from his mouth, and his eyes bulged from his head as if in horror. His weight had stretched the muscles and tendons so that his neck seemed absurdly long. His wife sat in the big easy chair, facing him. She was immaculately dressed as always, but she sprawled bonelessly in the chair like a sullen teenager, her head lolling to one side. She held a large-caliber handgun loosely in her right hand. There was a spray of blood and brains across the wall opposite. The smell of cordite, blood, and shit, the familiar odors of violent death, lingered in the air.

I knew what I would probably find, but I checked anyway. The computer room had been stripped, cables and cords hanging like veins and tendons from a clumsily severed limb. Someone had gotten here before me. Someone who knew what the Spellings had. Someone who wanted to make damn sure it never came to light. I didn't miss the irony of the fact that whoever had done this had accomplished exactly what I had wanted to do: tear the whole operation loose and rip it from the Internet. And they had made sure that Chuck and Linda wouldn't be around to be interrogated. Whoever had done this knew they'd never last, that they'd spill everything. I didn't know if the person or people who'd beaten me here had murdered poor Chuck and Linda and arranged it to look like a double suicide or if they'd offered them the out as an alternative to something much worse. I had a strong suspicion that Johnny's cousin Clay had been here, and Clay would definitely have been able to convince them that there were far worse alternatives than death by their own hands. As far as I was concerned, it was an academic question. I was blown. Screwed. In the open. It was time to run.

But it seemed that the day wasn't finished with me yet.

CHAPTER FORTY-FIVE

I WAS ON MY WAY OUT OF TOWN when I saw Clay's truck coming the other way. I looked in my rearview and saw the taillights flash. The truck slowed and began to turn around. I thought about trying to outrun him, but that might not work. Or maybe I was still hyped on adrenaline, I don't know. Anyway, I slowed, let him follow me out to farm country. I pulled onto a narrow two-lane feeder road and sat there as Clay pulled out behind. He got out and started walking toward the truck. His companion, Stoney, followed. When Clay got a few feet away, I swung out and trained the machine gun on his chest. He stopped.

"Axel," he said calmly, "what the fuck are you doing? Where's Johnny?"

"I shot him," I said. Then: *"Don't even fucking think about it, Stoney!"* as I saw Stoney reach into his jacket.

"You're making a big fucking mistake here, boy," Clay said. "Now tell me where Johnny is."

"First," I said, "you and Stoney are going to take those jackets off. Then you're going to put your guns on the hood and go stand on the other side of the road." They didn't move. *"Do it!"* I screamed. Slowly, they shucked off the jackets and dropped them at their feet.

"Guns out, between thumb and forefinger," I said. "Use your off hand."

"My what?" Stoney said. His shaved head glistened with sweat.

"Your left, Stoney," Clay said. "The one you don't shoot with."

With their guns on the hood, I motioned them over to the side of the road with the barrel of my weapon. I walked over to Clay's pickup and took his and Stoney's pistols. I was going to have enough stock to open up my own gun shop at this rate. I looked into the cab of the truck. There were two more duffels in there. I also noticed the gas gauge. The tank was full. I turned back to Clay and Stoney. "There's two duffels in the back of the Suburban," I said. "Get them out."

"You little pissant," Clay snarled. "You think you can fucking rob us? You think we won't find you?"

I raised the gun higher. "I think you won't be alive to find out, you don't get moving right fucking now." If looks could kill, Clay's glare would have left me in a bloody heap by the truck. But looks can't kill, and machine guns can, so Clay and Stoney did what I said. When they were done, I had them stand by the front passenger door of the Suburban.

"I'm going to find you, you cocksucker," Clay said. "I'm going to find you and I'm going to cut pieces off you and make you eat them. I'm going to make you last for fucking days, McCabe."

"I think you'd rather find Johnny," I said. "Right?"

Clay struggled to get the answer out. It was killing him to not know, but it hurt almost as bad for him to admit he needed something from me. "Yeah," he finally choked out.

"He's at the lab on Fire Tower Road," I said. "Florida Bob's with him. He's been shot. I don't know if he's still alive. You can maybe save his life. But you'll have to call someone else to do it." I raised the gun and fired. Clay and Stoney dove to one side. "Because you're not doing it in this car," I finished. They looked up from where they lay on the ground, staring at the shredded front tire of the Suburban.

I got in the truck and drove away. I kept driving until I got to Pine Lake.

CHAPTER FORTY-SIX

THE ROOM WAS SILENT when Wolf had finished speaking. After a moment, Gaby asked, "And you hid yourself at Pine Lake why?"

Wolf shrugged. "Seemed like a nice place."

"So how did you . . . I mean, you made a whole new identity for yourself."

"It's not hard," he said. "If you know what you're doing. And if you mostly deal in cash, you don't need much ID." He laughed. "One thing I had plenty of was cash."

"And you could have stayed here forever, not drawing any attention to yourself . . ."

"Yeah, well," he said. "Things didn't really work out that way."

"Because you saved those boys."

He shrugged again. "Didn't have much choice."

"No," she said thoughtfully. "No, I guess you didn't. Not you." She reached out and turned the recorder off. She put her hand on his. "What are you going to do now?"

He looked at her without expression. "Probably die."

She pulled her hand away. "Don't say that."

"Why not?" he demanded. "It's true. I could come in, but wherever they put me, there's somebody who'll find out. And they'll tell the Brotherhood. And they'll find me, and then Clay will kill me as slowly and painfully as he can. It's what he's good at. He enjoys it. I could run again, but it's pretty obvious I can't hide. Not with my picture everywhere." He took a deep breath. "No," he said, "I'm pretty well screwed, thanks to you. You and your friend killed me as sure as if you'd put a gun to my head." He picked up the pistol from the table and handed it to her, butt first. "Go ahead," he demanded. "Finish what you started."

She was crying now. "Stop. Please stop."

"*Go ahead!*" he screamed in her face. "It's a hell of a lot kinder than what the Trents and the Brotherhood will do to me." He shoved the gun at her again. She jumped up and slapped it away.

"*What do you want me to say?*" she screamed back into his face. "How the hell was I supposed to know? I was just doing my *goddamn job!*"

They sat staring at one another, the tears running down Gaby's face. Finally Wolf slumped back in the chair. "Fine," he said. He sounded weary enough to sleep for a thousand years. "Okay. It's not your fault. Your job. Right." She kept sobbing. "Okay," he said. "It's okay. Quit crying."

She took a tissue out of her purse and dabbed at her eyes. "Go to hell," she said, then blew her nose.

"Look, I'm sorry, okay?" he said. "In case you haven't noticed, I've been under a little bit of stress lately." He sighed. "You're right, though. It's not your fault. It's the Trents." He thought for a moment, then stood up. He bent over and picked up the gun from the carpet. "If I'm going to die, all that's left for me is to pick how to do it. And it won't be screaming for mercy." He racked the slide on the weapon. "I'm taking the truck," he said. "You've got a phone here. Do me a favor and wait an hour before you use it."

She looked up at him, startled. The man who had a few moments ago been slumped in his chair, defeated, was gone. He seemed to have never existed. "What . . . what are you going to do?"

His smile chilled her. "Break cover."

PART THREE

Breaking Cover

CHAPTER FORTY-SEVEN

S O ARE WE GOING to talk about this?" Brett Harper said.

Kendra Wolf thought of a number of evasive replies: *Talk about what?* Or *We have been talking about it,* referring to the investigation. But she knew it wouldn't work. Brett could be sweet, but he was dogged. Once he set his mind on something— the solution to a case, a promotion, her—he would keep going un- til he got it. She could tell from the look in his eyes and the set of his jaw that this was the conversation he wanted to have and by God, the conversation she was going to have.

She sighed and laid the transcripts of the witness interviews on the table. They were in her room in the old mom-and-pop "motor court" that was the best Pine Lake had to offer in the way of accommodations. It wasn't a bad place: Everything was clean, if a bit worn around the edges, and the proprietor had a plate of warm ham biscuits on the office counter every morning. The agents who'd taken over the place made jokes about Mayberry and Aunt Bee, but they always took the biscuits. The rooms, though, were tiny. Two people in one room with the curtain drawn felt as if they were right on top of one another.

"I don't know where to begin," she said slowly.

"Just tell me how you feel about this," he said. "You've been totally shut off from me since the news—"

"I don't know how I feel, Brett!" The words came out more vehemently than she had intended, more angry. She could see his jaw clench. *Great,* she thought. *This is really helping.*

"Look," she said a little more calmly. "Four days ago, I was convinced my husband was dead. Now I know he's alive. But I have no idea why he hasn't contacted me in four years. So I'm angry. I'm hurt. I'm worried. I'm confused. And the confusion makes me angry again because I don't like being confused."

He nodded. This last was something he could understand. Unanswered questions, he had always told her, seemed to bother him more than they bothered other people. They nagged at him, robbed him of sleep, made him irritable. It made him a good agent. It also made him a bit of a pain in the ass to work with. But Kendra had always had the same feelings. He was one of the few people, she felt, who really got that part of her. One of the other ones, of course, was Tony. Which brought her back to square one.

"I understand," Brett was saying. "You really need to know more facts before you know how to feel."

At first, she was appalled. What a bloodless way of looking at things, she thought. Not knowing how to feel until you had all the facts . . . that sounded like something an android would say.

Again, she thought of Tony. One thing he never had trouble with was knowing how he felt. It was one thing he had never had any trouble telling her, either. She had often wondered how two people so different had ended up together. She knew she had a reputation as an ice queen with her co-workers, while Tony had had a natural talent for being at ease with people. He had put her at ease with herself.

Suddenly, she missed him so badly it seemed as if her heart would burst. *Not now,* she said angrily to herself. *Not here.* You *have one more thing to do.*

"Brett," she said, trying to keep her voice steady despite the lump in her throat, "there's something you need to know."

He caught the tone in her voice and sat down in the rickety chair opposite her. "What?"

She couldn't look him in the eye. "I think I might be pregnant."

He didn't answer right away. She looked up. His face was still and expressionless, but he was blinking rapidly. *Processing the information,* she thought. *Trying to decide how to feel.* The flash of hatred she felt for him was brief, there and gone in an instant, but it staggered her as much as her earlier yearning. It vanished as quickly as it had come, leaving a burn of resentment behind. *How can you be so calm?* she thought. *For God's sake, react. Yell yippee! Scream at me. Punch the wall. Anything.*

Instead, all he said was "How did this happen?"

Her heart broke all over again. She realized that she did not love this man; she could never love this man; she had wanted to feel that again so badly, but this was not going to be the man she felt it for. He was, she thought with bitter amusement, just that little bit too much like herself for her to ever love him.

She forced out a laugh. "The usual way, I suppose."

He shook his head. "Don't joke about this," he snapped. "I thought we were being careful."

"You mean you thought *I* was being careful," she said, "and I thought I was. I don't know what happened."

He thought a bit more. "Are you sure?"

"No. I mean, I haven't been to a doctor. All I have is a home pregnancy test I took right before . . . before all of this."

He grimaced. "Wonderful timing."

"It's not the time I would have picked, no."

He stood up. "Well, there's no use making any decisions until we're sure." She could see him filing the problem away, putting it aside until he could get the facts that would tell him how he should feel. "When are you going back to Washington?" he said.

"What do you mean? I'm going back when this investigation is over."

"You think that's a good idea? To wait?"

"One way or another, we'll be through here in a few days."

He looked at her. "And what about the emotional ramifications of this?" he said coldly. "Do you think it's a good idea for you to be involved in this, all things considered?"

"Well," she said with equal coldness, "I guess I won't know what the emotional ramifications are until all the facts are in, will I?"

He flinched as if he'd been slapped. Then he turned on his heel and walked out, slamming the door as he went.

She took a deep breath, let it out. She walked over to the bed, slowly, as if she were afraid of falling. She lowered herself onto the bed, moving carefully as if she might break, until she was lying on her back staring at the ceiling. She took a deep breath, let it out. She took another. Let it out.

She wondered when she'd forgotten how to cry.

CHAPTER FORTY-EIGHT

THE ROAR OF THE BIG MOTORCYCLES rattled the store's front windows and shivered the bottles in the drink cooler. The girl behind the counter glanced up from her magazine, her eyes brightening with unaccustomed interest. She spent every day after school behind this counter, looking at the same faces, making the same small talk. Any change in the routine was something to savor.

She watched the bikes pull in, a dozen at least, along with a large white van. The riders were clad in black leather adorned with silver and black patches across the back. One by one, they throttled the bikes down and dismounted. They moved stiffly, as if they'd had a long ride. She put down the magazine, smiling shyly as the first of the bikers entered the store.

"Hey," she said.

The man stopped and looked her over appraisingly, his eyes glittering in a weather-beaten, bearded face. "Hey, yourself," he answered.

"I like your bikes," she said.

"Thanks," he said. Then the press of his companions behind

him pushed him farther into the store. For the next few minutes, she was busy, taking money for gasoline, beer, snacks, and cigarettes. It was the most business the place had done in months.

When the first guy came up to the counter again, he asked, "So what's your name, sweet thing?"

"Alison," she said.

He stuck out a hand. "I'm Pete," he said.

She shook it. "Hey, Pete," she said. "So where're you guys from?"

"Oh, here and there," Pete said. "Seems like a nice little town you've got here."

She made a face. "It sucks," she said. "Nothing ever happens here. It's soooo boring."

"So, Alison," Pete said. "You want to go for a ride?"

She sighed theatrically. "I've got to work."

"So what time you get off?"

She brightened. "Five."

"Well, then, I'll be back at five." Pete smiled. "Maybe you can show me around. Show me some of the sights."

"Welllll," she said, her reluctance so exaggerated it was clear she meant something entirely different, "I don't know . . ."

"C'mon, honey," Pete said, "it's only a bike ride. I'll have you home by dinnertime."

She knew it was a bad idea, but it was something to break the monotony. And despite the leather, Pete at least seemed like a nice guy. You couldn't just go around judging people by appearances. People had done that to her for years, making fun of her tongue stud and the way she wore her hair, calling her "freak" and "goth girl." Pete was older, and he'd probably been through a lot of the same things. "Okay," she said. "But not here." Nadine had the shift after her, and that dried-up old bitch saw her leaving with a biker, she'd be on the phone to Alison's dad as fast as her bony fingers could dial. "I'll meet you at the lake," she said. She gave him directions.

"Great," he said. "See you then." He stopped. "Hey," he said, "how old are you anyway?"

The lie came easy, like it always did. "Eighteen."

He grinned again. "Okay." He walked out.

In the parking lot, Pete stopped to stretch his back. Florida Bob came out behind him, carrying a plastic bag with two sixes of Bud. "Eighteen." He chuckled. "Right."

"Hey," Pete said, "if they're old enough to bleed, they're old enough to breed, right?"

Bob laughed. "And she's still got her baby fat."

"Just the way I like it, my man," Pete said. "You want a piece of her when I'm done?"

"Well, I don't much care for sloppy seconds," Bob said. "But if you had her after me, she'd be so stretched out it'd be like throwing a hot dog down a hallway."

"Fuck you," Pete said, laughing. "You want to share or not?"

Bob shrugged. "Maybe. We'll see what shakes out." He looked around the parking lot and shook his head. "Jesus," he said, "what a dipshit town."

"Hey," Clay yelled from the driver's seat of the van. "Let's get moving."

Pete, aka Pete the Perv, and Florida Bob acknowledged the summons with a wave and saddled up.

CHAPTER FORTY-NINE

WOLF ROLLED INTO TOWN just under the speed limit. He wanted to avoid traffic stops; some of the gear he was carrying under tarps in the back of the truck would take more explaining than he felt up to. He passed the liquor stores, the car lots assuring poor-risk buyers that their job was their credit, the pawnshops where TVs and bling shuttled in and out, bought and lost between paydays. He slowed down as he approached the Leopard Lounge. It was still there, same pale yellow windowless cinder-block walls, same gravel parking lot. It was early evening, between the happy hour crowd and the hard-core drinkers, so there were only a few scattered cars in the lot. He didn't see any bikes. He had no idea what Nathan or Clay was driving these days, but his cursory glance didn't turn up anything ostentatious enough to suggest either was there. He sped up and drove off.

On a whim, he drove to the neighborhood where he'd once lived. The little house was still there, a rusting pickup sagging low on its springs in the drive. It gave Wolf a creepy feeling, thinking that someone else was living in his house.

No, he told himself. *Axel McCabe's house. This house was never yours.* Still, he felt an unaccountable sadness, as if McCabe were a person he'd miss.

His last stop was the Spelling house. It was empty and looked as if it had been that way since he left. A faded FOR SALE sign with the Realtor's name rendered nearly illegible by time and the elements poked up from the shaggy lawn. The paint was peeling, and a screen hung half off one of the windows. It looked like someone had given up even trying to sell the place. Wolf figured that a notorious double suicide in the living room hadn't done much for the house's curb appeal.

He drove back out to the strip and found a mini-storage facility that provided twenty-four-hour access but didn't provide twenty-four-hour live security. He paid cash for a six-month rental. It was a smaller unit than he'd had back in North Carolina; he wasn't planning to stash the truck there. In point of fact, he wasn't planning to need it for six months. He'd be lucky to be alive six days from now, and he rated his chances of surviving six weeks as roughly those of his being selected for *American Idol*. But he wasn't going out quietly. Or alone. Knowing that, for the first time in years he wasn't afraid anymore.

He stashed the supplies he'd brought in the rental unit. He paid cash for a cheap room in a nearby motel and got a good night's sleep. He figured it was the last one he'd have.

CHAPTER FIFTY

BUCKTHORN PULLED HIS CRUISER UP to the small hut that served as a makeshift office for the Pine Lake Campground. As he got out of the car, he could hear the roar and rumble of motorcycles from down the hill. He glanced down the long slope toward the big lake that gave the town its name. Half a dozen tents nestled among the pine trees, unusual for this off-season, and doubly unusual for the middle of the week. Some tents had big bikes parked in front. A couple of men clad in leather and denim relaxed at one of the picnic tables, drinking beer. Others were building campfires. Several other men were riding their own machines up and down the gravel paths. Buckthorn could smell the exhaust from the top of the hill.

Buckthorn turned back to see Romy Watts, the owner of the campground, coming out of the hut. He was wiping his hands on his overalls.

"Evenin', Sheriff," Watts said. "Any trouble?"

"Nothing major, Romy," Buckthorn said. "Just got some concerned calls about a bunch of bikers coming through town. Looks like they decided to stay the night."

"Yessir," Romy said, ducking his head slightly, as if he had just barely stopped himself from bowing. "Paid for a few days, in fact. In cash. In advance."

"That so."

"But they ain't caused no trouble. 'Cept the noise." He looked nervously down the hill. "I can tell 'em to be quiet."

Yeah, thought Buckthorn. *That'll work.* "Noise ordinance doesn't kick in till sundown," he said. "They're all right till then. Assuming they behave themselves otherwise."

"Like I said, no trouble."

"Guess there won't be any objection to me goin' down there and saying hello, then," Buckthorn said. "Just to welcome our new visitors."

Romy looked unhappy, but he ducked his head again. Buckthorn took that as assent. He walked down the gravel path toward the campsites. He saw one of the men at the picnic table say something, saw the other one look in his direction. Others stopped poking the campfires and straightened up. Buckthorn silently counted. Looked like a dozen men, all told. Then he noticed the van parked on the concrete slab of the campground's handicapped accommodation. There was a man in a wheelchair sitting by the campsite's picnic table. As Buckthorn approached, one of the riders killed his engine, dismounted his bike, and strode over to the picnic table to stand beside the man in the wheelchair, who motioned to him impatiently. The rider bent down to hear what the man in the wheelchair had to say, nodding quickly as he listened.

That's the leader, Buckthorn thought, then he slowed, almost stopped, before picking up his pace again. *A man in a wheelchair,* he thought, *running a biker gang*. Couldn't be too many of those. He thought about the story Blauner had told him, of how Wolf had crippled the leader of the bikers he'd been investigating. If what Blauner had said was true, then these were some very dangerous people. Buckthorn suddenly wished with all his heart that he'd called for backup. But there was no way to back away now.

He had reached the handicapped site. The man in the wheelchair looked up at him, his face impassive. "Evenin'," Buckthorn said. There was no response at first; then the man nodded.

Buckthorn heard a couple more of the bikes throttle down, leaving only one rumbling along the lakeshore. He thought he could hear footsteps in the gravel behind him. He felt cold sweat beading on the back of his neck. "Just wanted to stop by and welcome you fellas to town."

The man who'd gotten off the motorcycle snorted. "Right," he said. The man in the wheelchair shot him a look before turning back to Buckthorn. "Thanks," he said.

"I'm Tim Buckthorn," he said. "Just wanted to make sure you fellas knew about some of the town ordinances. So there wouldn't be any, ah, misunderstandings."

"No," the man in the wheelchair said. "Wouldn't want that."

"I didn't get your name," Buckthorn said.

"Didn't tell you," the man in the wheelchair said. "But I'm Johnny."

The name removed all doubt. Johnny had to be Johnny Trent. These men were here looking for Anthony Wolf. Well, Buckthorn thought, the best way to get these thugs out of his town was to convince them that Wolf was gone. But to do that now would tip Johnny Trent off that Buckthorn knew who he was, and he didn't find the idea appealing right then. He decided the friendly-dumb-hick-sheriff routine was working fine.

"Pleased to meet you, Johnny," Buckthorn said. "We got a noise ordinance startin' at sundown, so you fellas want to keep the bikes quiet after then." He could hear the one motorcycle ripping and roaring behind him, as if mocking him. "You can drink your beers inside the campground, but there's a public display ordinance, too. So no alcohol on town streets. 'Course, no drinkin' and drivin'. We do run DWI checkpoints, and state law don't let us give no warnin's. Okay?"

Johnny Trent's gaze never wavered. *You're not fooling anyone with this cornpone bullshit,* that gaze said, *but I'll let it go.*

"Okay, then," Buckthorn said, absurdly pleased with himself at how steady his voice sounded. "You guys have fun here. And welcome to Pine Lake." He turned. There was a solid wall of bikers behind him. He didn't break stride, and the line parted at the last possible second to let him past. He didn't look back, but he concentrated all his attention on listening behind him. He didn't hear the sound of running footsteps, and to look back to see if anyone was sneaking up would be a sign of weakness. So he didn't.

He was so busy thinking of what was behind him, he didn't see the motorcycle until it pulled onto the path ahead of him. There were two people on the bike, a man and a girl. As the man gunned the bike up the path, the girl looked back at him, laughing. The smile on her face died as they recognized each other. *Oh, shit,* he saw her say, and he knew just how she felt. She turned back to the man steering the bike and said something to him. He slowed, stopped, turned the bike to face Buckthorn. He began gunning the engine as if he were going to peel out and run Buckthorn over. The girl was pounding on his shoulder frantically, saying something Buckthorn couldn't hear. He hesitated, and Buckthorn used the interval to step forward and grab the bike handlebars with his left hand. "Stop the bike," he said. The rider acted as if he didn't hear. He grinned and gunned the motor again. Buckthorn reached down and unsnapped his holster. The man's eyes widened. "*Stop the bike!*" Buckthorn yelled. The man hesitated, then killed the engine. The sudden silence was deafening.

"Get off the bike, Alison," Buckthorn said.

"Hey, asshole," the rider said, "she's with—"

"She's with who, *asshole?*" Buckthorn snapped. "Before you answer me, let me just tell you something. This girl is fifteen years old."

The man's jaw snapped shut with an audible click. He gave Alison a wounded look that would have been comical under other circumstances. As it was, the sound of heavy boots slowly crunching up the gravel path behind him squelched any humor Buckthorn might have found in the situation. "Now, *sir,*" he almost spat the last word, "you have anything else you want to say?" *Before that pack of wolves behind me kills me and eats me*, he thought. He looked at the girl. She was looking down sullenly, her shoulders slumped. "Look at me, Alison," he said.

She looked up. Her eyes were red and glassy.

"Now," Buckthorn said, "if I was to do a search incident to a lawful arrest for, say, failure of either you or your passenger to wear a helmet, I'm sure I wouldn't find any evidence anyone here has either been possessing controlled substances or providing same to a minor. Would I?"

"I ain't done nothin'," Alison mumbled.

"Shut up, girl," Buckthorn snapped. *And maybe I can get us both out of this alive.*

"No," the man on the bike said through clenched teeth.

"Good," Buckthorn said. He released the handlebars. He turned. The line of bikers had re-formed behind him, glaring at him with open hostility. Both sides stood there frozen, each waiting for the other to escalate things the next notch higher.

A man shouldered his way through the line. It was the same man who'd previously stood beside Johnny Trent. "Let her go, Pete," the man said. He grinned at Buckthorn, but there was no humor or friendliness in the smile. *The joke's on you,* that smile said.

"Aw, shit, come on, Clay," the man on the bike began, then stopped as that grin was turned his way.

"Let's go, Alison," Buckthorn said. He grasped her by the shoulder and started marching her back up the path. Once again, all his attention was turned to listening behind him.

"Why don't you leave me alone?" the girl muttered. "You ain't my daddy."

"Alison," Buckthorn said, "I've known you all your life. I was there when you were baptized. I even taught you in Sunday school. But girl, I'm telling you truly, if you don't shut up, I'm going to punch you right in the mouth." The threat stunned her into silence. As he bundled her into the patrol car, Buckthorn saw that the hut/office had a hand-lettered sign in the window. GONE TO SUPPER, the sign said. BACK IN AN HOUR.

"Thanks a lot, Romy," Buckthorn muttered. He started the car.

Alison slumped in the passenger seat, looking out the window. "I guess you're going to tell my dad," she said.

"I guess I am."

"I'll tell him you threatened to hit me."

"Go ahead. Girl, have you got any idea how damn stupid you're bein'?"

"You're just picking on them because of the way they look," she flared. "You're just like—" She stopped, then slumped back into the seat, like a marionette with its strings cut.

"Just like the kids at school who pick on you," Buckthorn said. "Don't look so surprised, Alison. I know what's going on. But there's a difference here. These are some very dangerous people you're playing with."

"So *you* say. Besides, they're so dangerous, why don't you arrest them? Huh?" Her face brightened with malice. "You're scared of them, is that it?"

The words stung. Fact was, Buckthorn *had* been afraid. He didn't like the feeling one bit.

"No," Buckthorn said. "They haven't done anything here I can arrest them for. Not yet. And I aim to see that they don't."

"They're my friends," Alison said. "You can't keep me from seeing them."

Buckthorn tried not to grit his teeth. His warnings seemed only to increase the teenager's attraction to the bikers. "I sure as hell can. If I have to handcuff you to the front porch."

"You can't do that. I got rights."

No, Buckthorn thought, *I really can't do that.* He wondered just what he could do to protect his town.

CHAPTER FIFTY-ONE

"PINE LAKE'S FINEST," Clay sneered.

"Hah," Pete said. "Did you see the look in his eyes? He was scared shitless."

"He was just checking us out," Johnny said. "Next time, he won't come alone. We'll worry about that when it happens. Speaking of checking things out, Clay, you find out anything?"

"Yeah," Clay said. "McCabe and those two kids are the only thing around here anybody's talking about. He was living out here under the name of Sanders. Rentin' a farm outside of town."

"You seen it yet?"

"No. But word is he had the place wired up. Even had a damn minefield."

"Bullshit," Pete said. "Where the hell'd he get mines?"

Clay shrugged. "That's what I heard."

"Stories get exaggerated," Johnny said. "But we can figure McCabe or Sanders or whoever the fuck he is is packing some pretty serious firepower."

"Yeah. Well, so are we," Clay said. "But McCabe's gone. We got any idea where?"

Johnny thought about his uncle Nathan's inside source. He'd known for a long time that the source existed, somewhere inside the Feds, but the precise identity had been a secret Nathan guarded jealously.

"Let me make a phone call," Johnny said. "I might be able to get some leads." No one moved. "A private phone call," Johnny said.

"Come on," Clay said. "Let's go get fucked up." As they moved away, Johnny pulled out his cell phone and dialed.

Nathan picked up on the first ring. "Johnny," he said.

"You hear anything?"

"Matter of fact, I have. Looks like the FBI's snooping around in the area for our friend Axel McCabe."

"They're here?"

"Yep. In force. And here's the good part. My person on the inside's done well for himself the past few years. He's gotten a lot more inside, you might say."

"And?"

"I know McCabe's real name." He paused.

"Well?" Johnny said. "You want me to play Twenty fucking Questions?"

"You might want to watch your tone with me, Johnny. Let's not forget it was you that brought McCabe into the Brotherhood."

Johnny's free hand gripped the wheelchair rail, white knuckled. "Sorry," he said through gritted teeth. The bastard wanted to play games, Johnny didn't have much choice but to take it, at least for now.

"It's okay," Nathan said indulgently. "You've been under a lot of stress."

Johnny thought how sweet it would be to put a bullet in his uncle's head right then. *Later*, he promised himself. *Soon.*

"Yeah. Okay," he said. "The name."

"Axel McCabe's real name is Anthony Wolf. He was FBI. They're really anxious to talk to him, too. Especially his wife."

"His *wife?*"

"Yeah. She's an agent, too." Nathan chuckled. "I wonder what Mrs. Wolf would do if she found out what her hubby was up to while he was undercover?"

Johnny's mind was racing. "Maybe I should ask her."

"Whoa. Whoa. Now wait a minute, Johnny. You do *not* go fucking around with an FBI agent. That is heat we do not need."

"Don't worry," Johnny said. "I won't do anything stupid."

"Okay. See that you don't. I know you want this bastard, but let me—"

Johnny cut him off. "I will. No problem." He shut the phone.

You don't get it, he thought. *Yeah, Uncle Nathan. I want your job. I want the Brotherhood. But more than anything else, I want the bastard who took my legs. I want to hear him scream when I cripple him. I want to hear him beg for his life, then I want to hear him beg for death. And I'll tear the Brotherhood down for that. I'll tear down the whole fucking world for that.*

NATHAN HUNG up the phone. He leaned back in his chair and stared at the wall. Johnny was beginning to worry him. Johnny had been his heir apparent for years before he went inside. Clay was too crazy to trust with anything but the most brutal kind of wet work, while Johnny had been the cool one. Now, his legs gone, his mind solely focused on revenge, Johnny was getting as crazy as Clay, while retaining his intelligence. That made him dangerous. Nathan Trent wondered if Johnny was thinking of taking a run at him. He hoped not. He liked his nephew. He would hate to have to kill him.

CHAPTER FIFTY-TWO

"YOU KNOW, CUZ," CLAY SAID, "I had a thought."

"Be nice to it," Johnny said. "It's in a lonely place."

"Fuck you," Clay said without anger. He took a long pull off the blunt in his hand and passed it to Johnny. After he held it for a moment, he blew out a long stream of smoke and went on. "No, seriously. Some of the guys have been checking this burg out. Man, it's like . . . I don't know." Johnny waited for the thought to percolate through all the smoke in Clay's brain. The campfire cracked and hissed in the silence. Somewhere in the darkness, somebody laughed drunkenly.

"Nobody runs this place, man," Clay finally said. "It's all small-time dealers. It looks like most of the product they make themselves. There's no . . . no . . ."

"Organization," Florida Bob piped up from the other side of Johnny. Johnny passed him the blunt.

"Organization, right," Clay nodded. "It's not run . . . ah . . ." He trailed off, looking into the campfire with half-closed eyes.

"Efficiently," Johnny offered.

"Right. Right. Not efficient."

"Duplication of effort. No maximization of profit."

Clay squinted at him. "Huh?"

"Nothing," Johnny said. "You think we should maybe set ourselves up here?"

"Could be," Clay said. "Lot of green to be made with the right guy running it."

And that won't be you, cuz, Johnny thought. *Not in a million years. But it's something to consider. Florida Bob might . . .*

There was motion just outside the circle of firelight. Pete stepped forward, his arm around a girl. "Hey, fellas," he said, his teeth bared in something that might have been mistaken for a smile. "Look who's back."

Alison smiled shyly. "Hey," she said.

"WE'VE BEEN over this and over this," Gaby said. "There's nothing more I can tell you."

"And she's already told you a lot more than she has to, Agent Steadman," the station's lawyer put in. "Plus, it's late. If you don't have anything else to ask, you need to let Miss Torrijos go."

The FBI agent took off his glasses and rubbed his eyes. "Tell me again about the storage facility. The one where he was keeping the cash and weapons. Were there any road signs, any indication where—"

"Pat," the blond female agent sitting next to him broke in. "She's right. She's been over this before. She doesn't know any more than she's told us."

Gaby couldn't stop the rush of gratitude she felt, even though she knew that the agents were probably just playing the ancient "good cop, bad cop" routine. There was a reason it was a cliché. Even when you knew you were being played, it was effective.

Steadman sighed. He got up and stretched. He stared off into space for a moment, then looked at Gaby. "Stay here," he said. "I'll be right back."

Gaby looked at the large mirror hanging on the wall of the interview room before looking back at the female agent. "He's going to ask permission to let me go, isn't he?"

The female agent, a slender blonde, looked startled for a second; then her face returned to the same impassive mask she had worn throughout the interview. "You need to let us ask the questions, Miss Torrijos."

"Straight out of the book," Gaby said with a tired smile. "But I am going to ask one more question. Sorry, it's kind of what I do."

The woman stared at her for a moment; then Gaby saw the barest hint of a smile. "Go ahead, then."

"Are you Tony's wife?"

The smile vanished. The woman stood up abruptly. "How do you—"

"He talked about you," Gaby said.

The mask had splintered. The woman—Kendra, Gaby now knew—had a look of pure need on her face, almost desperation. Normally it was the sort of moment a reporter lived for, the "gotcha" moment, but now Gaby felt like she'd ripped away the agent's clothing. "How . . . what did he . . ." She stopped, obviously struggling to get hold of herself, to piece the shattered armor back together.

"He's still in love with you," Gaby said. "I could tell. It was in his face whenever he said the words 'my wife.'"

The woman's face twisted. For a moment Gaby thought she was going to slap her. Then she said, "He's got a damned funny way . . ." She bit the words off and then, as if by magic, the mask was there again.

"He doesn't know who to—" Gaby began, but the woman had moved to the door and was gone before she could get the words out. Gaby sat in silence for a moment, staring at the door, before the lawyer spoke up.

"Want to tell me what that was all about?"

"Not really," Gaby said.

CHAPTER FIFTY-THREE

THE CELL PHONE'S RINGTONE brought Nathan up out of sleep. He rolled over and snatched the phone up to look at the screen. It was one of his contacts in the local police, a junior detective named Enloe. He snapped the phone open. "This better be good to wake me up," he snapped.

"Mr. Trent," Enloe said, "you need to come down to the club."

"Why?" Nathan snapped. "What the fuck—"

"Somebody just bombed it."

"What the fuck do you mean—"

"The fire department's there now. I don't know that they'll be able to save anything."

By the time Nathan got there, the building was almost completely consumed. There were still some spots blazing, but most of what was left was charred piles of soaked rubble. Fire trucks were parked haphazardly in the gravel parking lot, lights flashing in mad cacophony.

The fire chief stepped up to him as he exited his vehicle. "Sorry, Mr. Trent," he said in a voice that told Nathan he was anything but. "Doesn't look like you'll be openin' for business tomorrow night." The man was practically smirking at him. Nathan glanced at the man's lapel and saw the cross pin there. So that explained it. He fought back the urge to punch the sanctimonious fuck in the mouth. "What happened?" he said in a strangled voice.

The fire chief put on a face of such exaggerated thoughtfulness that Nathan knew the man was still laughing at him. *You better be right with God, you cocksucker,* Nathan thought, *because you may be going to meet him real soon now.*

"Well, now, we won't know for sure till the investigators are all done," he said, "but from the way the fire spread, it looks like there were at least three places where it started, at roughly the same time. That means it had to have been deliberately set. And from the damage at those points, I'd say some kind of explosive device was used." The chief looked at Nathan shrewdly. "Your insurance all paid up?"

"I don't have any," Nathan said, "so you can drop the idea I did this."

"Huh." The chief was openly grinning now. "Well, I guess you must've made somebody mad, then."

A yellow-coated firefighter trotted up to the chief and whispered something in his ear. The grin vanished. He looked at Nathan. "We got another call," he said. "The address 479 Greenhill Road mean anything to you?"

The Brotherhood's clubhouse, Nathan thought. He felt sick. "What about it?"

"It's on fire, too." The fire chief shook his head. "You and your boys must've made someone *really* mad."

T HANKS FOR COMING, TIM," Jeff Slocum said.

"No problem." Buckthorn took off his hat as he came inside. "What's going on?"

"It's Alison. She snuck out after we went to bed last night. This morning, she come in and . . . well, look for yourself."

Buckthorn walked into the living room. Alison was seated on the couch, a blanket around her hunched shoulders. Her eyes were vacant, staring at the morning show on the TV. As Buckthorn got closer, he could see scratches on her face and what looked like small bruises on her neck. He sat down next to her. He realized that what he was seeing was bite marks. "Alison?" he said. She didn't answer. He reached out to touch her shoulder. She flinched away with a panicked whine. She looked at him, her eyes wide with fear; then the dullness came over them again. "Alison?" Buckthorn said again.

"I'm fine," the girl said in a barely audible voice.

"Alison, did you go back out there?" She shook her head. Buckthorn turned to Jeff. "Is she hurt, you know, ah . . . anywhere else?"

Jeff looked helpless. "I don't know. She won't let me or her mama touch her."

Buckthorn turned to Alison again. "Tell me the truth, girl," he said in his best stern-cop voice. "Did you go back to where those men were?"

She didn't answer at first, but her eyes widened with fear. Her lower lip trembled as if she were about to cry. "No," she whispered.

"I think you're lying to me, Alison. I think I'll go back out there and talk to—"

She rounded on him, her eyes suddenly wide and panicked. "No," she said frantically. "Please don't tell them I said anything. Please."

"I have to—"

"No!" she was shrieking now, nearly hysterical. "You can't. You CAN'T!"

"Did they threaten you? Tell me!"

"Please! Please! No!"

"Answer me!" Buckthorn shouted back. "What did they do?"

"Tim!" Jeff was hanging on to Buckthorn's arm. Alison collapsed on the couch, sobbing piteously. "For God's sake, Tim," Jeff whispered. "She's not a criminal. It's like you're interrogating her."

Buckthorn pulled away, his face red with frustration. "She needs to get to a hospital," he said. "They need to do tests."

"No," Alison spoke up from the couch. "I'm fine. I'm okay."

Buckthorn turned to Jeff. "If she won't make a complaint," he said stiffly, "there's nothing I can do. But you need to talk her into going to the hospital."

Jeff looked at him, his eyes almost as panicked as his daughter's. "Like you said. If she says she's okay . . ."

Buckthorn growled deep in his throat and walked to the door. He turned back. "You let them get away with this," he said, "they'll do it again. Maybe even to you."

"You can't stop them," Alison whispered.

Buckthorn put on his hat and left. He was shaken by the naked fear he had seen in the girl's eyes. He knew what had happened, and he had a pretty good idea of what she, and most likely her family, had been threatened with to make her keep quiet. He needed to get his people together. And he needed to talk to the FBI again. It hurt his pride to admit it, but he was going to need some backup.

CHAPTER FIFTY-FIVE

ALL RIGHT," NATHAN SAID. "I want answers, and I want them *right fucking now.*"

The bikers gathered in front of the burned out ruins of the warehouse that had been the Brotherhood's headquarters for the past ten years looked at each other nervously. No one wanted to be the first to speak to Nathan when he was in this state. He was pacing up and down, his jaw working furiously, his hands clenching and unclenching. It was the closest to being out of control that most of them had ever seen him.

"I talked to an old buddy of mine who's vice prez of the Bandidos," one of the bikers, a Hispanic who went by the nickname of Chop, offered. "He swears on his mama's grave they didn't have anything to do with it."

Nathan turned on him. "You believe him?"

Chop thought a minute, then nodded. "Yeah."

"What about the Angels?" someone spoke up.

That caused a brief, uncomfortable silence. If the Hells Angels, the biggest, best-organized, and most vicious of the nation's motorcycle clubs, had turned their hands against them, the Brotherhood was in deep shit.

Nathan shook his head. "No," he said. "I talked to the president of the nearest chapter. They've got no beef with us." He looked around at the circle of blank faces. "Who, goddammit!?" he shouted. "Who the fuck would do this!?"

"Hell," Tiny spoke up, "who *could* do this?" He gestured at the smoking wreckage with one huge hand. "I mean, look at this shit, homes. This didn't happen 'cause someone left the oven on. Somebody blew us the fuck up."

The phone on Nathan's belt rang. He snatched it up and looked at the number on the caller ID. Stoney. He snapped the phone open. "What'd you find out?"

"More than you might think," a familiar voice said.

Nathan felt the blood drain from his face. He couldn't speak for a moment.

"Stoney's fine, by the way," Tony Wolf said. "Good of you to ask."

Nathan got himself under control. "So I guess you're the one I need to talk to about the club. And the clubhouse."

"And a couple of labs I found out in the woods. Oh, and your car."

"My *car?* My car's right—"

There was a loud *whump* from the street. All heads turned at once. Nathan's Suburban was on fire, burning brightly. As the group watched, dumbfounded, a pair of motorcycles nearby went up, one after the other.

"Holy shit!" Tiny yelled. "He's here!"

A couple of the bikers went for pistols concealed in their jackets or waistbands, but the sudden eruption of gunfire from behind the fence across the street sent them diving for cover. When they finally dared raise their heads, two more bikes were burning. There was no sign of Wolf.

"What the fuck was he firing at us?" Chop asked.

"Sounded like a goddamn cannon," someone said.

Nathan got slowly to his feet. His face was nearly purple with rage. He snapped his phone open and hit speed dial. "Johnny," he said. "Wolf 's here. He's got Stoney's phone. You still have that number?" A pause. "Good. Do whatever you have to do. Whatever." He shut the phone.

S O, STONEY," WOLF SAID, "where's Johnny these days?"
"Fuck you," Stoney snapped back. He was handcuffed to
a pipe running from floor to ceiling in the garage of the
Spelling house. Wolf had taken the gag out of his mouth when
he'd pulled his truck back into the garage after paying his visit to
the clubhouse. The garage door was shut.

Wolf shrugged. "Suit yourself." He took a box out of the back
of the truck. Several bottlenecks showed above the edges of the
box. Each bottle had a rag stuck in it. Stoney licked his lips nervously.

Wolf took one of the bottles out of the box. He produced a cigarette lighter from his back pocket.

Stoney's eyes zeroed in on the lighter as Wolf flicked it on.
"What the fuck, man?" he said, his voice quavering.

Wolf touched the flame to the rag in the bottle. It caught
quickly.

"Man, you're crazy. You'll burn, too."

Wolf ignored him. He walked into the house through the open
door from the garage. Stoney pulled desperately at the pipe, trying

to dislodge it. The pipe didn't budge. He heard the smashing of glass, then a dull thump, followed by the crackling of flames.

Wolf came back into the garage, humming to himself. He took a couple more of the homemade firebombs and set them a few feet away from Stoney on the concrete floor of the garage. "Okay," he said cheerfully. "It's been nice seeing you again, Stoney." He started to get into the truck.

"*Wait!*" Stoney yelped.

Wolf stopped, half in and half out of the truck. "What?"

"Man, you can't leave me here like this. Not with the house on fire."

"Stoney," Wolf said patiently. "I *am* leaving you like this. With the house on fire."

"I'll burn!"

"Probably. But look on the bright side. Maybe smoke inhalation will get you before the fire reaches those bottles." Wolf shook his head. "Don't look so amazed, Stoney. I mean, let's be honest. You'd do the same thing for me, right?" Stoney didn't answer. He was starting to cry. "*Right?*" Wolf yelled.

"Look, McCabe. Or Tony. Or whatever. Come on, man. Please. Please?"

Wolf's voice was calm again. "It's nothing personal, brother. It's business."

"I can tell you where Johnny is!"

Wolf took the handcuff key out of his pocket. "Yeah?"

"Yeah. Just . . . just let me go, man." The sound of flames was louder now. Smoke was beginning to waft into the garage.

"Where?"

"Let me go!"

"I haven't got time to argue. You may have noticed the house is on fire." Wolf got into the truck and started it. He hit a button, and the garage door began to rattle upward. The smoke was getting thicker.

"He's in Pine Lake!" Stoney shrieked. "That town you were hiding in! He's looking for you!"

Wolf leaned out the window. He tossed the handcuff key at Stoney's feet. "See?" he called out as he started backing up. "That wasn't so hard, was it? Oh, and good luck explaining things to the fire department." As Stoney dropped to his knees, scrabbling for the key, Wolf backed the truck out of the garage and was gone.

CHAPTER FIFTY-SEVEN

T HOSE GUYS YOU WERE INVESTIGATING? The Brother-hood? They're—"

"Here," Steadman said. "Yes, Deputy Buckthorn, we know."

"I need to know if I can count on the FBI. Those guys are here in force."

"Yes, sir," Blauner said. "We're aware of that as well."

Buckthorn looked at the faces around the rickety conference table. The room was barely big enough to hold the table, much less the bodies around it. Sheriff Stark sat at the head, looking uncomfortable. Buckthorn was at his right. The FBI contingent—Steadman, Blauner, Ross, the blond woman who Buckthorn had been told was Wolf's wife, Kendra, and some kid who barely looked old enough to shave—were crammed elbow to elbow around the table. "Well?" Buckthorn demanded.

"Well, what?" Steadman said, his face bland.

"Look, I—" He shot a glance at the sheriff. "We could use some help."

"That's being taken under advisement—" Steadman began.

Buckthorn cut him off. "And just what the hell does *that*—"

"Tim," Stark broke in.

Great, Buckthorn thought. *Now he speaks.*

"The kidnapping investigation is closed," Steadman said. "We've pretty much gotten everything we're going to get here on our missing agent. And there's not a current operation pending against the Brotherhood. It was shut down after Agent Wolf 's"— he glanced at Kendra—"disappearance."

"Well, reopen it!" Buckthorn said.

"We're looking into the possibility of doing just that, Deputy Buckthorn," Steadman said. He leaned on the word "Deputy" just a little and glanced at the sheriff. Stark reddened slightly. "But these things have to be approved. We've got to figure out whose budget—"

"For God's sake," Buckthorn exploded, "my county's being invaded by the goddamn Mongols, and you're talking budgets!"

"Not the Mongols," the kid spoke up.

Buckthorn turned to him. "What?"

"The Mongols," the kid said. "They're a different gang. They work out of California."

Steadman was massaging the bridge of his nose, his eyes closed in apparent pain. "Thank you, Agent Harper," he said.

"Look," Buckthorn said, trying to keep his voice level. "I think these punks sexually assaulted a teenaged girl last night."

"What?" Stark said, sitting up straight. "Why didn't you—"

"She won't talk," Buckthorn said. "She's terrified. Near hysterical. They threatened her somehow."

"That's . . . unfortunate," Steadman said, his face once again expressionless. "But we don't have any jurisdiction. Sexual assault isn't a federal matter. It's a local one."

"He's right, Tim," Stark broke in. "I think we can handle a bunch of roughnecks."

Buckthorn just stared at him. The punch line of the old Lone Ranger and Tonto joke ran through his mind: *What's this "we" shit, white man?* He stood up. "Yes, sir," he said. He walked out.

Duane Willis was waiting in the hallway, fussing around at the water cooler. He straightened up as Buckthorn approached. "What's the word, boss man?"

"For right now," Buckthorn said, "we're on our own."

"Shit."

"Couldn't have said it better myself. I want someone on those bikers 24/7, Duane. At least two-man teams. Constant surveillance. And don't be sneaky about it. I want them to know we're watching."

Willis's brow furrowed. "That's gonna run into some overtime."

"I don't care. We are on those bastards like white on rice from now on. I don't want them feeling comfortable doing so much as taking a piss without turning around to see if we're watching."

"How long we going to keep that up?"

"Until they get tired and leave."

"Or till one of 'em gets pissed and decides to do somethin' about it."

"They do that," Buckthorn said, "and we land on them with both feet."

"Roger that, sir!" Willis barked out. Then he looked sheepish. "Sorry, sir," he said, "I wasn't tryin' to be a smart-ass."

"No problem, Duane." Buckthorn smiled. "You keep in that wild-ass marine frame of mind. Something tells me we're going to need it."

Willis grinned. "Yes, sir." He looked as if he were about to salute, then chuckled and walked away.

Buckthorn turned to see Kendra Wolf leaning against the wall. She had her arms crossed across her chest and the merest ghost of a smile on her lips.

"What?" Buckthorn barked.

The ghost vanished. "Why do you do it?" she said.

"Do what?"

She jerked her chin back toward the now empty conference room. "You're ten times the cop your boss is." Her lip curled. "He's more like the head of the chamber of commerce. Why aren't you in charge?"

Buckthorn shrugged. "He's good at what he does."

"Which is what, exactly?"

"Winning elections."

She thought about that, then nodded. "And you'd suck at that."

Buckthorn laughed out loud. "Yeah," he said. "I don't seem to have what they call the gift of gab."

"Me, either. I'm staying, by the way."

"Staying where?"

"Here. I'm going to be keeping an eye on things here while Agent Steadman does what he's good at."

"Which is what, exactly?"

"Working the bureaucracy."

"So he's really trying to get something going. He's wasn't just blowing me off."

"Pat Steadman is a lot of things, Deputy Buckthorn, but he's not a liar. And he wants these bastards as much as you do. He's just a little more calm about it."

Buckthorn grimaced. "I blew it in there, didn't I?"

"Like you said." The slight smile was back. "Don't worry," she said, "you're good at what you do. And we'll give you what help we can until Steadman can do the Bureau voodoo dance."

"We?"

"Agent Blauner's staying, too. He worked some on the original investigation. He knows the players within the Brotherhood. We're staying at the motor court, just outside town. I'm in room seven. Blauner's in eight."

"Okay. Good. I'll take what help I can get till the cavalry arrives."

"Well," she said, "it may not be the cavalry you expect."

"What do you mean?"

She hesitated. "I think my . . . I think Agent Wolf may be coming back here. Once he figures out where Clay and Johnny Trent are."

"Why would he do that?"

"He's devoted a lot of his life to destroying this organization. Then he had to hide from them for four years." She smiled sadly. "Tony Wolf is not the kind of man that would enjoy hiding. I don't think he'll go back to it. He doesn't trust us. Which leaves him with one choice."

"To go after them."

"Exactly."

"Look, Agent Wolf—"

"Kendra."

"Look, Kendra. I don't mean your husband any disrespect, but the last thing I need is some crazed vigilante rolling through, shooting everything up."

"If I see him, I'll let him know."

"You still don't have any way of contacting him?"

She shook her head. "I wish I did."

"Well, if he gets in touch with you, tell him to stay away. We'll handle this."

"I hope you can."

"Yeah," Buckthorn said. "Me, too."

CHAPTER FIFTY-EIGHT

"COME ON, DUDE," the long-haired man whined. He knelt on the cheap carpet of the single-wide trailer. Sweat ran down his face and soaked his T-shirt. "I ain't done nothin' to you."

"Didn't say you had . . . what was your name again?" The man didn't answer. Clay pushed the 9 mm pistol a little harder against his ear. "Bobby Lee Sessoms!" the man blurted out.

"Well, Bobby Lee Sessoms," Clay said in a voice that was an oily parody of an infomercial host's, "we're not here because we're mad at you. We're here, Bobby Lee Sessoms, to offer you, and your lovely lady over there on the couch . . . what's her name, by the way?"

Bobby Lee shot a despairing glance over to where his girlfriend, a short-haired blonde, sat between two grinning bikers. One had an arm draped casually around her shoulders. Her eyes were wide with terror. "Barbara," he whispered.

"Bobby Lee and Barbara. That's so cute I can't hardly stand it. Well, Bobby Lee and Barbara," Clay said, "we're here to offer you an exciting business opportunity. A chance to be part of a nationwide organization, not just a small-time meth cooker in a dipshit town."

Bobby Lee swallowed. "I ain't got no idea what you're talking about."

"Now, now, Bobby Lee, this isn't a good way to start a business relationship." He shook his head. "Your dealers gave you up, bro. Pete over there didn't even have to break anybody's fingers for them to do it. He was kind of disappointed. Right, Pete?"

Pete nodded, his face sorrowful. Clay went on: "See, that's one of the things we need to change. You'd been running things right, your dealers would've been so afraid of you that Pete would've had to do some serious damage to get them to talk. But I tell you what, Pete." His voice hardened. "This little redneck fucker lies to me again, you and Florida Bob can take little Miss Barbara and her perky tits into the bedroom and do a lot more than break a couple of fingers. How's that sound?"

Pete nodded. "Sounds fair."

Bob nodded as well. "I can live with that."

"Please, man," Bobby Lee said, "don't hurt her."

"That all depends on you," Clay said. "Now listen up, Bobby Lee. This is the way it's going to be from now on. Your output next month is going to double."

"I can't do that," Bobby Lee protested. "I ain't got the makin's—"

"Don't worry," Clay said. "We'll get you the ingredients. And we can get 'em in bulk. Just think, no more running around to drugstores and shit buying cold tablets. All you have to do is cook. Bob over there will be running your dealers. The good news is that if you do what you're supposed to, you'll be making a lot more money. The bad news is that if you don't make your quota, your ol' lady over there works it off in a motel room out on the interstate. You hear me?" Bobby Lee didn't answer. Tears were running down his face, mixing with the sweat. Clay sighed. "Pete, Bob. Looks like it's time to put Babs to work."

"Okay! Okay!" Bobby Lee cried out.

"There you go, then," Clay said. He straightened up. "Now we best leave and let Bobby Lee get to work. He's got some catching up to do."

Pete leered at Barbara. "I guess this means a blowjob is out of the question." She shrank away from him with a small whimper.

"Deal's a deal, Pete," Clay said. "Let Babs alone. She's a little old for you anyway. But cheer up, maybe your little friend from last night will come back."

"See you soon, Bobby Lee," Florida Bob said cheerfully. "It's gonna be great working with you. And Babs. You'll see."

CHAPTER FIFTY-NINE

"MR. TRENT," BUCKTHORN SAID. "I'd like a word with you."

Johnny looked up from his wheelchair, a bored half-smile on his face. "What, Sheriff," he said, "we're not on a first-name basis no more?"

Buckthorn looked out over the campground. Tents were coming down, and bikers were securing packs and bedrolls to the backs of their motorcycles. "You fellows packing up to leave?"

"No. Just got a little tired of camping out."

"Where you planning on staying?"

"We had our eyes on a little place outside of town. An old farmhouse. I hear the previous occupant skipped out on his lease. There was some kind of shootout. Sound familiar?"

Buckthorn turned to look at him. "You wouldn't be talking about the old Jacobs place?"

"That what it's called? I'm not from around here. But maybe that's it. I have one of my associates talking to the nice real estate lady right now."

Buckthorn kept his voice flat. "So you're staying."

Johnny smiled insolently. "No law against it, is there?"

"You don't want to wear out your welcome."

"You know, Sheriff, I didn't know better, I'd think you were threatening me. And the way you and your officers've been breathing down our necks, handing out tickets for crap like littering for flicking a cigarette butt . . ."

Buckthorn smiled tightly. "It's been a dry season," he said. "High risk of forest fire."

"See, it's that kind of attitude that makes me feel like there's some harassment going on. I've even had a talk with our lawyer about whether our civil rights might be bein' violated."

"Your civil . . ."

"See, Sheriff, all these years of people treating us like second-class citizens, just 'cause we dress different and live different from them, we get a little touchy when people treat us like criminals."

Buckthorn gestured at the van. "I guess if I searched that van," he said, "I wouldn't find any guns. Or drugs."

"Now, I'd be pretty stupid to carry that sort of thing around, wouldn't I, Sheriff? Not like we've given anyone any kind of probable cause to do any kind of search."

Buckthorn stared at him, teeth clenched. He could almost feel the enamel grinding away.

Johnny smiled. "Calm down, Sheriff," he said. "You're gonna give yourself a stroke if you don't learn to relax. Besides, not all of us are staying. I've got business back home. Me and some of the boys'll be staying at the motel."

"The motel?"

"Yeah," Johnny said. "That old house isn't exactly handicapped

friendly. And now that all those FBI types are moving out, I bet
the motel could use the business."

Damn, Buckthorn thought. *I need to warn Kendra. Get her out of
there.* The intensity of the feeling startled him. *She's a colleague*,
he thought, *that's all.* But he remembered what she'd said: *You're
ten times the cop your boss is.* Even now, the words gave him a flush
of pride. Well, so what if it did? She was, from what he could see,
a good cop in her own right. Nothing unusual with being pleased
about praise like that. Even if she was a fine-looking woman. *No*,
he thought as he turned without another word and walked away
from the smirking man in the wheelchair, *nothing unusual about
that at all.*

CHAPTER SIXTY

COUNTRY LIVIN'," FLORIDA BOB said as he stood on the front porch of the house that had recently been occupied by Tony Wolf.

"Yee-fucking-haw," Clay said sourly. "What's next, humping sheep?"

"I'll leave that to Pete," Bob said. "But you've gotta admit, Clay, our boy McCabe had a good setup here. Damn near impossible to get up here without somebody seeing you coming. He'd be crazy to try to come after us here. Hell, he'd be nuts to try to come after all of us anywhere."

"Don't worry about that," Clay said. "He'll come running. We'll make sure of that."

———

EVER SINCE the kidnapping, Lisa Powell had taken her boys, Evan and Earl, to school herself. The bus, she thought, was too dangerous, too open. She wanted them close to her all the time now, and she would have kept them out of school entirely if she could. She was even looking into the qualifications for home-schooling them. At first the boys had enjoyed not having to meet the bus so early, but after a few weeks, they began to chafe under their mother's constant vigilance and her incessant reminders to be careful, to not talk to strangers, to tell her about anything suspicious. She didn't care. Someday, they'd understand.

As she walked out of the school building, she held out her hand. Earl pretended not to see it. "Earl," she said.

"Mo-om," he said under his breath.

"Take my hand, Earl."

"Mom," he said a little desperately, "the guys are gonna see."

"I don't care. Take my hand for the walk to the car."

"Mom!" He started to whine. "The guuuuys . . ."

"Earl!" She stopped walking, her attention suddenly drawn away from her son. Her Lincoln Navigator was parked in the school parking lot. Behind it, blocking it in, was a large black motorcycle. No, she saw as she slowly drew to a halt, two motorcycles. With two very large men astride them. Both bikes were running, the low rumble of the idling engines sounding like distant thunder. They were looking at her. No. They were looking at Earl. *Oh, no,* she thought. *Oh no dear God, not again, please no, God you can't it's too cruel . . .* She reached into her purse, fumbling for her cell phone. As she pulled it out, almost dropping it, she saw a cell phone appear as if by magic in the hand of one of the motorcyclists. Instead of putting it to his ear, however, he raised it and seemed to point it at them. She let out a small moan of uncomprehending fear. Then she realized, *He's taking a picture.* As soon as the thought crossed her mind, the man with the cell phone dropped his arm and the phone disappeared into the pocket of his denim jacket. The second man, who hadn't moved or spoken since she'd seen them, raised his hand in a cheery wave. Then the rumble of the bikes increased to a roar, and the two men sped away.

"Wow, Mom!" Earl was practically jumping up and down beside her. "Did you see those bikes? Were those guys bikers? Wow, that was so cool!" She didn't answer, just walked numbly to her car with Earl bubbling and jittering beside her. She even forgot to insist that he take her hand.

GABY SWORE under her breath as the car in front of her slowed and stopped again. She was already running late, and a wreck on Interstate 40 had reduced the multilane highway to a parking lot. She drummed her fingers impatiently on the steering wheel. The car in front moved forward a few feet, stopped. Gaby sighed. She flipped open her cell phone and hit the speed dial. "Howard," she said, "I'm hung up in traffic on 40. Can you get the word to . . ." She trailed off as a large motorcycle pulled up beside her on the shoulder of the highway, the vibration of its engine rattling her windows. The man seated astride the motorcycle turned his head to look into her window, straight at her. He smiled. She felt a chill run through her.

"Gaby?" Howard's voice came over the cell. "You there?"

"Howard," she said, "there's some guy on a motorcycle who just pulled up next to me. He's just staring into my window."

"Hang up. Now. Dial star-four-seven. That'll get the Highway Patrol. Do it now. Gaby? Gaby, can you hear me?"

She was staring at the man on the bike, who had something silver in his hand. He pointed at her. *Gun*, she thought, and started to flinch away. But then she made out the object. Just a cell phone. The man pressed the button, then snapped the phone shut. He blew her a kiss and sped away, the bike's fat tires kicking up a rooster tail of dirt and grass from the shoulder of the road.

"Gaby?" Howard's voice was sharper now. "Answer me!"

"He's gone, Howard," she said, her voice shaking. "He's gone. All he did was take my picture."

She heard Howard let out his breath, as if he'd been holding it. "Thank God," he said. "Just a fan, you think?"

"I don't know," she said. "I . . . I didn't like the way he was looking at me."

"Get in here, girl," he said. "Soon as you can. I'll call the Highway Patrol."

CHAPTER SIXTY-ONE

THE PARKING LOT OF THE PINE Lake Motor Court was filled with motorcycles. A pair of men in jeans and leathers lounged in cheap plastic chairs outside the door of one of the rooms. They watched Buckthorn as he got out of his cruiser. One of them raised a plastic tumbler in a mock salute. Buckthorn briefly contemplated going over there, smacking the tumbler out of the smug bastard's hand, then letting things develop from there, but he reined himself in. He walked up to the door of the room Kendra had told him she was staying in and knocked. There was no answer. He knocked again. Nothing. He moved over to the next room, Blauner's. There was no answer there, either. He glanced at the men outside the room. They were halfway down the long line of doors facing the parking area, between Buckthorn and the hotel office. They were watching him and grinning. He had to go past them to get to the office. He didn't look at them as he passed by. Behind him, he heard one of the men whisper to the other, then a quick bark of laughter. He spun around and gave them a hard look. They gave it back. He turned and walked into the office. Mae, one of the owners, was behind the counter. Her lined face was tense and drawn. He noticed the usual plate of biscuits was gone from the counter.

"Afternoon, Mae," Buckthorn said. "Business looks good."

"I guess," she said.

"These boys giving you any trouble?"

She sighed. "Nothin' I can't handle, I reckon. They're just loud. Them motorcycles wake me up at night, then I can't get back to sleep."

"Well, you know we're keeping an eye on them. You see anything out of the way, you call me, hear?"

She smiled tiredly. "Thanks, Tim. You know I will."

"Those FBI folks check out?"

"Most of 'em. Couple stayed behind. That blond lady, and one other fella. The one with the German name."

"Blauner."

"That's the one. Ev don't like him much, 'cause of the German name. Ev was in the war, you know."

Buckthorn knew. Ev Carter, Mae's husband and the other co-owner of the motel, rarely let anyone forget it.

"I stopped by their rooms. They weren't in. They tell you where they were going?"

"Naw. Didn't see 'em leave, neither."

"Well, when they come back, ask them to call me, would you?"

"Will do, Tim," she said.

When Buckthorn walked back out in the parking lot, the men were gone from in front of the room. He walked back to the patrol car, feeling uneasy.

CHAPTER SIXTY-TWO

THE PHONE WOLF HAD TAKEN from Stoney rang. He kept one hand on the wheel as he flipped it open.

"We need to talk," Johnny Trent said.

"Don't think we have much to talk about, Johnny," Wolf said.

"You've got my uncle pretty pissed off."

"Imagine how sad that makes me."

"You might want to be a little more worried," Johnny said. "Considering."

"Considering what?"

"Considering that some people have a lot to lose, even if you think you don't. You sound like you're in a car. You in a car, Tony Wolf? You coming to see me?"

"Thought I might pay a visit. Once I get done here."

"Well, we're moving your travel plans up a little bit. Pull over. And check out the pictures I'm getting ready to send you."

Wolf hesitated, then pulled the truck to the shoulder. He glanced at the screen. The first picture that appeared was a young boy, walking hand in hand with a blond woman, apparently his mother. It was hard to make out features on the tiny screen, but he could see the woman's mouth open in an O of surprise. It took him a moment to recognize the boy as Earl Powell. Wolf gritted his teeth and thumbed to the next picture. It was Gabriella Torrijos. She had the same shocked expression as Earl's mother. Wolf put the phone back to his ear.

"We can get to them, anytime we want, Tony. Anytime."

"So?" Wolf said. "They don't mean anything to me."

"You're lying, Tony. You blew your cover to rescue the boy. And you can't tell me you didn't get to like that hot-assed little reporter. But that's okay. They're not the only people we can get to." There was a brief rustle; then Kendra's voice came on. "Tony?"

Wolf felt the blood pounding in his temples. "Kendra? Are you okay?"

"Tony, for God's sake don't come, they're going to—" She was abruptly cut off. There was a pause; then he heard her scream. It was a sound of raw agony, and it tore through Wolf's guts. He put his head on the steering wheel and bit back the sobs that threatened to erupt from his chest.

Johnny came back on the line. "Clay just cut off one of your wife's fingers," he said. "Just to let you know we're serious. Don't worry, though. It was just a pinky. And we'll make sure she doesn't bleed out. You'd better get here, though, before we start cutting off something else."

Wolf raised the phone to his ear. "I'm going to kill you," he said, his voice toneless.

"You missed your chance at that," Johnny said. "You should have shot me in the head. I actually wish you had. But all you took was my legs. And when you get here, I'm not going to kill you either. See, I'm a fair-minded guy. I'm just going to take your legs from you. Let you know what it's like to live like a cripple. Or, you don't show up, I can take your wife's legs." He chuckled. "That'd be a shame, 'cause they look like pretty nice legs. But it's your choice. We're at your old house. Be there by noon tomorrow. Alone, no cops. And unarmed. Or Clay goes to work on your bitch here with an ax. And after that, everyone you ever tried to protect dies screaming for mercy." The phone went dead.

Wolf stared at it for a moment. Then he slammed it against the dash. The plastic case splintered, shards flying throughout the truck cab. He did it again, cracking the interior works of the phone in half. A voice resonated in his head.

Mad now, boy? That's why you gonna lose. You get mad, you lose. Get icy, boy. Get icy.

He took a deep breath. He dropped the destroyed phone onto the floorboard. Then he pulled back onto the road and started to drive.

CHAPTER SIXTY-THREE

SHE SWAM BACK UP THROUGH THE DARKNESS, the pain in her left hand flashing in her fogged mind like a beacon. Consciousness returned to her abruptly, welded to the sick realization of what had been done to her. She was seated at the kitchen table. Blood covered the battered Formica tabletop. A stout rope around her waist held her to the metal chair. Another bound her right hand to the chair. For a moment, she didn't dare look at her free hand, at the damage that had been done. Finally, she glanced down.

The tip of her little finger was gone above the first knuckle. It had been tightly wrapped in a bandage. The bandage was soaked with blood. The blood was bright red. Kendra's head abruptly started spinning. She leaned over and vomited on the kitchen floor. The man standing next to her jumped back, but the splatter caught his pants legs. "Goddammit!" he yelled. "Fucking bitch!" He yanked her upright by the hair. He reached for the bloody cleaver on the table.

"Clay," Johnny Trent said. "Leave her alone." He turned to the bearded man standing beside his wheelchair. "Bob," he said, "get her some Oxys out of the truck. The blue pills, from my bag." Bob nodded. He didn't speak or look at her as he started out the door.

"No," Kendra said, her voice still fuzzy with shock. "No drugs." She thought of the baby inside her. She didn't know what a powerful painkiller would do. She couldn't take the chance. But she didn't want them to know why. God knows what the man in the wheelchair would order the other one to do. They were both clearly insane, each man's madness feeding off the other's. Some of the others, rough and brutal as they were, seemed almost sane by comparison. The one called Bob, for example. He seemed stunned by what he had just seen. Maybe, she thought, she could play on his sympathies, on whatever humanity he had left. But he had been the one who, at Johnny's orders, had grabbed her hand and stretched it out across the table, holding it steady for the cleaver. No, maybe she couldn't trust him. If only she could think clearly through the agony in her hand. Tears of frustration stung her eyes. *Oh*, some savage part of her snarled deep inside, *now you cry. Now, when you need to think.* "Please," she croaked, "can I have a glass of water?"

Bob moved quickly to the sink.

"Clay," Johnny said. "Get a mop. Clean this mess up."

"Get the bitch to do it," Clay snarled. "I ain't a goddamn maid."

"Clay," Johnny said patiently, "to do that, we have to untie her. We had enough trouble getting her here. Now, you don't want to clean this up, find someone else to do it. But get it fucking done, okay, cuz?"

Clay continued grumbling under his breath as he walked out. Johnny followed, leaving Kendra alone with Bob.

Bob came over and held the water to her lips. She took a long drink, trying to wash the taste of bile from her mouth. "Thanks," she whispered. Bob didn't answer. He pulled a chair out from beneath the kitchen table and sat down. He didn't look at her.

A few minutes later, Clay came back in with a mop and a bucket. His face was red with anger. He began mopping up the blood and vomit on the floor. "You're gonna pay for this, bitch," he said in a low, savage voice. "I ought to make you clean this mess up with your tongue. Johnny says no, though. I'm supposed to leave you alone." He stopped mopping and leaned over, bringing his face to within inches of hers. "But you're only safe till your darling hubby gets here. Then you and me, we're going to have some fun. At least I am. I'm thinking you won't enjoy it much." He straightened back up. He didn't speak again until he'd finished the job. Then he hauled the bucket to the back door and tossed the water out. He turned to her. "You and me, babe," he said. "You. And. Me." He walked out.

She looked at Bob. "He's going to torture me to death," she said, keeping her voice even. He didn't answer. "That doesn't bother you?"

"Shut up," he said.

"I'm a federal agent," she said, making her voice a little stronger by sheer force of will. "That's a death penalty if you're convicted, Bob. Even as an accessory. There's about five ways I can think of, off the top of my head, that what's going on here is pointing you straight at a gurney and a needle. And for what?"

"I said shut the fuck up," Bob muttered, his tone more miserable than angry.

"You can get out from under this, Bob," she said. "You help me out, I can help you out." It was the same vague promise she'd made in a hundred interrogations, dangling the glimmer of hope just out of reach if the guy in the chair would just give up what he knew. But this time it was her in the chair, and she was trying to keep the glimmer of hope alive for herself. It sputtered and died, however, as Bob took a roll of duct tape out of a kitchen drawer and ripped off a piece. "No," she said. "Wait—" She tried to turn her head away, but he grabbed her under the chin and held her firmly. He pulled the tape tight over her mouth and fastened it there. He took a length of rope and fastened her maimed hand to the chair. With her arm pointed down, the blood rushed into the stump of her finger. She could feel it beginning to bleed again, wet and sticky, saturating the bandage. *If I'm lucky*, she thought, *maybe I'll bleed to death before Clay comes back.* God, she thought, despair dragging at her, *please let me die.* Then the voice came again, strong and savage and clear inside her skull. *No*, it said. *Like hell you're giving up now. Not with all you've got to lose.* It was only then that the tears began to spill down her face. She couldn't just accept the death she knew was coming. She was going to have to keep fighting, for herself, for Tony, and for the life she had within her.

But she was so very, very, tired.

CHAPTER SIXTY-FOUR

THE PATROL CAR PICKED WOLF up on the outskirts of town, falling in behind him at a discreet distance. Wolf swore. This time, he couldn't run. Before, he had been headed out, with all the world in which to lose himself. Now, he had only one place to go. They'd follow him there, and Kendra would die. He had to think of something else. He looked over at the weapon propped up in the floorboard of the passenger seat, did a mental inventory of the knapsack resting in the truck seat. The explosion of blue lights in his rear window interrupted him. Wolf gritted his teeth and pulled over.

BUCKTHORN SAW the truck ahead of him slow and pull over onto the shoulder. He picked up the microphone and activated the loudspeaker. "*Out of the car,*" his voice boomed out in the stillness of the country road. "*Hands in the air.*" There was a brief pause, and the driver's side door opened. Tony Wolf got out, slowly, hands held above his head. "*On the ground,*" Buckthorn ordered. "*Don't move.*" Wolf complied. Buckthorn had radioed for backup, but that was at least ten minutes away. He got out of the car and drew his weapon. He approached slowly, the barrel of the pistol never wavering from Wolf's prone form. "Hands behind your back," he said.

Wolf didn't move. "*Hands behind your back!*" Buckthorn screamed. Reluctantly, Wolf crossed his wrists behind his back. Buckthorn holstered his pistol and took a pair of plastic zip cuffs out of the pouch on his belt. He looped them quickly around Wolf's wrists and pulled them tight. There was no key; the only way to get them off now was to cut them off. He stepped back. "Your wife said we could expect you back here," he said.

"They're going to kill her," Wolf said.

"Who?"

"You know who."

"We'll talk about that in a minute. Right now, I need to know if you have any weapons in the vehicle."

Wolf hesitated. "Yeah," he said. "AA-12 automatic shotgun on the floorboard, 9 mm Beretta in the glove box."

Buckthorn glanced over at the truck. He could see the silhouette of the shotgun. He stepped around the vehicle to the passenger side and pulled the door open. Something that had been wedged between the seat and the door dropped to the ground between him and the truck. He looked down. There was a cylindrical object lying between his feet. A metal lever lay next to it. *Grenade*, Buckthorn barely had time to think before it went off.

CHAPTER SIXTY-FIVE

VENTUALLY, EXHAUSTION OVERCAME FEAR, and Kendra dozed, still upright in the chair. She was awakened when Clay came back in. He had a submachine gun slung over one shoulder. He held another in his right hand. He was carrying a toolbox in his left. Bob stood up as Clay tossed the gun to him. "Go downstairs," Clay ordered. "Into the basement. There's some kind of tunnel or some such shit down there. He may try to get in that way. You and Pete watch for him. Fred-dog and Tiny are upstairs watching the outside." Bob glanced at Kendra, and Clay grinned nastily. "Don't worry, we'll save you some. The fun doesn't begin till he gets here. Just remember. Take him alive. You kill him before we get a chance to take his legs, and Johnny says you get the ax in his place."

"Clay," Bob said, "this shit is fucked up, man." Clay said nothing, just stared at Bob with narrowed eyes. "Come on, brother," Bob said, his voice a little desperate. "I know Johnny wants payback. I'm down with that. All the fucking way to the end. But you get down to threatening brothers, people you've ridden with for years . . . man, what the fuck? I mean, really . . . what the fuck?"

"Just get down there," Clay snapped. Bob shook his head but walked out the swinging door. Clay took the seat he had just vacated, setting the toolbox down beside him. He kept his eyes on Kendra without speaking. Something in those eyes caused her to shrivel inside. She knew what was going on behind them. Images of her in agony, images of torture and rape and pain. He was planning how best to make her suffer, running through fantasies in his head, refining them. She didn't want to think about what was in that toolbox. When she tried to speak, her voice sounded rusty, as if it had been unused for a long time.

"Blauner," she said.

The name seemed to jar him out of his dark reverie. "What?"

"Your guy on the inside. It's Blauner, right? He was there when I interviewed the reporter. She told me about the tunnel. I had written it up, but I hadn't sent the report in yet. So if you know about the tunnel, you probably know about it from Blauner."

"Nice work, Agent Wolf," Blauner said as he came into the room. He was pushing Johnny Trent ahead of him in his wheelchair. Johnny held a stubby cut-down shotgun across his lap. "I can see why you've gone as far as you have," Blauner said.

"You son of a bitch," Kendra spat at him.

Blauner just smiled as he parked Johnny next to Clay. He sat down. "Sorry it had to end this way," he said. He shrugged. "I don't suppose it would make any difference if I told you this wasn't what I'd planned. I guess it's always that way when you make a deal with the devil." He looked at Johnny. "No offense."

"None taken," Johnny said. He turned to Kendra. "Aren't you even curious as to why?"

"Not really."

"Bullshit," Johnny said without heat. "Of course you're curious. That's why you're a cop. You can't help but stick your nose in other people's business." He turned and looked at Blauner. "See, Agent Blauner here's a longtime customer of ours. He has a taste for some of the more, ah, extreme product we put out." Blauner looked away.

"We like to keep up with our customers," Johnny went on. "Check the mailing lists and whatnot. Keep abreast of our customers' other interests so as to serve their needs better. When we found out that one of the people who particularly enjoyed videos of little girls sucking dick was an FBI agent . . . well, my uncle Nathan is too good a businessman to waste an opportunity like that."

Blauner reddened. "That was supposed to have been between—"

"Uncle Nathan finally told me everything," Johnny interrupted. "I can see why he'd want to keep a card like you up his sleeve and well hidden. But once a card is played, there's no use in secrets anymore." He turned back to Kendra. "Of course, that was just the hook," he said. "Once Agent Blauner here saw there was more money to be made working with us than he could make in twenty years at a government salary . . . plus, maybe be in on the production of some of the movies he likes so much—"

"Just give me my money," Blauner said, "and let me get out of here."

"Yeah, well, about that," Johnny said. Another pair of men came in and took up positions on either side of Blauner's chair. "Uncle Nathan and I had a talk about that final payment. I suggested that since you're a card that's been played, it doesn't make any sense to throw any more money your way."

Blauner tried to stand up. The two bikers on either side of him grabbed his elbows and yanked him to his feet. Johnny leaned forward, his eyes bright and feverish. "You ever read about the Vikings?" he asked.

"Wh-what?"

"They had a special punishment for traitors," Johnny said. Clay stood up. He had taken a mallet and a chisel out of his toolbox. He had that grin on his face again. "They called the punishment the Blood Eagle." Johnny nodded to the two men holding Blauner. "Use the dining room table," he said. "It's sturdier. Better built. We'll do Wolf there, too." The men dragged Blauner out of the room. He was struggling frantically.

Johnny turned to Kendra. "I've got to tell you," he said, "I really like some of the furniture they've got in this place. They just don't make stuff like that anymore. Built to last."

From the next room, the screaming began.

CHAPTER SIXTY-SIX

THE FIRST SENSE BUCKTHORN recovered was smell. The acrid scent of burnt fabric filled his head. Then he felt the pain in his lower legs. *Holy shit, I'm on fire*, he thought. The fear shocked him back to full consciousness.

He was sitting in the front seat of Wolf's truck. They were moving. The sun had gone down, and Wolf had the headlights on. Buckthorn's hands were fastened in front of him with a pair of silver handcuffs. They were the old-style police cuffs, not the plastic kind, so they weren't Buckthorn's. *At least the bastard didn't lock me up with my own cuffs*, Buckthorn thought. The thought gave him only the slightest comfort. He looked over at Wolf's wrists. He'd cut his own cuffs off in a hurry, and it must have been clumsy work. He'd wrapped his wrists with torn bits of fabric that were spotted with blood.

"Sorry about your pants," Wolf said from the driver's seat. "The flashbang set them on fire. I had to put them out. They're pretty well fucked, I'm thinking. And you've got some burns on your legs, but they're not serious. Still, you'll want to have those looked at."

"A flashbang," Buckthorn repeated stupidly.

"Yeah. Stun grenade. Sets off a hell of a noise—"

"I know what a goddamn flashbang is!" Buckthorn snapped. "I also know you're not supposed to use them at that close a range."

"Yeah. Sorry. I didn't have much time. I had to improvise."

"Kidnapping and assaulting a law enforcement officer is a felony, Wolf. A serious one."

"No shit, Sheriff," Wolf said. "I'm really not thinking that far ahead right now, but I don't expect I'll need to."

A memory came back. "You said they were going to kill her. You mean the Trents?"

"Yeah. And their little army. They're dug in up at my old house."

"You ever consider that maybe you should let the real police handle that?"

"Like you handled me?" Wolf paused. "Okay, that wasn't fair. I saw your guys work. You've got some moves. Pretty impressive for a bunch of country boys."

"I hope you don't expect me to thank you."

That got a reluctant chuckle. "No, I guess not. But let me ask you something. If I hadn't stunned you and cut these cuffs off, what would you be doing right now about this little situation?"

"I'd call in the Rapid Response Team. Get a tac plan in place. Get out there and—"

"And my wife would die. Guaranteed. See, Sheriff, here's the thing you don't get. All your doctrine and tactics assume that the subject in the house doesn't want to die."

"And Johnny Trent doesn't care, is that what you're saying?"

"You're not listening to me!" Wolf pounded the steering wheel in frustration. "He does care if he lives or dies. But dying's what he cares about doing."

"How do you figure?"

"He told me himself. He told me he wished I'd killed him. Right now, the only thing he wants more than his own death is to see me suffer. He wants to do it directly. But if he can do it by killing my wife, or making her suffer in my place, he'll do it. He already cut off one of her fingers."

"What!?"

"Or more likely he had Clay do it."

Buckthorn was silent for a moment. "So what are you going to do?"

"First, find someplace safe to stash you, where you won't be able to do some by-the-book cop thing that's going to get my wife killed. Then I'm going to give myself up to them."

"They'll just kill you."

"Probably. But they'll want to play with me a while first."

"You stopped to think that maybe they won't let her go? That they'll hurt her and you?"

"Oh, yeah. Believe me, I've thought about it. But I have a couple more surprises." He looked over at Buckthorn. "Tell me, how long have they been in the house?"

"Couple of days. No more."

Wolf nodded. "Good. After I got out, what'd you do with the place? You process it as a crime scene?"

"Yeah. Of course."

"You see anything unusual about the walls?"

"The walls?"

"Yeah. The interior walls. Notice anything about the plastering?"

Buckthorn scowled. "No. Nothing. Why?"

"Good." Wolf drove on for a little while in silence. Then he pulled the truck onto a dirt path off the main road. It bumped and jolted over the ruts. Finally, they came to a stop.

"The house is over that way, through the woods," Wolf said. He got out. He pulled the shotgun and knapsack from behind the driver's seat. He reached into his shirt pocket and pulled out the handcuff key. He stepped out and tossed it underhand, into the darkness down the road where they'd just come. He leaned back into the cab. "It'll take you a while to find that," he said, "and a while longer to get to a radio. By then, everything will be resolved. One way or another. Nice knowing you, Sheriff." He started to leave, then stuck his head back in. "Oh, by the way," he said, "if you're tempted, there's not really a pistol in the glove box. It's another flashbang with the arming lever wedged down." He grinned. "I couldn't be sure you'd open the passenger side door. Good luck finding the key, Sheriff. But not too good." Then he was gone into the darkness.

"THIS IS FUCKED UP," Florida Bob said.

"I know, man," Pete the Perv said glumly. They sat in the gloom of the basement, submachine guns across their laps. They'd found an old pair of rickety wooden chairs that creaked and threatened to collapse into splinters at every moment. A battery-powered lantern hung by a hook from the low ceiling. "Sittin' down here in the fuckin' basement," Pete went on, "guardin' a fuckin' hole in the wall, while Clay and Johnny party with that fine-lookin' blonde . . ."

"Not that, man," Bob said. "It's Johnny. I think he's gone bugfuck."

Pete snorted. "Johnny's always been nuts, bro. You just don't notice it as much when Clay's around."

Bob was getting exasperated. "That's not what I mean, either. Did you hear him up there? If we don't bring McCabe or Wolf or whatever the fuck his name is in alive, he's gonna have Clay cut our legs off instead." He shook his head. "We're brothers, man. Full members. That's not right."

"Aw, man," Pete said. "He's just sayin' that. He ain't really gonna do it. He's just, you know, bein' motivational and shit."

"No, I thought that, too. At first. But you weren't looking at his eyes when he said it. I was. He ain't just woofin', man. He doesn't care about the Brotherhood anymore. All he cares about is gettin' even."

"Hey, ain't nothin' wrong with that."

"It ain't right," Bob repeated. Pete didn't answer. The only sound was the chairs creaking under them when they moved. Then they heard the screaming begin from upstairs.

"Huh," Pete said disgustedly. "Looks like they started without us."

"Naw," Bob said. He cocked his head, listening. "That's not the bitch." The voice was pleading now. They couldn't make out the words, just the desperation. Then the words were cut off and the screaming began again, louder.

"Who the fuck *is* that?" Pete said.

"I don't know," Pete said, "but sounds like Johnny and Clay aren't too happy with him."

They were both looking up, fascinated and terrified at the howls and sobs of agony from above. Then they saw the dark stain seeping through the old wooden floorboards. As they watched in shock, the stain spread and deepened in color.

"Fuck," Pete whispered.

WOLF CREPT to the door of the barn. He stopped, pressed against the rough wood wall, and listened. He thought he could hear shouting—no, screaming—from the house. He felt himself dying inside. But the screaming stopped for a moment, followed by a voice, pleading. It didn't sound like a woman. Then the screaming started again. He clenched his fists. He couldn't rush in, no matter how much he wanted to. He'd only succeed in getting both himself and Kendra killed. He couldn't hear any movement from inside the barn, though.

The sounds from inside the house stopped. He didn't want to think about what that might mean. He pulled the barn door aside, wincing as it groaned along its track. He gave himself just enough room to slip through.

Inside, he waited for his eyes to adjust to the deeper gloom. When he could just barely make out the shapes of objects, he picked his way carefully to the workbench. He propped the shotgun against it before locating the drawer he needed by touch and easing it open. He felt around inside until his fingers closed around a familiar shape. He took it out of the drawer and stuck it in his back pocket. He picked up the shotgun and slung it on his back. Slipping back out as silently as he came in, Wolf made for the toolshed.

When he had reached the bottom of the ladder and the entrance to the tunnel, he could see a dim glow at the end. Someone was waiting in the basement. Wolf reached into his pocket and took out the object he'd taken from the barn. He fumbled in the darkness until his thumb found the switch he wanted and pressed down, then released it. There was a click and a low, almost indistinguishable whine. A red LED glowed in the darkness like a baleful eye. He found the second switch and pressed down with his thumb, this time holding the button down. The red light went out and a second one came on, this one green. He raised the device above his head like a torch and started off down the tunnel, toward the light.

CHAPTER SIXTY-EIGHT

L ISTEN," FLORIDA BOB SAID.

"I hear it," Pete replied. They stood up, machine guns at the ready, pointed at the dark mouth of the tunnel, fingers tensed on their triggers. Pete's shoulder jostled the light hanging from the ceiling, causing the shadows to jitter and waver drunkenly. They waited, listening to the sound of footsteps approaching.

Before long, the man they had known as Axel McCabe appeared in the mouth of the tunnel. He held a small black plastic object in his right hand. A long gun was slung across his back. He didn't seem surprised to see them.

"Evening, Bob," he said calmly. He nodded. "Pete."

"Drop it, McCabe!" Florida Bob snapped.

"You don't really want me to do that, Bob," the man said. "And the name's Wolf, by the way."

"I don't give a fuck if it's Princess motherfucking Diana," Bob said. "Drop whatever that is you're holding—"

"If I do that, this place goes up like a Roman candle." Wolf said. He held the object out. "Deadman switch, boys. Connected to a pound of C-4 in each of the downstairs walls. Shoot me and it all goes bang."

"Bullshit," Pete said.

Wolf looked at him calmly. "Try me." He smiled tightly. "Besides," he said, "I'm betting Johnny told you to bring me up alive. Right?" Pete and Bob looked at each other uncertainly. "So why don't you take me on up there?" Wolf said. "Johnny and me, we got a lot to talk about."

There was another moment's hesitation. Then Bob nodded. "Yeah," he said. "Okay. But you give us whatever gun that is on your back."

Wolf shrugged. "Sure. Not like I need it." He slid it from behind his back and lowered it to the floor.

Pete retrieved it, then poked Wolf in the back with his machine gun. "Up the stairs, asshole."

Bob went first, Wolf in the middle, Pete bringing up the rear. They exited into the kitchen. "Johnny?" Bob called out.

"Dining room," Johnny called back.

Bob entered the dining room, then drew up short. "Oh, Jesus," he said. He stood aside as Wolf came up behind him.

Johnny was in his wheelchair at the far end of the table. He held a shotgun across his lap. Clay stood to one side, dressed in a coverall that had probably once been yellow but was now stained and spattered with blood. He held a bloodstained ax in his hand. His eyes were somewhere far away.

Stretched out on the table like an obscene feast was the body of Agent Blauner. He was facedown, his face turned away from Wolf. He was fastened to the table by leather straps across his wrists that looped around the table legs. His back had been cut open, the wounds crude and jagged. Wolf could see splinters of bone protruding from the edges and the white ridge of the spine down the middle. Two dark, blood-sodden lumps of tissue extended from the wounds and lay across the dead man's shoulder blades like stunted wings. Blood soaked the table and the floor.

"The Blood Eagle," Johnny said. "Nice work, huh?"

"Why?" Wolf said.

"Why what?"

"Why kill him? And why like that?"

Johnny shrugged. "I don't like traitors. And he wasn't any use to us anymore."

Wolf held up his hand, the deadman switch still clutched in it. "Where's my wife?" he said.

"What the hell is that supposed to be?"

Wolf gestured with his chin at the wall behind Johnny. "While I was living here, I rigged up some surprises for anyone who might want to come looking for me. You're sitting right in front of one of them. There's about a pound of C-4 plastered up inside that wall. And the wall of the kitchen. And the front parlor. This is the detonator. Rigged to blow as soon as I release this switch."

"Bullshit," Johnny said. "You're bluffing."

"Pull that picture away," Wolf said. He gestured at a bland, old-fashioned print of a still life, hanging on the wall by the window. "And see if you still think I'm bluffing."

Johnny stared at him, considering, then gestured to the man beside him. "Tiny," he said. "Check it out."

Tiny hesitated, then reached out and gingerly lifted the print off the wall. There was a patch of plaster behind the print, about a foot in diameter. It was unpainted and looked newer than the plaster around it.

"There's another bomb behind the calendar hanging on the kitchen wall. And another in the wall of the front parlor. There's enough to bring the whole building down."

CHAPTER SIXTY-NINE

W HAT THE FUCK FOR?" Pete blurted out.

"Shut up, Pete," Johnny snapped.

Wolf answered anyway. "There's worse things than dying. Right, Johnny? Things you'd rather die than see happen. Things you'd be willing to blow the whole place up rather than have happen to you. Now, Johnny. I'm going to ask one more time. If you don't answer, I'm going to assume you killed her like you did this poor dumb son of a bitch here. And if that happened . . . well, that's one of the things I'd rather not live with."

Johnny looked hard into Wolf's eyes. Then he spoke. "Pete," he said. "Go get the bitch. Bring her in here." He gestured at the body on the table. "Fred-dog, Tiny, get this out of here." They moved slowly, reluctantly, but they dragged Blauner from the table. Grunting with the effort, they hauled him between them and out of the room. A few moments later, Pete came back in, pushing Kendra in front of him. She was pale, and her hand was wrapped in a bloody bandage, but she was alive. She gasped when she caught sight of Wolf.

"Hey, honey," Wolf said. "I'm getting you out of here. Just hang tough."

"I don't think so," Johnny said. He looked at Clay. He was still staring off into space, absently shifting the ax in his hands. Johnny turned back to Wolf and smiled. "Fiona says hi, by the way." Wolf didn't answer. Johnny glanced over at Kendra and smirked. She stared straight ahead. Johnny turned back to Wolf. "Must be something about you, buddy," he said. "She never got over you."

"Johnny," Wolf said, "you're going to let us walk out of here. Bob can go with us, unarmed. When I get to my vehicle, I'll give him the detonator. Then the rest of you can get out of here."

"I've got another offer to make," Johnny said. "I let the bitch go. Then Clay and I do what we came here to do. She lives. You live, sort of. And I get what I want."

"I don't think much of that deal, Johnny."

"Then blow the place up," Johnny said. "I don't give a fuck."

"Hey," Pete said.

"Wait a minute," Florida Bob protested. Johnny raised the shotgun and fired a barrel of double-aught buckshot into Pete's chest. The shot slammed him against the wall. His face went blank with shock as he began to slide to the floor.

"Shit!" Bob screamed and raised his own submachine gun. Johnny fired again, and Florida Bob's face disappeared into wet red pulp. The gun clattered to the floor. Johnny cracked the shotgun open and began to reload.

Clay seemed to come alive for the first time. He snarled and raised the ax over his head. He started around the table toward Wolf, his eyes wild. Wolf threw the detonator aside. Kendra screamed. Wolf scrabbled for the machine gun, but Clay was on him before he could bring it up. Wolf rolled aside as the ax came down between him and the gun. Clay's strength buried the head of the ax inches deep into the heart-pine floor. Clay struggled briefly, wrenched it loose. The effort threw him off balance, and Wolf came up off the floor, smashing the heel of his hand up under Clay's chin. It was the blow that had killed Furry, but Clay had the table to break his fall, and he went sprawling across it. The ax flew from his grip. Wolf leaped atop the table and grabbed Clay by the throat. He slammed Clay's head against the table, his fingers pressing against the windpipe. Clay's hands grabbed at Wolf's wrists, trying to break the death grip. Wolf heard a metallic click. He looked up into the barrels of Johnny's shotgun.

CHAPTER SEVENTY

THE AX HAD LANDED AT KENDRA'S FEET. Johnny snapped the shotgun closed and took aim at Wolf. Kendra bent down and snatched the ax from the floor, screaming again as the action sent lightning bolts of pain through her maimed hand. The missing finger interfered with her grip, and her first stroke smacked Johnny in the chest with the flat of the blade. It was enough to throw his aim off, however, and the double load of buckshot destroyed the hanging light fixture over the table. It blasted apart in a shower of metal and glass fragments, plunging the room into semidarkness, the only illumination the light from the next room. Pieces of the shattered fixture rained down on Wolf and Johnny. They rolled off the table to crash onto the floor. Kendra sobbed with pain and terror and rage as she drew the ax back and swung again. This time, her grip was better, her aim true. The blade bit deep into the soft flesh of Johnny Trent's neck, not stopping until it lodged between the vertebrae. The severed jugular and carotid spurted dark red, the breath leaving his lungs through the windpipe in a hoarse gurgling squeal, air mixing and bubbling though the gouts of blood. She pulled the ax back, still screaming. Some rational part of her knew he was mortally wounded, but her rage at the way he had callously mutilated her was in control of her now, blotting out any thought of mercy. She struck again, and the ax sliced easily through ragged flesh, bone, and tendon. Johnny's head came off and thumped on the floor. Kendra fell to her knees, sobbing. She tossed the ax away in horror.

The door to the dining room was yanked open. Tiny stood there, his mouth gaping in comical surprise. He looked at Johnny's body, in the light from the hall. The body was slumping sideways, the fountains of gore already beginning to slow their rhythmic pulsing. She saw him standing there and grabbed frantically for the shotgun. "You know what?" Tiny said. "*Fuck* this." Then he was gone.

WOLF HAD landed on top of Clay, his fists working like pistons as he tried to smash the other man's face in. But Clay got a knee up that caught Wolf in the balls. He grunted in agony, the strength suddenly draining from his arms as everything south of his chest exploded in sickening pain. Clay tossed him aside easily, and he landed on the floor. Clay turned his head slightly in time to see Johnny's head hit the floor and roll beneath the table.

"*Johnny!*" he screamed and lurched to his feet. He saw the body crumple to the side. His eyes were wide, the whites showing. "Fucking *Bitch*," he growled. He started after her, stumbled in the blood on the floor, fell to his knees. "*Johnny*," he screamed again. This time there was a sob in his voice, as if his heart were broken. He staggered to his feet again. "Fucking. Kill. You." Wolf was still trying to get his breath as he rolled to his hands and knees. He saw the machine gun still lying next to Florida Bob's prostrate body. He gagged with pain as he clutched for it. Clay was stooping, grabbing the ax, raising it high above Kendra's kneeling form, ready to bring it down and split her skull. Wolf fired wildly, one-handed, the room lighting up again with the strobing muzzle flash. The shots went wide, cutting a line of holes in the wall before shattering the dining room window. The air was full of flying fragments. Clay stopped, the ax in midair. Some instinct for preservation took over, and he bolted for the dining room door, where Tiny had been a moment before. Then he, too, was gone, leaving Wolf and Kendra alone in the dining room that had been turned into a slaughterhouse. The only sound was her weeping. Wolf crawled to her and took her in his arms. She collapsed into his embrace, sobbing.

"Shhhh," he said. "It's okay. It's okay." She didn't answer at first. Then she said, "He's still alive."

"Yeah," he said, "it's okay."

"No," she said, "he'll be back."

"No, honey," he soothed. "He's headed for tall timber."

"He'll be back," she insisted. Her voice was desperate. Her eyes were full of nightmares. "You've got to get him, Tony. You've got to kill him. He'll be *back*."

"Okay. Okay." He got slowly to his feet. He was beginning to feel as if he might be able to walk again.

She looked up at him. "There weren't any bombs."

"No."

She looked at the new plaster. "So what's that?"

"That's where I patched the holes in the walls," he said. "This place was a damn wreck when I got it."

"So what was that in your hand?"

"Project I never finished."

"Huh," she said. Then she drew his head to hers and kissed him. "I missed you so much," she murmured against his lips.

He kissed her back, then drew away slightly. "I missed you, too," he whispered. "But I've got to go."

"Yes," she said, and her eyes narrowed. The line of her mouth hardened. The fear and panic were gone, replaced by cold rage. "Find him. Find him and kill him."

"On the way," he said. "There's a phone in the kitchen. Call 911." He walked over and grabbed Pete's machine gun up off the floor. "You remember how to use one of these?"

She took it from him. "I think it'll come back to me."

"Any of those bastards come back," Wolf said, "take them out."

"Not a problem."

CHAPTER SEVENTY-ONE

BUCKTHORN TRUDGED SLOWLY along the dirt road, back in the direction of the truck. His eyes swept the ground, back and forth, looking for the telltale glint of the handcuff key. *Screw it,* he thought, as he reached the truck. *I'll just walk back to the road. Someone'll see me.* He hated the thought of having someone see him handcuffed, but he'd paced up and down looking for the key several times without success.

He heard someone crashing through the underbrush in the nearby woods. There was a thud and a curse, then more sounds of footsteps in the dry leaves. "Wolf?" Buckthorn called out.

It wasn't Wolf who came out of the woods, though. It was Clay Trent, like an apparition from a horror movie. He was wearing a yellow coverall stained with blood, and he was carrying an ax. His eyes were wild; Buckthorn could see the whites from where he was.

"They took the goddamn van," Clay said, as if Buckthorn should have known what he was talking about. "Fucking cowards. They ran off. They took the goddamn van. I'll fucking kill them for that."

Buckthorn tried to keep his voice soothing. He started backing away from the truck slowly. "That's too bad. Why don't you—"

But Clay had caught sight of the truck. He strode over to it, set the ax down, and yanked the driver's side door open. He turned back to Buckthorn. "Where's the keys?"

"I don't know," Buckthorn said. "I guess he must have taken them."

Clay covered the ground between himself and Buckthorn in a few swift steps. He punched Buckthorn in the stomach. With his hands behind him, there was no way for Buckthorn to avoid taking the full force of the blow in the solar plexus. He fell to his knees, retching in agony. Clay kicked him, again in the stomach. Buckthorn fell over, writhing on the ground. *"Where are the fucking keys?!"* Clay screamed. Buckthorn couldn't catch his breath to answer. Clay picked up the ax. "Tell me where they are," he said through gritted teeth, "or I'll start cutting pieces off you till you do."

Buckthorn rolled over, looked up at him. He finally managed to draw enough breath to answer. "Okay," he wheezed. "Okay. Just don't hurt me anymore." He looked Clay in the eye. "They're in the glove box."

WOLF HEARD the shouting, heard Clay's voice raised in maniacal rage. Then he heard the bang, followed by screaming. He came out of the woods near where he had left the truck. Clay was on the ground behind the vehicle, flopping like a fish, his hands over his face, his vision seared by the flash grenade. Buckthorn was staggering to his feet. He walked over to Clay, drew his foot back. He stopped and put it back down. He looked over and saw Wolf standing there.

"Go ahead," Wolf said. "You want to kick his fucking teeth in, I'm the last person to stand in your way."

"No. Thanks anyway," Buckthorn said. "I'd appreciate it if you'd help me look for the keys to these damn cuffs. I think we're gonna need them in a minute."

"Yeah." Wolf fished the key out of his back pocket and started walking toward Buckthorn.

"Hey," Buckthorn said. "I thought you tossed it out in the road."

"Yeah. Well. Sorry about that. I needed to keep you occupied. I figured if you thought the key was around, you'd want to look for it rather than have somebody else get you out of the cuffs."

"You son of a—" Buckthorn stopped. He sighed. "Just get me out of these things."

"You got it," Wolf said. He stepped behind Buckthorn. He didn't immediately unlock the cuffs. "You're probably going to want to deck me when you get loose," he said. "And I don't really blame you, Sheriff. But now's not really a good time."

"I know that, son," Buckthorn said. "I've done some stupid things lately, but I'm not a total idiot."

"What I'm saying is, I'll give you a chance. One clear punch. Just not now."

"Goddammit, boy, will you stop jawin' and take the damn cuffs off?"

"Just so we're clear." He worked for a moment and the cuffs fell away. There was the sound of sirens in the distance, coming closer. Buckthorn quickly got Clay Trent into the cuffs. He straightened up. "Anthony Wolf," he said, "you're under arrest. For assault on a law enforcement officer. For resisting, obstructing, and interfering with a law enforcement officer in the course of duty. For kidnapping in the first degree. I'll probably think of a lot of other things, but that'll do for now."

Wolf looked amused. "You realize I still have the gun here."

Buckthorn didn't smile. "I realize that, after all this, you're still a sworn officer of the law. You may've had a reason to do what you've done up to now. I'll let the courts straighten that out. And I'll tell them the truth, straight up, and . . . well, they'll do what they'll do and I'll be content. But now all that's done. You turn that gun on me just to get away . . . well, you took the measure of me pretty good, Mr. Wolf. But I think I took the measure of you, too. I don't think you're a lawless man."

Wolf stared at him for a moment. Then he set the machine gun down. "Well, there you're wrong," he said. "But I'm damned if I can bring myself to shoot you." He stepped back. Buckthorn picked the gun up. "Can I ask a favor, Sheriff?" Wolf said. "My wife's going to the hospital. I'd like to make sure she's okay."

Buckthorn rubbed his chin. "You'll come down when you're done?"

"And make a full statement," Wolf said.

"Yeah. Okay." Buckthorn looked down at Clay, who was sitting up, looking around him with a blank expression.

"I can't see," Clay said in a small voice. "I'm blind."

"It ain't permanent," Buckthorn said. "Get up, you son of a bitch, before I change my mind about kicking your ass."

CHAPTER SEVENTY-TWO

THE WAITING AREA OF THE GIBSON COUNTY Hospital's tiny emergency room was cramped but brightly decorated with pastel colors and flower posters on the walls. A slight smell of disinfectant hung in the air. Wolf sat in an uncomfortable plastic chair and thumbed through a months-old *People* magazine. A young black woman sat a few chairs away, a child asleep on her shoulder. The woman rocked back and forth gently, her eyes focused on nothing.

A balding dark-skinned man in a doctor's white coat entered the room. He scanned the room with his dark brown eyes until he saw Wolf. "Mr. Wolf?" he said, his words clipped and precise, with only a trace of accent. Wolf stood up. "I am Dr. Bhagram," the man said. He didn't extend his hand. "You are Mr. Wolf?"

"Yeah," Wolf replied.

"The husband, correct?"

"Yeah. How is she?"

The doctor nodded in satisfaction. "We have cleaned and sutured the wound. There was some blood loss, but we have given

her a unit of whole blood. There is no sign of infection. And"—
he smiled broadly—"the baby is fine."

Wolf stared at him. "The baby."

"Yes," Bhagram said, still smiling. "I have advised her to see her
usual ob-gyn, but there is no sign of—" He stopped at the look on
Wolf's face. "You didn't know?"

Wolf sat down slowly. "I've been away for a while."

The doctor scowled briefly in disapproval. He quickly composed his face into his professional mask. "Well, congratulations."

"Thanks." Wolf stood up. "Can I see her?"

"Of course." Bhagram turned and led him through a set of
double doors. There were a number of private areas separated by
white curtains. Bhagram led Wolf to one of them. "We gave her a
mild sedative," he said in a hushed voice. "She is resting. We will
discharge her soon, if you are able to drive her home."

"Yeah. Okay." Wolf pushed the curtain aside.

Kendra was lying in a bed, propped up. Her face was still pale
and washed out in the harsh fluorescent light, and her eyes were
heavy-lidded and dull. She turned her head slightly as Wolf came
in. "Hey," she said.

He let the curtain fall behind him. "Hey." He paused. "The
doctor said the baby's fine."

She turned her head away. A single tear coursed down her
cheek. "I'm sorry," she whispered.

"I just want to ask one thing," he said, barely keeping his voice
controlled. "How long was it before you gave me up for dead?"

She turned her head back to look at him, without raising it
from the pillow. A glint of anger cut through the haze behind her

eyes. "I don't know. But it was after you disappeared without even letting me know where you were. And I'm no math whiz, but I guess that makes it long after, what was the name? Fiona."

That stopped him.

Kendra sighed deeply and closed her eyes. "We're not going to get this straightened out tonight, Tony. We may never get it straightened out. But right now, I just need some rest." She didn't open her eyes again. Wolf stood there, staring at her face. Even in the hard light it was still the most beautiful face he'd ever seen.

A blond-haired nurse stuck her head around the curtain. She looked worried. "Mr. Wolf?" she said. "There's a Lieutenant Buckthorn here to see you."

Buckthorn was sitting in the waiting room, his feet out in front of him, hands folded over his belly. He stood as Wolf walked in.

"You didn't think I was going to show up?" Wolf said.

"The thought had crossed my mind." Buckthorn nodded toward the double doors to the treatment area. "How's she doing?"

Wolf hesitated. "Tired," he said, "but she'll be okay."

Buckthorn nodded. "Okay, then," he said. He took a pair of zip cuffs out of his back pocket. "Let's go see the magistrate."

Wolf looked at the cuffs. "Those really necessary?"

Buckthorn considered it, then shook his head. "Ah, hell," he said. "I broke more rules tonight than I have in twenty years of law enforcement. What's one more? But I do have to do this." He put the cuffs back. "You have the right to remain silent . . ."

CHAPTER SEVENTY-THREE

CHAPTER SEVENTY T

T HE GIBSON COUNTY COURTHOUSE, like most of the ones built in the late nineteenth and early twentieth centuries, was a square, high structure made of native brick. When originally built, it was situated in a large open commons and designed with doors on all four faces of the building, both for ventilation in the pre-air-conditioning era and so that people coming to go to court, to record deeds, or to pay their property taxes would have access from any direction. Now the town had closed in around it; there were shops on both sides and a diner across the street that did a booming business on court days. Only the side facing the main street still had the broad sweep of grass before it. And now, in a more paranoid era, three of the four heavy, brass-handled double doors were locked from inside, turned into emergency exits opened by metal bars that would set off a piercing alarm if opened. The one entrance that remained open to the public was guarded by a bored elderly man in a deputy sheriff's uniform, seated behind a metal detector. It was 9:00 A.M. on Monday, and a long line of people was shuffling through the narrow aisle of the detector, placing keys and other metal objects in a small Tupperware container, retrieving them on the other side. From time to time, a particularly large belt buckle or forgotten cell phone would cause the detector to beep harshly, whereupon the deputy would sigh, haul himself arthritically to his feet, and scan the offender with a metal wand while the rest of the people in line waited with varying degrees of impatience. The people were dressed in jeans, overalls, and the occasional pair of shorts that would draw a stern lecture from the presiding district court judge and occasionally result in a trip home to change before that person's business before the court could proceed.

A large bearded man in a denim jacket stepped up to the detector. He dropped his keys and cell phone into the container. He also unhooked a portable CD player from his belt and dropped it in beside the keys. The deputy passed them along the table outside the detector. The bearded man passed through without incident.

A few minutes later, another man dropped a CD player into the container with his cell phone and keys. The deputy paused. He looked at the man standing under the arch, a short, wiry man with a lined face, as if he were used to working outdoors. Not an unusual look for Gibson County. The deputy shrugged and passed him through.

"ALL RISE," the deputy standing by the bench called out. A few early arrivals in the audience got to their feet, looking slightly confused. Court wasn't supposed to start until nine thirty, and it was just after nine.

"Oyez, oyez, oyez," the deputy intoned, pronouncing the Latin words as "oh yes, oh yes, oh yes." As he spoke, a middle-aged man in a black polyester robe stepped up onto the bench. "This honorable court for the County of Gibson is now open and sitting for the dispatch of business. God save the state and this honorable court. The Honorable Horace Martin, judge presiding. Be seated."

"Thank you, Mr. Bailiff," Judge Martin said. He was a ruddy-faced man, still sporting the brush cut he had worn as a marine colonel. Despite an outwardly stern demeanor, he was generally well liked by both the prosecution and the defense bar, known for being willing to say "not guilty" if the facts allowed, but fearsome in his sentences once guilt was decided.

Martin picked a sheaf of papers up off the bench. "Before we get started with district court, I understand we have some ninety-six-hour hearings?"

"Yes, Your Honor," the assistant DA answered. She was young and pretty, not six months out of law school, and still a little uncertain.

A door to one side of the courtroom opened, and a line of men shuffled in, each dressed in an orange jail jumpsuit and shackled at ankles and wrists. Each was here for his first hearing before a judge after being jailed. One of them was Tony Wolf.

"Okay, gentlemen," Judge Martin said in a voice that indicated he'd said the words thousands of times before. "You're here on your first appearance. You'll be informed of the charges against you and informed of your right to a lawyer. If you can't afford counsel, it will be provided for you. You need to understand, anything you say can and will be used against you. Let's start with . . ." He picked up a piece of paper. "Anthony Wolf, a.k.a."—he peered over his half-glasses—"Anthony Sanders." He looked up again. "A.k.a. Axel McCabe."

Wolf stood up.

"Mr. Wolf, you're charged with first-degree kidnapping, assault on a law enforcement officer, resisting, obstructing, and delaying a law enforcement officer, and"—the judge peered at the paper more closely—"possession of a weapon of mass destruction, to wit, a machine gun. You understand these charges?"

"Yes, sir," Wolf said.

"What do you want to do about a lawyer?"

"I'll represent myself, sir."

The judge paused. "You sure about that, sir? These are some very serious felonies."

"Yes, sir."

"Your Honor," Tim Buckthorn spoke up from the audience. "May I address the court?"

"Of course, Lieutenant Buckthorn," the judge said.

"Your Honor," Buckthorn said. He paused. "This is kind of an unusual situation."

The judge took off his glasses and leaned back. He spread his hands. "I'm listening."

Buckthorn looked uncomfortable. "Your Honor, may I approach the bench?"

"Certainly." He leaned forward as Buckthorn and the assistant DA walked up to the bench. "Tim," the judge said in a low voice, "what the hell's going on? Oh," he said, "and good morning, Ms. Taylor." The DA nodded, looking like a deer caught in headlights.

"Your Honor," Buckthorn said, "Mr. Wolf offered substantial assistance in the apprehension of the young man you're going to be doing a hearing on right after these fellows. He's also, well, sort of a federal agent."

"Tim," the judge said, "how is a person 'sort of ' a federal agent?"

"It's a long story, Your Honor."

"I'll bet. Just tell me it's not going to come back and bite me in the ass later."

"No, sir," Buckthorn said.

"Uh-huh. So what kind of bond do you want?"

Buckthorn looked uncomfortable. "Written promise to appear, Your Honor."

The judge's face went blank. "On a Class B felony." He turned to the DA. "What says the prosecutor's office?"

"Your Honor," the DA said, "our office received a call this morning from the FBI in Washington. We . . . we concur with Lieutenant Buckthorn's recommendation."

The judge leaned back and stared at them. Then he shook his head. "All right," he said. He turned to the clerk beside him. "Mr. Wolf waives counsel and will represent himself. He may be released on his written promise to appear. Next case is . . ."

CHAPTER SEVENTY-FOUR

AFEW MORE PEOPLE HAD PASSED through the metal detector before a man in an expensive suit stepped up. He was bearded, but his beard was neatly trimmed, as was his hair. He was dressed in an expensive-looking suit and carried a metal briefcase. The deputy looked up as the man stood before him. "You a lawyer?" he asked, looking at the case.

"Yes, sir," the man said. "Ted Pagliano, from Wake County."

"C'mon through," the deputy said. A few longtime members of the local bar had grumbled at the indignity of having their briefcases and files rummaged through just so they could gain access to the court where they appeared daily. The sheriff, mindful of the campaign contributions some of the lawyers put into his war chest come election time, quietly passed the word that lawyers could pass without being searched. They were, after all, officers of the court.

The man with the briefcase set the case on the table. The deputy slid it down. The lawyer walked under the metal arch of the detector.

"Go 'head on," the deputy said.

"Thanks, Deputy," the lawyer said. "Can you tell me where criminal court is being held? I've got a client being arraigned this morning."

The deputy pointed to a staircase off to one side. "Up those stairs. Courtroom Two."

"Thanks," Nathan Trent said, smiling as he picked up the metal briefcase.

"OKAY," JUDGE Martin said, "does that do it?" He had finished the first-appearance hearings on the five men shackled to Wolf and was looking at the clock. People were filing into the courtroom, and it was getting close to the official starting time for court.

"We have one more, Your Honor," the DA said.

The bailiff stood the line of shackled men up and herded them out the door to the holding cell behind the courtroom. From there they would be processed, back to the jail or, in Wolf 's case, back to the outside. Wolf glanced out into the crowd. He stopped. The man behind him bumped into him. "Hey," he mumbled.

"Deputy," Wolf said, "I need to talk to Buckthorn."

"Keep movin', boy," the jailer said. "You caught one break to-day. Don't be actin' like you're golden."

"Buckthorn!" Wolf called out. Buckthorn looked up, but before Wolf could say anything else, the aggravated jailer shoved him out the door.

THE LINE at the metal detector was getting sparser, the late ar-rivals passing through without incident. The deputy looked out the door past the last few people. He saw a dark-haired woman standing on the green in front of the courthouse, holding a microphone down by her side. A middle-aged black man was setting a camera on a tripod a few feet away. "Huh," the deputy said to no one in particular. "Wonder what the TV folks are doing here."

—

THE NAME on his birth certificate was Charles (NMN) Wells. He had been abandoned the week after his birth by the mother who hadn't bothered to give him a middle name or to provide a name for any potential father. He had grown up in a series of foster homes until he had aged out of the social services system and been deposited onto the landscape, rootless and angry. The Brotherhood was the closest thing to a family he had ever known. He would die for it, and today, he fully expected to. He picked up the CD player and opened the cover. Inside, nestled in the space where a music CD would normally be found, was a machined steel disc with a razor-sharp edge around its entire circumference. He reached into a jacket pocket and pulled out a thick leather glove. He pulled the glove on. The task was made more difficult by the small circle of Kevlar sewn into the lining of the palm. He held the metal blade between the ungloved fingers of the other hand, careful not to cut himself on the edge. Charles No Middle Name Wells, who was known now by his Brotherhood nickname of Chuckles, looked across the courtroom aisle to where another member, whose slightly protruding eyes and small mouth had earned him the nickname of Guppy, was pulling on a similar glove. Guppy looked over and nodded.

—

"HOLD STILL, dammit," the jailer was muttering.

"I need to talk to Lieutenant Buckthorn," Wolf insisted. "There's two members of the Brotherhood in the courtroom. In the audience."

"I don't know nothin' about no brotherhood," the jailer said. He worked the key, and the cuffs fell away from Wolf 's wrists.

A few feet away, another deputy opened the heavy solid steel door of the holding cell. Clay Trent stepped out, shackled at wrists and ankles. He looked over at Wolf. "Today's the day you die, fucker," he said, and he smiled. "And your bitch with you."

"Shut up, boy," the deputy said. "You're in enough trouble as it is. I hear the Feds are here to take you." He led Clay, shuffling, past Wolf toward the courtroom.

CHAPTER SEVENTY—FIVE

F IVE . . . FOUR . . . THREE . . . TWO . . . HOWARD Jessup's outstretched fingers counted down the seconds till the camera rolled. When he reached zero, he pointed at Gaby, who raised the microphone.

"Bob, just two weeks after a tense standoff resulted in the escape of fugitive FBI agent Anthony Wolf, violence has come again to the small Gibson County town of Pine Lake. In what one source described as a bloodbath, members of the outlaw motorcycle club known as the Brotherhood—" She stopped. A low rumble in the distance was steadily growing in volume.

"What the hell . . ." Howard said.

"Good thing we're not live," Gaby said. As she spoke, a pair of heavy motorcycles came into view at the far end of the long main street. They were followed by another pair, then another.

"That can't be good," Howard said.

From inside the courthouse, they heard the sound of gunshots.

———

DEPUTY TRAVIS Persons had never liked courtroom duty. He liked being on the road, out in the county, catching criminals. But it was his turn in the rotation, so he dealt with the boredom with as much good humor as he could muster. Every now and then something interesting would happen. Not often, but sometimes, like now, as they brought a stocky young man with dirty blond spiked hair into the courtroom. Word was this was one real bad character.

—

PERSONS'S ATTENTION was distracted by a bearded man in a suit walking into the courtroom, carrying a metal briefcase and talking on a cell phone. He sighed. Lawyers. They always thought the rules didn't apply to them. He stepped over to tell the man to shut it down. He heard footsteps behind him; then someone grabbed him from behind. As he instinctively pulled forward, he felt something like a line of ice drawn quickly across his throat. The cold immediately turned to heat, then pain. The hands around him were gone, but it felt like someone was tugging at his belt. He slapped down with his hand, felt someone's fingers fumbling at his buttoned holster. He tried to turn, but something seemed to be wrong with his vision. And the front of his uniform was wet. He looked down in horror to see the blood—his blood—pumping from his throat. He tried to cry out, but no sound came. He looked up in bewilderment as the bearded man flung open the briefcase and pulled out a submachine gun. Then Persons dropped to his knees, pitched forward onto his face, and died.

—

CHUCKLES DROPPED the metal blade and yanked the deputy's automatic from his holster. People were screaming, leaping up from their seats. He turned to aim at the other courtroom deputy, but he was already down, Guppy leaning over his prostrate body, fumbling for his man's weapon. Chuckles turned his gun on the jailer standing beside Clay Trent. He was standing there in shock, his mouth open. Chuckles shot him, and he fell. Then something seemed to hit Chuckles in the chest like a hammer. He turned. Another deputy, this one with a mustache, had his gun out and pointed at him. That was the last thing he saw.

———

BUCKTHORN DROPPED the man who had just killed two deputies with a second shot from his Beretta. He glanced up at the bench. The judge was nowhere to be seen. Hopefully he was under cover and Buckthorn would have one less thing to worry about. He was turning toward where the other biker was now unlocking Clay Trent's handcuffs when he saw movement out of the corner of his eye. Instinctively, he threw himself down between two rows of seats. There was the distinctive stutter of an automatic weapon, and the wooden seat backs above him exploded into splinters.

———

"WHAT THE . . ." the jailer muttered. He started for the door, then hesitated. Wolf's paperwork wasn't done, and he couldn't leave a man alone who was still technically a prisoner. Wolf made the decision for him. He shoved the man aside and ran toward the courtroom door. "Hey!" the jailer yelled, following.

———

PEOPLE WERE running out of the courthouse screaming. Howard instinctively turned the camera toward them. Gaby, however, was still watching the line of bikers. The pairs split apart, taking up positions on either side of the street. The first biker in line reached down beside his leg. He came up with a blocky-looking machine gun. Other bikers were drawing weapons of their own.

"Howard!" Gaby yelled as the first rounds caught him in the chest.

———

WOLF BURST into the courtroom in time to see Clay and Nathan Trent disappearing out the back door. The smell of blood and gunpowder filled the air. He saw a deputy lying on the floor by the railing separating the area of the judge's bench from the audience. As he started toward the fallen officer, Tim Buckthorn popped up from behind some seats that looked as if they'd been chewed on by an enormous angry animal. His weapon was trained on the center of Wolf 's chest, and his eyes were wild. Wolf threw up his hands. "Hey!" he said. "It's me!"

The jailer came in right after Wolf and grabbed his shoulder angrily. "You get your ass—"

"It's okay, Tom," Buckthorn called out. "He's on our side."

"I am?" Wolf said.

"You better be," Buckthorn said grimly. "Because we've got a goddamn war going on out there."

The radios on Buckthorn's belt and those of the fallen deputies were going crazy with the babble of panicked voices. The sound of gunshots could be heard through the walls, echoing eerily over the radios.

"Tom," Buckthorn told the jailer, "get to a weapons locker. Grab as much as you can carry. Then follow us." He pointed at where two men lay dead in the courtroom aisle. "There's a weapon there," he told Wolf. "Come on."

CHAPTER SEVENTY-SIX

GABY WAS PINNED DOWN. Most of the bikers seemed engaged in shooting up as much of the now-deserted main street as they could reach with their weapons, but a small contingent concentrated their fire on the courthouse. She could hear the bullets zipping by overhead, hear them ricocheting off the brick walls. Opposing them was a lone gray-haired deputy with his service pistol, crouched to the side behind the shattered frame of one of the doors. At short intervals, he would pop out from behind the doorframe and fire a couple of shots, only to be driven back inside by a hail of gunfire.

A white van pulled up to the curb in front of the courthouse. It was unmarked, nondescript. Two gunmen took up positions at the front and rear bumpers. The others dropped their weapons to the ground and began gunning their engines, ready for a quick departure. As soon as the van pulled away, they'd scatter down the back roads, trying to lose themselves in the countryside.

Gaby crawled over to where Howard lay on his back. His breath came in great wheezing gasps. He turned his head to look as she reached him. His eyes were glazed with pain.

"Get out of here, girl," he whispered. "Go on. Go."

She ignored him. "Help!" she called to the deputy inside. "There's someone hurt out here!"

"Stay down, miss," the deputy called back. "I've got a call in for backup. We've got people—" There was a flurry of gunshots from inside and a cry of pain. Then two men burst out of the door. One was a bearded man in a suit; the other was a younger man dressed in an orange jail jumpsuit. Both were armed, the bearded man with a small machine gun and the man in the jumpsuit with a pistol. The firing stopped, and a ragged cheer went up from the men in the street. The two men bolted for the van. The man in the jumpsuit pulled up suddenly as he noticed Gaby and Howard on the ground. He strode over to them.

"Clay," the bearded man said, "what are you doing?"

"Insurance," Clay said. He reached down and grabbed Gaby by the hair. She cried out as he yanked her to her feet.

"We haven't got time for this!" the bearded man yelled.

"Come on, bitch," Clay grunted.

"No! No!" Gaby yelled. She kicked out at him frantically. He slammed her across the face with the barrel of the pistol.

"Sonofabitch!" Howard gasped from the ground. He reached out and grabbed Clay around the ankles. Clay tried to pull away. Howard clutched tighter, groaning with pain. He dragged himself closer and wrapped both arms around Clay's lower leg.

"Get off me, nigger," Clay shouted down at him.

"Now . . . you're . . . just makin' me angry . . ." Howard mumbled. Clay snarled and pointed his pistol at Howard's head.

Anthony Wolf slammed into him like a linebacker on a quarterback.

Clay lost his grip on Gaby. They went down in a tangle on the ground. Howard let go and rolled over, gasping. The bearded man stepped back and took aim, the gun barrel wavering, searching for a clear shot.

"*Put the weapon down!*" a voice called out. Nathan Trent turned. Tim Buckthorn was down on one knee, his weapon trained on Trent's head.

Trent turned to the gunmen by the van. "*Shoot him!*" he screamed.

They hesitated. Trent was between them and Buckthorn. If they fired, they risked hitting their leader.

—

ANOTHER VOICE boomed out, harsh and electronically amplified.

"*POLICE! Don't move! Weapons down!*" The gunmen stood, frozen in shock, and used up the only chance they had of survival in the face of a dozen well-armed and terrified cops. Half a dozen police rifles fired in a ragged volley from deputies in tac gear who had taken position on either corner of the courthouse. Another half dozen blasted from hastily prepared positions in the shattered windows. The men in the street crumpled. Trent screamed and raised his own weapon. Buckthorn's shot hit him full in the face and knocked him over backward. One biker reached down to pick up the weapon he'd discarded. A flurry of bullets cut him down. A pair of others tried to run and were shot down. A few tried to throw their hands up in surrender, but that time had passed and the killing fury was on the men behind the guns, just as it had been on the men now before them. They were shot down with the rest.

———

CLAY HAD discarded his pistol. Nothing would satisfy his rage except to kill his enemy with his bare hands. His face was purple with fury as he locked his fingers around Wolf's throat and began to squeeze. Wolf gagged, his vision blurring from the lack of oxygen. He punched as hard as he could at Clay's gut, but the two of them were too close together and the punches were too short to do any damage. He was losing. He was going to die. A voice came back to him. *Ice, boy. Ice. Remember your training.* He took both hands and placed his palms together as if he were praying. With a short, quick upward thrust, he drove his hands like a spear between Clay's biceps, then spread his arms apart abruptly. Clay's grip broke. Wolf brought his cupped hands together as hard as he could against Clay's ears. Clay screamed with pain as an eardrum ruptured. He fell away.

Wolf rolled to one side, gagging. He could hear the staticky roar of a police PA system, then the rattle of shots. He knew what it meant. He rolled over and looked at Clay writhing on the ground. "Hey, faggot," he said, his voice sounding rusty and strangled. Clay rolled over, staring at Wolf with hatred in his eyes. "Sorry my wife killed your boyfriend Johnny," Wolf taunted. "I know you were queer for him. Must suck to be killed by a girl, though."

One ear must have remained undamaged. Clay screamed and

grabbed the gun. He got to one knee, then staggered to his feet. He raised the gun. A hail of bullets blew him off his feet. He crashed to the ground, his eyes still fixed on Wolf.

Wolf got to his knees. He raised his hands above his head. "See," he gasped, as the rage and the life faded from Clay's eyes. "You get mad, you lose. You always lose."

CHAPTER SEVENTY-SEVEN

BUCKTHORN STOOD AS DUANE WILLIS trotted up. He was dressed in a Kevlar vest and his black tac gear. "Sorry for the delay, sir," he panted. "We got here as fast as we could." A pair of EMTs had moved into position and were crouched over the black man on the ground. He was unconscious but still breathing raggedly.

"You did fine, Duane," Buckthorn said. His voice was subdued. "We're going to need some more EMTs, though." He was looking at Nathan Trent's body.

Willis followed his gaze and grinned. "Don't expect that fella's gonna need an EMT, sir. Undertaker's more likely."

Buckthorn looked at him for a moment, then smiled weakly. "Guess you're right, Duane." Suddenly he felt more tired than he ever had in his life. He walked unsteadily over to the courthouse steps and sat down.

"You okay, sir?" Willis asked.

Buckthorn waved him away. "I'm fine, Duane. Go on and secure the scene."

As Willis walked off, barking orders, Buckthorn looked back at

Nathan Trent lying on the ground. Wolf came and sat down beside him.

"Those the first men you ever killed?" Wolf asked after a moment.

"Yeah. Haven't had much call for it here."

"It was what you had to do."

"To protect the people I'm supposed to protect . . . yeah, it is. But it's not something I want to get used to."

"Good."

"I guess it won't come as any surprise . . . I want you out of my county, Mr. Wolf. Or Sanders. Or whatever the hell your name is."

"No problem," Wolf said. "Sorry for all the trouble I brought you."

Buckthorn didn't look at him. "Yeah, well, your saying you're sorry don't help me much. It don't help me tell the wives and parents of a bunch of good deputies that their husbands and kids ain't coming home. It don't help me tell Travis Persons's children the only thing they're going to know about their daddy is the stories someone else tells. And it's all because you brought your war here. You think your sorry's gonna make that easier? For me or for them?"

"No. But it's all I've got."

"It ain't enough. Now get out. And if I see you in this county again, I don't care what name you're using, I swear by sweet Jesus, I'll see you in jail."

Wolf sat there for a moment before he got up. He started to walk away, then turned. "You think it wasn't going to come here eventually?" he asked. Buckthorn didn't answer. Wolf gestured at the tree-lined street. "It's a nice town, Sheriff. Pretty. Nice people. But you're drilling your men in antiterror tactics and meth interdiction. The last time I had time to sit on my porch and read the local paper, there were two main stories on the front page. One was about the new pastor at the Freewill Baptist Church, and the other was about your sheriff going to the county commissioners and asking for funds for a bomb-sniffing dog. Seems the drug-sniffing dog you already have wasn't properly trained to pick up explosives. This is the way the world is now, Buckthorn. No safe havens. We all might as well get used to that." He turned and walked away. Buckthorn watched him go.

CHAPTER SEVENTY-EIGHT

AND THE AWARD FOR BEST Investigative Report goes to . . ." The heavily made-up presenter paused dramatically while she opened the envelope. "Gabriella Torrijos, WRHO NewsNow, Raleigh, North Carolina."

The room erupted in applause, with one or two exceptions. One of those was a sullen-looking dark-haired man seated at the table from which Gaby had risen to make her way toward the dais.

"I can't believe it," Brian Mathers muttered. "That story had no visuals. It was just some guy talking on tape. I had—"

"Brian," Michael Ellis snapped, "shut up." He stood, as did the other reporters and producers around the table. All across the darkened ballroom, people were rising from their seats and applauding. Gabriella took the stage. She looked down at the podium, nervously shuffling a few index cards in one hand. Gradually, the applause died down.

"Thank you," she said softly as the room quieted. "First of all, I want to dedicate this award"—she gestured at the clear plastic statuette beside her on the podium—"to my videographer,

Howard Jessup." She stopped and cleared her throat. There was a scattering of applause. "Howard's got a long road of recovery still ahead of him. But I know he'll make it. Because of all the brave men it's been my privilege to meet . . ." Her voice caught for a moment, and she looked down. When she looked back up again, her voice was steadier. "Of all the brave men I've met, Howard Jessup is the bravest." She picked up the award and held it up. "This is for you, Howard!" The applause was longer this time, and it went on for a full minute as she left the dais.

After the ceremony, at the cocktail party, an ever-changing group swirled around Gaby. She accepted their congratulations and compliments with a professional smile. The smile slipped a bit when she took a flute of champagne from a red-jacketed waiter. She excused herself and followed him. She caught up with him in the outside service corridor.

"If you'd let me know where you were," she said, "I'd have sent you an invitation."

Tony Wolf smiled. "I got used to not letting people know where I am," he said. He set the tray down on the floor and picked up one of the champagne flutes. "It got to be a habit. Anyway, congratulations." He held out his glass to hers.

"Thanks." She clinked glasses with him, then touched the sleeve of the red waiter's coat. "But why the masquerade?"

"Like I said. Some things get to be a habit."

She laughed, a little uncomfortably, and took a sip of her champagne. "So how did things work out with your wife?"

The smile vanished. "We're not together."

"I'm sorry. I didn't know."

"No way you could have."

"No," she said, "that's not true. I could have followed up. But I moved on to the next story, and I didn't. And I'm sorry."

He shrugged. "Things happen."

"That's all you've got to say?"

The smile was back, this time sardonic. "Still trying to get the story? 'Where are they now?' "

"No," she snapped. "I want to know because—" She stopped. "Never mind." She took another sip. "You saved her life. You almost got yourself killed doing it."

Another shrug. "You can't build a marriage on gratitude. Plus . . ." He took a deep breath. "No," he said, almost to himself. "Leave it there." He looked at her for what felt like a long time. Then he said, "She told me she didn't know who I was anymore." He looked away.

"Ouch," she said.

He shrugged. "It's okay. Sometimes neither do I. Occupational hazard." He took the red waiter's coat off and slung it over one shoulder. "I'd better be going," he said. "The guy this belongs to has got to be getting pretty frantic about now. Congratulations again." He started to walk away.

"I think I do," she blurted.

He turned. "What?"

"I think I know who you are. I think I saw who you are in that motel room when I was interviewing you. At least, I'd like to find out."

He stood there, regarding her. "Meaning what, exactly?"

"Meaning first, you come back inside with me. We have a few drinks. We talk."

"Off the record?"

"Totally off the record."

"Okay," he said finally. "But you're making a mistake."

"Maybe. I'll deal with that if you're right. But right now, get rid of that costume. Give that silly coat back to the man it belongs to, come in here, and have a drink. I have some friends I want you to meet." She took his arm. "It's time you broke cover for real."